SALTUS

Saltus

TARA GEREAUX

NIGHTWOOD EDITIONS

2021

NIGHTWOOD EDITIONS

P.O. Box 1779

Gibsons, BC VON 1VO

Canada

www.nightwoodeditions.com

COVER DESIGN: Angela Yen
TYPESETTING: Shed Simas / Onça Design

Nightwood Editions acknowledges the support of the Canada Council for the Arts, the Government of Canada, and the Province of British Columbia through the BC Arts Council.

This book has been produced on 100% post-consumer recycled, ancient-forest-free paper, processed chlorine-free and printed with vegetable-based dyes.

Printed and bound in Canada.

LIBRARY AND ARCHIVES CANADA CATALOGUING IN PUBLICATION
Title: Saltus / Tara Gereaux.
Names: Gereaux, Tara, 1975- author.
Identifiers: Canadiana (print) 202003531IX | Canadiana
    (ebook) 20200353128 | ISBN 9780889714007 (softcover) |
    ISBN 9780889714014 (HTML)
Classification: LCC PS8613.E734 S25 2021 | DDC C813/.6—dc23

for gavin and jack
my own two superheroes

Preface

SALTUS IS A FICTIONAL ACCOUNT of a real event that happened in my hometown. When it happened, I had been living outside the province for several years, but it still rocked me. I was stunned by the harrowing act of desperation and by all the factors that may have led to such a decision. I was also fixated on the people in town who may have been involved. As years passed, I continued to think about this, and about my own experiences growing up in that town and hanging out in that hotel. I started to wonder how such an event might have impacted the lives of the people involved and the decisions they might make. How would it reverberate? This is how the story began.

Embarking on writing this novel forced me to think about how to tell it. Although it's fiction, it is based on real events and that makes it delicate and complex. I made the decision early on not to write from Erin's point of view. Erin's story (and that of the real-life Erin) is a different one than my experiences as a cisgender writer, and outside of the perspectives I wanted to explore. I recognize this creates a silence or gap within the novel. Although Erin's direct point of view is not included, her character is very much present. To ensure that I captured and represented her experiences appropriately, I worked with a sensitivity reader who also grew up in a small town on the prairies and related to Erin's situation.

I also recognize that the experience at the story's centre remains a very real issue today. Limited access to gender-affirming health and medical care for trans and gender-diverse individuals, especially those living in rural and remote areas, continues to be a problem. In light of these considerations, I am committed to donating 10 per cent of the author's proceeds from sales of this book to a local or regional non-profit agency or agencies that provide gender-affirming supports and services to transgender and gender-diverse individuals.

While this novel was inspired by a real event and has grown out of my own experiences growing up in that same small town, the characters are entirely fictional. They also use language and terms that are not appropriate in today's world, but that are intended to reflect the mindset of some people in that time and place.

Prologue

June 1992
Beauville, Manitoba

THE CATTLE ARE ALL THAT'S NOTICEABLE on the landscape. The darkness is still so rich it mutes everything else around them and they stand in stark contrast. Scattered on the other side of the fence, some of them lie on the ground, others stand in small groups, clusters here and there. Massive and imposing. Even the calves at just over three months old already weigh two hundred pounds. The sheer size of them makes Al feel compact, contained. Like he takes up no more space than he's supposed to.

Earlier, before the hint of dawn and hours before he was scheduled to arrive, Al left his motel room in Beauville and drove out here to Sherman's farm. Took the grid roads that line the property until he found the herd.

He climbs out of his truck and stands near the fence. The animals turn their heads and sniff. Their tails twitch perceptibly. The calves are the first to lose interest in him, but the cows continue to eye him, alert, as all mothers would be when strangers are near their young. Al stands tall but relaxed and doesn't make eye contact, letting them be in control. He stays a long time. Long enough for them to get a sense of him, learn his smell and decide he's not a threat. When calm finally returns to the herd and the cows are comfortable with him, Al returns to his truck and heads up to Sherman's house to wait for the workday to start.

THE SUN NOW UP and the day warming quickly, Al watches the youngest hired hand, the one who's here specifically to learn from him. The kid was cocksure and smug before, swaggered around the pen in boots far too flashy. But now he's fallen silent and obedient as he waits for instruction.

Al kneels on the ground beside the calf, recumbent on its side. Its back end is held by Sherman, and its head by another hired hand. Al feels the heat from the calf through his knees, which rest along the animal's lower vertebrae. He pats the calf's front leg, massaging it, then bends it gently at the joint and tucks it against the calf's body.

"Here," he says to the kid, "hold it like this."

The kid crouches down and does what he's told.

"That'll prevent him from escaping. Not too tight," Al tells him. "You want to hold him, not hurt him."

The calf's breath is short and shallow. Al runs his hands down the calf's side, a few smooth strokes. Its back leg kicks twice and then stops. Intention is everything, but that's not something Al can teach easily. So much can't be explained.

Al washes his hands in the nearby bucket of chlorhexidine, then reaches into the bottom of the bucket for the knife, the one his father gave him when he was a kid himself. The only one he's ever used. He steadies himself on his knees, still touching the calf. It's important to maintain physical contact. That's more important than anything he might say. He leans over slightly and takes the scrotum in his left hand and, ensuring the testicles are up high and not in the lower part of the sac, slices straight across the bottom. Once the scrotum opens, he gently squeezes out a testicle and pulls on the membrane to reveal the spermatic cord. With the knife at a slight angle, he scrapes the cord as if shaving it until it breaks. A clean cut would only cause the animal to bleed out. He completes the procedure on the other testicle with only a small, quiet bleat from the calf. In less than two minutes he's done.

Al leans back and the men let go of the calf. It shoots up onto its legs and skitters off to the edges of the pen.

"Barely even fought," Sherman says as he gets on his feet too, wiping his brow.

A woman on the other side of the pen opens a gate and the calf canters out in search of its mother.

"No stitches?" the kid asks.

"A dry, clean field is all they need now. Wound will heal on its own."

Al stands and stretches his legs, readying himself for the next calf.

"You available again in a few weeks' time?" the other hired hand asks. Al was introduced to him earlier but doesn't remember his name.

"You got cattle?"

"A friend of mine two hours from here has a herd about half this size."

"How old?"

"A month older than these, maybe two."

"Weaned?"

"Not sure."

"I don't do weaned calves."

"Why's that?"

Sherman answers for him, "Greater weight loss and chance of infection if they've been weaned."

5

The woman at the gate leans against the fence, arms folded across the top bar, one foot resting on the lower. Her coppery hair a scratchy cloud around her head. No cowboy hat or baseball cap, and wearing a pair of high-tops. An odd sight for work like this. She nods at Al like they know each other but he's never seen her before. Sherman's wife, maybe? He nods back, then dips his hands and the knife back in the bucket to disinfect for the next.

THEY BREAK JUST BEFORE ELEVEN and gather in the shade of the barn. Sherman hands out pre-wrapped homemade sandwiches. On a fold-out table there's a box of fruit and a cooler filled with pop cans and juice boxes. The men help themselves. There's small talk in between mouthfuls of food, but the barn falls silent when the copper-haired woman walks in. She grabs a sandwich and a cream soda, then heads back outside and sits in the sun by herself.

No one says anything until the kid pipes up. "Isn't that the mother of that fucked-up boy?"

Sherman smacks him on the arm.

"It's true, isn't it?" A piece of roast beef falls from the kid's bun and he catches it, shoves it in his mouth. "What's she doing here?" he asks while chewing it.

"Returning a favour," Sherman says. "Her brother-in-law owns a cartage company in Brandon and shipped some equipment for me for cheap." More silence. Then someone brings up the weather and the conversation doesn't stop. Al listens, nods his head a few times, tsk-tsks when it's required.

6

At the end of the day, on his way to the house to use the john, he crosses paths with the woman on her way to her car.

"That was not at all what I expected," she says, stopping in front of him. "Didn't know what to expect, honestly. I'm a townie. Rarely been on a farm, much less worked on one. But that," she says, pointing to the pen, "how'd you learn to do that?"

"Grew up watching my father do it." It's both true and not true. It's true he watched his father do it, but what he learned was not to do it the way his father did. He was rough and force- ful. The calves would buck and scream, and Al would race to the house to hide. But as he grew older and understood that the procedure was necessary for the safety of the cattle themselves, he was determined to find a method that was less traumatic. He studied others, and developed his own technique over time, mastering a style that was swift and smooth.

"Is this all you do, hire yourself out? Or do you have your own farm?"

"Retired now. Just help others out here and there."

She watches him, as if sizing him up.

"You came all the way from where in Saskatchewan?" she asks.

"Saltus."

"Down in the valley there?"

Al nods. Something about her seems jittery. Thoughts whir in her eyes, but then she just ups and walks away. As he heads to his own truck, she drives by him in a rust bucket about fifteen years old and slows, rolls down her window.

"Nice to meet you, Al," she says and sticks her arm out toward him so he's forced to step forward. "Name's Nadine."

She waves as she moves off and he tips his hat. She's not hitting on him—he'll be seventy in less than a year, and she's got to be thirty-some years his junior—but there is something there. Something he can't pick up on. But then he's only ever been good with animals.

September 1992
Winnipeg and Beauville, Manitoba

"So, WHAT EXACTLY ARE YOU SAYING?" Nadine adjusts her denim purse from her right leg to her left and its long, fraying tassels stretch across her thighs like hair. Behind a hefty oak desk, Dr. Goertzen reads through Aaron's file and avoids eye contact. Beside Nadine, Aaron sits hunched, his back so curved that his dress's Peter Pan collar is tight against his throat. The dress is a pale yellow with white flowers and short petal sleeves. His taste in clothes is so feminine and pretty. Different from all the black jeans and band T-shirts that fill Nadine's dresser drawers.

"We'd like Aaron to have a few more sessions with his therapist first, and then we'll reconvene."

"A few more sessions? We've had six months of sessions already, and another four with a therapist before that who, it turned out, thought Aaron was doing all this just for attention."

"That was not a therapist we referred you to."

"No, but it was the only one I could find in Brandon who

would take us. It's two hours to Brandon, and another two to get here to Winnipeg. I can barely afford one trip a month, never mind once a week."

"If you want, I can see if there's another therapist in Brandon, an appropriate one, and refer you there. Though I think Ms. Webster is a good fit. What do you think, Aaron?"

He's unresponsive.

"Another referral means another six to eight weeks' wait." Nadine's aware her voice is rising.

"Aaron," says the doctor, "can you answer me?"

"I'll stay with Ms. Webster." His voice is just a whisper.

Nadine reaches out and touches Aaron's forearm. "It's been two years of this now. Appointment after appointment, and all you guys do is refer us to someone else."

"I'm not referring you to anyone else in this instance. Aaron will continue his sessions with Ms. Webster, and we will reassess in a little while."

"How long is a little while? And what more do you need to assess?"

"According to Ms. Webster's notes, there have been a number of events in Aaron's life recently that she considers to be major stressors. She recommends taking the time to work through these events and stabilize things first. I agree with her. After things are stabilized, then we can look at the best course of action for hormone therapy."

"Events?"

"I understand that Aaron has been going through some stages of puberty in the last while that have been..." He pauses. "Impactful." The doctor is unsure or unwilling to explain further.

9

Nadine knows full well what he means, though. When other kids Aaron's age started to show signs, Nadine wondered if Aaron was caught in some strange limbo, which was only further proof that he wasn't like everyone else. But just over a year ago, his voice started to change, and since then it's felt like an endless series of puberty-related episodes. Hair growth, muscle growth. Each of these things set Aaron off and he'd cover his emotions by blasting grunge behind locked doors. Eventually, sometimes days later, he'd calm down and they'd talk about it. She bought him his own Lady Schick razors, and a bottle of hair removal cream. But they have yet to talk about the underwear she's been finding in the trash for the past several weeks. She's told him about wet dreams before, but now that they're actually happening, he avoids any kind of discussion about them.

"Ms. Webster also indicates that Aaron is no longer attending school but doing his studies by correspondence."

"That was not our choice. The principal at Beauville is just as small-minded as the parents."

"I'm sorry to hear that." Dr. Goertzen clicks his pen a few times. "But isolation can add to what seems to be a very challenging time right now." He stares at Aaron and Aaron's chin quivers, but he clenches his jaw and stops it.

"In addition to the continued sessions," Dr. Goertzen continues, "I'd like to recommend that we start Aaron on a course of antidepressants."

"Antidepressants?"

"They will help alleviate some of this inner turmoil, and ultimately, we hope, help him cope with these challenges."

"I don't believe this."

"What are your concerns?"

"My concern is that you don't understand at all." She twirls a purse tassel in her fingers. "This turmoil you say he's going through, these stressors, his emotional state—these are all the result of one thing. If you would just fix that one thing, then there wouldn't be any of these 'other things.'"

"Miss Gourlay—"

"Stop with the 'Miss Gourlay' shit," she says. "Please."

"I am trying to help you in the best way I know how."

"How? The one thing we've come to you for is the one thing you won't give us. And because you won't, things have gotten worse. And now you're throwing solutions at us that don't make sense."

"Hormone therapy is not a decision to enter into lightly, especially for someone who is only fourteen. And if sex reassignment surgery is still the intended end goal," he says, closing the file, "well, it's not something that's reversible if the client decides they were wrong."

"I don't know what's worse," Nadine says, leaning back in her chair, "the hicks back at home, or you people with all your education and money who think you know better than us."

"Miss Gour—" He stops himself. "Nadine."

"None of you know what the fuck you're doing, do you? Two bloody years of this nonsense. All those framed certificates and degrees that are supposed to impress people," she says, pointing at the walls, "they don't mean dick when you can't do what they say you're supposed to, which is help people."

"Getting upset doesn't help the situation. In fact, it makes things worse for Aaron."

Nadine falls silent. "You think I'm making things worse for my own child?"

"No, I recognize that you're trying your best to help Aaron. However, I know things must be challenging for you as well. Money is tight and finding a job in your hometown is difficult. And you've mentioned you're intentionally remaining single because of this situation."

Nadine hugs her purse to her stomach.

"I think it would be beneficial if you were to discuss some of your challenges with a therapist as well. It doesn't have to be the same as Aaron's. In fact, it'd be better if you were to see someone other than Ms. Webster. I can put a referral in the system today."

—

NADINE FOLLOWS AARON OUT THE DOORS of the medical building. Rush hour. Endless cars, streams of people. A grey blur. She follows him down the sidewalk, in the opposite direction of their parked car.

"Aaron?"

He walks faster and then tucks into a narrow space between another building and its neighbour. There's a faint odour of spray paint and urine.

"I'm so sorry," Nadine says, and puts her hand on his shoulder.

"I keep thinking I'm getting closer but each time it just feels farther and farther away." His voice is strained, crackly with emotion.

"I know, hon. I don't know what to say. I thought we were getting the prescription today." His head collapses onto her shoulder and she stretches up to put her arms around him. He's had two inches on her for a while, but now his shoulders are broader too.

"He said just six more months." Nadine squeezes him tighter. "We can do that, right?"

"There's no guarantee he'll write a prescription then, though."

He's right, but she doesn't say so. "We can find another doctor," she says instead.

"He's the fourth one, Mom."

"Goertzen is a pompous ass but he has gotten us this far." The first three doctors they saw diagnosed Aaron with developmental disorders, ADHD, Asperger's, even undernutrition.

"But how long is it going to take?"

"We'll get there. I promise." Footsteps and car horns bounce off the walls around them, almost deafening.

When Aaron's sobs have died down, she pulls away from him. "Want to hit Shanghai Garden before we head home?"

"I'm not really hungry."

"Come on. Deep-fried wontons with sweet and sour sauce?"

"I just want to go home."

When he was younger, Winnipeg was a safe place for him. But as he grows, each time they come there are more stares, more comments. Nadine imagines punching the concrete walls around them with her fists.

Aaron pulls away and his bangs hang over his eyes. Nadine removes his bobby pin, uses her fingers to comb them smooth to the side, and re-pins them.

THE TEMPERATURE DROPS THAT EVENING and when they arrive home in Beauville, Nadine turns the furnace on for the first time since last winter. Tonight, she doesn't care about the cost. Aaron changes into his favourite B.U.M. Equipment sweater and fuzzy leggings, while Nadine heats the Shanghai Garden takeout and prepares the TV tables.

When *Quantum Leap* is half over and there's a commercial break, Nadine mutes the television. "When is your next appointment with Ms. Webster?"

"Two weeks."

"I was thinking..." She pauses. "What if you did get a prescription? For antidepressants."

Aaron turns to her. His mouth open but nothing coming out.

"We just have to get through the next few months so why don't we bite the bullet and keep the damn doctors happy?"

He still doesn't respond.

"If you get the prescription then both Dr. Goertzen and Ms. Webster will see that you're following their advice and might be more inclined to start you on hormones."

In a surge that startles her, Aaron kicks his TV tray and it topples over. The food that he barely ate falls to the floor. Sticky sweet and sour sauce spatters the rug. He pulls his knees to his chest and tucks his head between them.

"You're changing your mind," he chokes out the words.

"No, no, Aaron. Not at all. You don't even have to take the pills. You could just fill the prescription and pretend that you are."

"That'd be like admitting that they're right and they're not. You said so."

"I'm just thinking of it like a compromise."

"Why are you taking their side?"

"I'm not, it's just to get you your hormones. It'll only be a few months."

"What if I get them and then they still don't give me the hormones? What if they think antidepressants is all I need? They could do that."

"Then we find someone else."

He punches the couch cushion. Another and another.

"Stop." She tries to pull him into her, but he pushes her away with more strength than either of them expected. They sit in stunned silence.

The show returns to the screen. "Can we just forget about it?" Aaron un-mutes the television and picks up the mess he made on the floor.

"How about some hot chocolate?"

Aaron nods. Nadine carries the dirty dishes to the kitchen. When she returns, she puts the hot mugs down on the coffee table.

"I thought this might be nice in our mugs as well." She dangles a bottle of peppermint schnapps.

"I'm only fourteen," he says with a smile.

"Fifteen in two months," she says, not mentioning anything about the bottles of beer that have gone missing here and there. She dribbles some in his cup and pours a good amount into hers. Before she's halfway through, she tops hers up again. More peppermint than chocolate. When the credits roll, Nadine rises to go to bed and offers a hand to Aaron, but he declines, says he's going to stay up and watch more television. Tipsy, Nadine kisses the top of his head and moves off to her room, a hand on the wall for balance.

SOMETIME IN THE MIDDLE OF NIGHT, Nadine rolls over and opens her eyes, suddenly alert after being sound asleep. It takes her a moment to realize that something woke her. A noise from down the hall. She pulls the covers back from her face and turns her head so both ears are off the pillow, attuned. There's nothing but silence. She can't recall exactly what the noise was. A bang, or a thud. Maybe it was just the fridge popping again; it's on its last legs. But her heart's beating fast. Even her skin is alert.

Nadine puts a sweatshirt on and stands in the doorway of her bedroom. The flashing blue light on the VCR reaches all the way into the hall, a muted strobe. A shiver runs through her. Turning, at the other end of the hall, a sliver of light from under the bathroom door. Across the hall, Aaron's door is wide open and the room is empty.

She knocks on the bathroom door and tries the knob at the same time. Locked, and no answer. Without calling out, and running only on instinct, she races outside to the shed, not even bothering with her high-tops. The ground is both icy and damp on her feet. There's no light in the shed and it's impossible to see anything. She grabs at the tools she knows are leaning against the east wall and carries them out to the lawn, throwing them down to look at them in the moonlight. Outdoor broom, two shovels, a broken rake, a spade. Many of which they've never used in the eight years they've been renting the place. Finally, the crowbar.

Nadine wrestles it in the bathroom door jamb and pries it open. The wood around the door frame cracks and splinters. She drops the tool in the hallway and pushes into the room.

He's in the bathtub, lying crossways, legs dangling over the edge, his back against the far wall. His head's bent forward onto his chest so it's not noticeable at first, but the broken shower rod and the shower curtain that's bunched and crumpled at the corner of the tub add up to one thing. It's then that the trail of leather belt down the other side of his neck comes into view.

Nadine falls onto her knees at the edge of the tub and reaches over, clawing at the buckle. "Aaron. Fuck." She loosens it but the prong gets caught in a hole and the loop is still too tight to pull over his head. As she fights with the prong, Aaron stirs.

"Wake up. Come on, honey, wake up!" The belt comes off and she throws it behind her where it clangs against the metal waste bin. "Sweetie, come on." She cups her hands around his face and holds it up. She'd try to pull him out if she could. Instead, she climbs in beside him. He opens his eyes and immediately starts to cry.

"It's okay," she tugs on him so they're both lying lengthwise, his head on her chest.

He tries to say something but starts coughing and can't get it out, just alternates between coughing and choking. Nadine strokes his back, shushes him. She's scrunched and uncomfortable. Soon her muscles cramp and pinch and she welcomes the pain.

THERE'S A CRACK IN THE CORNER of the window. It's not a small crack, either. The tiniest of gaps is visible in the pane, and Nadine runs her finger over it, feeling the sharp edge. Hospitals shouldn't have broken windows.

The door opens and two people in scrubs enter carrying coffees and takeout breakfast in paper bags. They sit in the opposite corner of what was once a cafeteria but is now just a room with tables and chairs. The section where the kitchen would be is shuttered and locked, the food display cases empty.

Aaron begged her not to bring him here. She didn't want to, either; she wanted to curl up with him in his bed while he slept, but he wouldn't stop swallowing and holding his throat. She brought him a glass of water, but it was too painful to drink. It was then he allowed her to bundle him up in the quilt from the couch, put him in the back seat of the car and drive forty-eight kilometres to Laurette, the nearest town with twenty-four-hour emergency care.

The doctor told her it was only some bruising and swelling and he would be fine in a couple of days. But they wanted him to stay there until the afternoon when the psychologist would arrive. Aaron is asleep, with the help of a mild sedative. When he wakes, he'll piece everything together. He'll know that the hospital will notify Dr. Javid in Beauville, who's listed as his family doctor, and that Dr. Javid will notify Dr. Goertzen in Winnipeg. Aaron will not be fine at all.

Part 1

Part 1

AT THE HARVEST GOLD INN and Restaurant off Highway 53, Trish carries two plates of the Salisbury steak special to the corner table when she spots him. He's in his horse and cowboy pyjamas with his winter jacket unbuttoned. Bare feet stuffed into his runners, dirty laces trailing behind. He stands by the desk at the entrance, in front of the stairs that lead up to the hotel rooms on the second floor. His hands hang limply at his sides. Who knows how long he's been there. And he's just watching her. Her stomach pulls on her insides. She sets the plates down and quickly walks up to him.

"Jase, you've got to stop coming here. It's late and you've got school tomorrow."

"I had a bad dream."

"Does Dad know you're here?"

The boy shakes his head.

"Jesus Christ," she says to herself.

"Go take a seat and I'll bring you a glass of milk." She watches her son amble to a booth and climb in, then reaches for the phone behind the desk and dials. "Sean. He's here again." She hangs up before anything else can be said.

She imagines her son leaving the house, closing the front door behind him. Sees him on the sidewalks, the sky already dark and the streetlights flickering. Wrinkled pyjamas, bed-head, all by himself. It kills her. He's not small for his seven years, and he's not struggling in school, but there's something about him that's so frail. Weak. Trish has no idea what to do about it.

In the kitchen she pours a glass of milk. "How's it going back there, Reggie?" she asks the cook.

Reggie doesn't answer, which means all is good. He'd only answer if something was wrong. He's been the evening cook here forever. No one knows how old he is but he's long past retirement age. He often disappears for chunks of his shift when it's slow and leaves early every day even when it's not. No one complains because he still works for minimum wage and doesn't get the tips the waitresses do. It's an unspoken agreement between them all. Trish half expects that he'll die back there by himself. The others would only notice when their orders weren't sitting on the counter waiting for them.

Lenore enters the kitchen and looks out the pass-through window at Jase, hunched over and resting his head in his folded arms. "Another nightmare?"

"Third one this month."

"I know I've said this before, but why don't you ask to go back on day shifts? You could be home in the evenings."

But Trish likes the quiet of the house during the days when Jase is at school and Sean is at work. Those are the only moments that keep her going. "It's better when we work opposite shifts. There's more coverage for Jase when he's at home and we don't have to pay a babysitter." Trish puts the milk back in the fridge and heads back out to her son.

"Jase, honey." Trish nudges his arm a little. "You sleeping?"

"No." He sits up but there's telltale drool on the side of his mouth.

"Are you hungry?" She sits across from him.

"No. Dad made hot dogs."

"Your favourite again, hey?"

Jase nods.

"He didn't give you too much pop, did he?"

"Only this much." He indicates about an inch with his fingers. Trish watches him for a moment, waiting, and sure enough a smile erupts.

Sean, always trying to be the friend instead of the father. "That's why you're having trouble sleeping at night."

Jase's smile disappears and he picks up his milk and gulps it all down. Clunks the glass on the table and looks around the place as if for the first time. After a moment, he slumps back in his seat, his mood changed. He's quiet. Sullen, almost. "Mom, are you going to die?"

The question stops her. Sometimes, more than feeling her son is too easily breakable, she feels he's a complete stranger. This person in her life who arrived so fast and unexpectedly. Like he came before she had a chance to think about it. But that's not really true because they did talk about it. Or, rather, Sean talked and Trish listened, believing that his dreams must be hers too.

"Everyone dies, Jase." She never wants to sugar-coat things like Sean does, but she also knows it sounds harsh.

"That's why I can't sleep at night."

"Because you think of me and Dad dying?"

Jase shakes his head. "Just you."

She takes a quiet breath. "I'm not going to die for a long time. Not until you're all grown up." And you stop needing me like this, she wants to say, but the thought makes her feel bad. These moments are the most difficult ones. The ones that gnaw at her gut. That tell her she should be doing things differently. But no matter how much or how hard she thinks about it, the answer eludes her. "Look, there's your dad." She sits up, relieved at the interruption.

Sean, in his ratty old sweatpants and his jean jacket that's far too light for the weather. The elastic hems of his sweats are shot and they drag on the carpet. He's a tall man, but petite. In the beginning, she liked that about him. She liked that she could cup his ass cheeks in the palms of her hands like they were scoops of ice cream.

Sean walks toward their table wearing that shit-ass grin of his. "Hey little buddy, you can't leave like that. That shit's not cool, you know? You scare me when you disappear." He sits beside his son.

"Sorry." Jase leans into his father when Sean puts his arm around him and kisses the top of his head. They could almost be twins, right down to the cowlicks near their left temples. Aside from age and size, the only real difference is the shade of their hair. Sean's is the same glistening black as his Chinese mother's, and Jase's is a vague brown, watered down by Trish's genes.

"I waited with him until he fell asleep," Sean says to her. "I didn't hear him get up." He's apologetic.

The three of them sit there in silence. A few tables down, two truckers finish their meals. Knives and forks screech across the plates as the last of the mashed potatoes and peas are scraped up.

LENORE FLUSHES THE TOILET and tucks her blouse into her dress pants. White shirt, black pants, five days a week, sometimes even six or seven, for a number of years she doesn't care to think about. Of course, the styles have changed, and at points along the way she got into the habit of skirts, but now she finds hose too uncomfortable and there's no way she could go bare-legged anymore. Customers wouldn't appreciate the sight of that with their meals.

Lenore pulls out her small, shiny cigarette case from her purse balanced on the back of the toilet. Lights up. Some would think it's silly she smokes in the staff washroom, but out in the restaurant someone always wants something. Even on her breaks others will interrupt, or worse, they'll join her and start in on a mindless conversation. She's better off locked away and alone.

She never used to be like this, hiding away. When she was in her twenties she was always around people. Parties, concerts in the city, camping trips, rodeos, powwows. But after Daniel things were different, and she started making excuses to stay home. Then seven years ago on her fortieth, she bought her own two-bedroom bungalow on Tallis Street behind the Anglican church. She never thought she'd be able to buy her own place but she did, and in the years since, she's been spending more and more time alone. And not minding it. Not usually, anyway.

Lenore watches herself in the mirror as she smokes. Her lips pucker around the filter as she takes a drag, creases more and more evident. She knows she's aging more quickly because she's a smoker. Her skin's even going the colour of ash, but at least she makes an effort. Trish doesn't put on any makeup, and sometimes she doesn't wash her hair for days so it's greasy and stringy. Lenore's surprised no one's complained. But Trish does have a lot going on at home. What would it be like if Lenore had a son herself? Her gut aches but she allows herself to think about it. What would his name be? Carl, or Troy. Steven, maybe. But she doesn't really like any of those names; they're what other people would pick.

She studies the skin on her neck. Pushes it up and back. When he'd be all grown up, would Carl come over for dinner on the weekends? And bring a girlfriend? Would his father still be in the picture? Lenore could have married. In fact, after Daniel, she'd had two proposals, in her mid-thirties no less. Kenneth Coulthart and Stanley Rooke. At the time, Lenore had no real reason to say no except for a feeling in her gut that she couldn't explain. Now, years later, she wonders if that feeling was really fear. Fear that it would never be as good as it was with Daniel—or, as good as it was with Daniel at the beginning. But then if she had married, she could have easily ended up like Trish with Sean. It's hard to make that comparison, though, because there's hardly any similarity between herself and Trish. Trish, so quiet and detached. Keeps everything so tightly wound up inside.

Lenore shrugs off her thoughts and grabs her purse. She teases and spritzes her bangs. Then she turns the tap on and sticks her cigarette underneath, enjoys the quick sizzle as it's snuffed out.

—

HIDDEN FROM VIEW by the rickety *Saltus Welcomes You* sign, Roger scans the highway traffic. He's perched in his patrol car at the bottom of the dirt road that forks off from Highway 53 and rises up the hill to the cemetery behind him. The hills at his back ascend sharply, like they're bearing down on him. Across the highway in front of him, the town stretches out until the hills on the other side hem it in, trapping it.

Saltus. A beat-up old place. It's been a long, slow death. Mostly due to machinery. Used to take an entire family to farm a quarter section, now it takes one person with a lot of metal to farm thousands. When Roger was first stationed here in the sixties, the town's demise was already in progress. He was thirty-three then and thought he'd be long gone by now and wouldn't see its final end. But sometimes dying takes a long time. And sometimes life takes you places you never thought of, or it doesn't take you any place at all.

Roger looks at the string of houses that curve around the edge of town closest to him, the highway cutting between. It snakes through them and then rises, continuing beyond the valley, flat and straight, heading for other towns, other cities. Places Roger's never been.

It's his last night patrolling. A few days of office work and then he's done. Just like that. Thirty-six years of service and now nothing but empty days ahead of him. He reaches for his Thermos of coffee resting in the passenger seat. A sadness in his belly. He twists off the lid and pours a steamy cup. Occasionally, a set of headlights or tail lights streaks past. It's almost nine already. Nights are getting shorter, and longer days usually lift his spirits but he's still waiting. Roger turns the volume up on his walkie and glances at his pager. No messages.

Then, at the top of the hill, a car begins its descent. It's already moving visibly faster than the limit and if the driver doesn't correct its speed, it will keep accelerating as it approaches town. Roger cracks his door open and pours out his coffee. He's still in the game for now.

—

"IS THAT IT?" Aaron looks down into the valley. The open map in his lap crumples as he leans forward. During the entire eight-hour trip, the map has been spread out over his legs. As they passed each town, he'd cross it off with a pencil. A string of *X*s trails down the paper, forming a soft, backwards *L*.

The car begins to enter the valley. A bowl of blue light before them, streetlights sparkling here and there. Nadine's skin tingles. She never expected something so stunning on the prairies. A strange kind of anomaly. Side two of *Copperhead Road* ends and the cassette pops out of the player, startling them both. They ignore it and drive in silence. There's nothing but the hum of the engine as they finish their descent and the car straightens out on the flat basin floor.

"Mom."

"What?"

"Mom!"

But she's already slowing the car. Aaron shifts to accommodate the quick change in pace. Nadine glances in the rear-view and sees the flashing lights.

"Fuck," she says. "We're just going to get a ticket, that's all." She pulls the car to the shoulder and rolls down her window. The cold air gusts in and the map flaps in Aaron's lap. He starts to fold it up but he can't get the creases in the right order and gives up. He watches the car behind them. It's parked now too, lights still flashing, but the officer hasn't stepped out. In between the blasts of the outside air, the heat from the vents wafts over them.

"What's taking him so long?"

"It always takes forever. In addition to fining you, they also try to teach you a lesson. Fuckers."

"Mom," he pleads.

"I'll be nice," she says, flaunting a smile.

"I'm serious!"

"Relax, even if we are a little late I'm sure he'll understand." The car clock says 8:52 p.m.

"You said you'd call between eight and eight thirty." Aaron's voice is tight.

"Nine," she lies.

"Even so, he's just not going to reschedule." He slaps a hand on the dash.

"He's coming now," she says, shushing him.

The officer asks for her licence and calls her *miss*.

"Do you know how fast you were going?"

"It's Steve Earle's fault," she says, tapping on the tape deck.

"It was twenty-five over the limit."

She shrugs her shoulders—there's nothing she can do about it now.

"In a hurry to get somewhere?"

"No, just been a long day of driving."

Beside her, Aaron tucks his hair behind his ears, which is long enough now he doesn't need pins. He smooths it into soft curves, again and again.

The officer examines Nadine's licence. "You coming from home?"

She nods.

"Beauville, Manitoba?"

"That's what it says."

The officer stares at her. "Ma'am."

He's already changed from *miss*. "Yes, officer?"

"I'm just asking a few questions here. Do we have a problem?"

"No, we don't. Well, I do—I'm getting a bloody ticket I can't pay for. But I think you're good."

"Ma'am."

Aaron tenses beside her.

"I'm just cranky," she says. "It's been a real long day."

"Where you headed?"

"Calgary. But we were just talking about stopping for the night."

"What's waiting for you in Calgary?"

"Doctor's appointment." She taps Aaron's leg.

The officer leans over and looks in the vehicle with his flashlight. He runs the light over Aaron. Up and down. An equation he can't solve. "You all right, kid?"

"We just need to get some dinner in us and rest tonight," Nadine says.

"I'll be back." The officer returns to his patrol car.

"Why'd you say Calgary?" Aaron asks.

"If I said Saltus, he'd ask why we were here. Seemed better to say we're passing through." She pauses. "You do look pale."

He picks up her purse and digs through it. "Do you have the phone number?"

"I think so."

"You think so?" Panic rises in his voice. "What did you do with the paper I wrote it down on?"

"He's listed, Aaron."

But he doesn't stop rifling.

"Try the side zipper."

Aaron finds it. While Nadine waits for the officer to return, he cups the slip of paper between his palms, interlocks his fingers into a knot.

—

AL HANGS UPS THE PHONE. He puts the lid on the shoebox. Snaps a large elastic band around it to keep it shut. The shoebox as a container at first seemed odd. Wrong, even. But it's the perfect size. The tools he placed inside jangle, metal clinking against metal. He tugs on his baseball cap and tucks the shoebox under his arm. He heads out to his truck and climbs behind the wheel and repeats the room number in his head: 203, 203...

He feels a sense of something deep in his gut. Not excitement. Purpose, maybe. He used to feel it all the time when he still had the farm. Before he sectioned it off and sold it, along with the cattle and the poultry. Before the high blood pressure, the arthritis in his hands and arms, and all the medication. He's kept a few acres to himself, a hobby in retirement, but it's not the same. A hobby farm doesn't mean anything; he doesn't have to get up in the morning if he doesn't want to.

The sun has long since dipped below the horizon. It's a short drive from his farm to the town in the valley. Aaron's voice on the phone was soft but certain. During these past few months of letters and phone calls between them, Al is finally going to see what this kid looks like in person. It's silly to hope for some kind of resemblance; they're not related in any way. Still, Al wonders.

In town, the streets are filled with dirty slush, spring forcing itself in but winter not quite ready to leave. He crosses Main Street, empty, and turns west toward the Harvest Gold. The whole way, that feeling never goes away. That feeling he had in the early mornings when there were animals to feed, fences to repair, spraying or seeding to do. When he would be exhausted at the end of the day, and barely able to make dinner and get it down before collapsing into sleep. That feeling that kept him going his whole life.

The Harvest Gold is shabby, always was. Even the new wallpaper and antique-looking decorations can't disguise it. The tabletops still display the carved names of depressed teens. Each vinyl seat is cracked open, their foamy, tobacco-stained insides bulging out. Al walks past the restaurant and up the stairs. Takes a final moment before knocking on the door.

Aaron's mother answers. A mass of angry hair crowds her face. She's lost weight, at least from what he remembers. Her cheeks look sunken, like she's so thin she's hollow. Nadine doesn't say anything, just turns around, walks back into the room. Al follows, closes the door lightly behind him. The room is dim. The heavy drapes pulled shut, a single lamp on the night-stand sheds the only light. Beside the lamp, a large bottle of Coke, unopened and covered in water beads. Then Al sees him.

Aaron sits in an armchair near the far wall, holding a packet of ice wrapped in a towel between his legs, as Al had instructed. He's got a T-shirt on but nothing else, and he's all bones and sharp points like a grasshopper. It's hard to see his face in the dim light but he doesn't look fifteen. His left heel jackhammers the floor.

Al has to break the silence. "You doing okay?"

The boy nods. "I'm ready, thank you," he says. The polite-ness is strange but Al appreciates it.

"That armchair won't work. I'll have to ask you to move to the bed."

Aaron doesn't hesitate and hobbles over to the end of the mattress, still holding the ice tight against himself.

"And we'll need some more light."

His mother flicks on both light switches and grabs the table lamp, sets it on the armchair and drags it to the bed. The silence between mother and son sets Al on edge. He thought they'd all talk a little beforehand, but they both seem to want to get this over with. And really, what would they talk about? This certainly isn't the time for him to lay out the idea he has, what he's been thinking about this whole time. It's probably ridiculous anyway.

Al kneels in front of Aaron and the boy spreads his legs. Removes the ice. Al looks at his genitals. Skin red, frozen. A flicker of doubt passes through him. He realizes only now that the animals lie on their side on the ground and he can't ask Aaron to do that. That would be wrong in a way he can't explain.

He'll have to come at this from a different angle. An angle he's never tried before.

Aaron's leg starts bouncing again.

"You can't move while I'm doing this," Al says, and looks up. Aaron stops. Al watches him a moment, sees his eyes. A pale green. The subtleness is startling. The shade is lighter than his, but something inside Al catches. He wants to ask the boy once again if this is what he wants. If this is really the answer to his problems, to crippling self-awareness and a life of second guesses. He wants to ask again if he's sure this will make him happier. Instead, he asks, "Did you eat?"

"A burger on the way in."

"He barely ate any of it," his mom says behind them.

"You'll need to eat well these next few days. Drink lots of water." Al pats Aaron's knee. He slides the elastic off the shoebox and stretches rubber gloves over his fat fingers. Reaches in for his knife.

—

"No." JASE PULLS AWAY from his dad's reach. Jase wishes his dad wasn't here at all but he knows that's mean.

"We have to go, little dude. We have to let your mom work." His dad tugs on his pyjama sleeve but Jase doesn't move. "You have to get some sleep."

"I don't want to go home." Jase leans back in his chair and folds his arms across his chest. He's wide awake and wouldn't be able to sleep anyway.

"If I take a longer break and sit with you for a while, will you go home with Dad and go straight to bed?" his mom asks.

Jase wants to wait until she's done work and go back home with her, but he nods anyway.

"You sure?" his dad asks his mom. "We should get outta your hair."

"It's okay."

"You got any decaf brewing back there?"

His mom goes to get some and comes back with some paper and a jar of crayons too. Drawing is his favourite thing. There aren't as many crayon colours at the restaurant as he has at home. Many of them are broken too, and don't even have the paper labels on them to tell him what the name of the colour is. But he can always figure out something to draw with them. He grabs a goldy-brown crayon and scratches away at the bottom of a piece of paper. A sandy beach. He can't wait for the summer, when school's over.

"Little bugger's not gonna quit, is he? How many times is this now?" His dad dumps some sugar in his cup, not even measuring. "I've been trying everything you've said," he says, slurping up some coffee.

Jase reaches for the blue crayon to colour the water even though the beaches around town are green and slimy.

"I've been reading until he's asleep," his dad goes on, "and giving him a glass of warm milk a half hour before bed, no sugar after six—"

"Except that pop he had tonight."

His dad looks at him, and Jase tries to keep focused on his drawing, pretending not to hear.

"You ratted me out?" his dad asks, poking him in the ribs.

Jase can't keep a straight face anymore and he laughs.

"You crossed your heart and hoped to die and everything."

"Sorry, Dad." He mostly is too. He doesn't know why he'd rather lie to his dad than his mom.

"It was just tonight, I swear," his dad says, turning back to his mom. "Pop's all gone now and I'm not buying any more. I'm cracking down on this little turd." He ruffles Jase's hair.

"Jesus, Sean," his mom says.

"I am, Trish." His dad's silent a moment, and then his voice goes quiet. "I will."

Jase wishes he could understand what's going on between his mom and dad. He doesn't, though, and it makes him feel bad. He decides he'll draw himself playing in the water with a beach ball, and his mom lying on a towel on the sand, reading.

—

AL'S TRUCK RUMBLES up the hill as he leaves the valley. The shoebox of tools slides across the bench seat as the road curves. He can't believe it's over. He was in and out of the room faster than it takes to drink a coffee. He thought there'd be so much more to it.

He takes the long way home, following the grid roads that zigzag west and south, west and south. They lead him past the old Nielsen farm, and he stops there for a moment. The house off in the distance a shadowy mass. He wonders where Raymond is now. Where he is in the world. Near or far. That summer was so long ago, ancient times, really, but it still sits inside of Al. Long after he dies, someone could dig up his body and find traces of the summer of 1944 etched in his bones.

When he pulls into the driveway at home, the thought of entering an empty house doesn't appeal to him. He lingers in the truck awhile, just sitting there.

The boy didn't squirm at all, though Al could tell he was in pain. He saw sweat forming on the boy's forehead so handed him a towel from the small pile that he had stacked beside him on the floor. The boy's arms and legs started to shake too. His mom got on the bed behind him and he leaned back into her, his arms falling limp at his sides. She squeezed him tight and didn't look when it was happening. Al was calm through it all until it came time for the stitches. Just before he threaded the needle, he saw Aaron staring at the translucent ovals on the floor. Al quickly dropped another face cloth over them but there was a look on the boy's face, an intensity that unnerved Al. It took him a few tries before he had the needle prepared.

When it was all over, Al didn't want to go. They had been through something big, something important; only it wasn't over yet, it was just beginning. After this, things would be under way for Aaron and the doctors would have to listen. They'd finally have to do something.

Al wanted to stay and present his offer. That was his plan. He was going to tell them what he's been thinking over the last few weeks while preparing for this night. But he picked up his things, including the face cloth and what was inside, gave the boy some aftercare advice that he thought would apply and closed the door behind him.

If he regrets anything, it's what he did next with that face cloth. He should've taken it back to his farm and buried it. That would've been the right thing to do, it would've been respectful. But the whole time he'd been making plans, he didn't think about this detail. He's ashamed he didn't. Instead, he drove around to the back of the hotel and deposited it in the metal trash bin. He'll have to live with that now.

He wonders what's happening in room 203 at this very moment. If they're asleep, what time they'll leave tomorrow, and whether he'll receive any more letters. Or maybe, after months of almost weekly correspondence there'll be nothing but silence. Maybe it's not too late to tell them his idea. Maybe he'll ring their room in the morning. He turns the ignition off but before he even removes the key, he starts it back up again. The tires spit up some gravel as the truck backs out a little too quickly and heads back to town.

—

LENORE BALANCES THE TRAY on her hip and knocks on the door of room 203.

Trish had checked them in earlier and though she was in the kitchen when their orders were ready, she handed them to Lenore. It's not like Trish can't handle the assholes and the weirdos, but Lenore is better at it. Maybe because she enjoys it.

"There's a kid, though," Trish said, cautioning Lenore. "A kid and his mom."

"What'd they do?"

"She was just rude as hell and..." Trish searched for the words. "Intense. Something was off and it kind of creeped me out."

There's murmuring behind the door. Lenore glances down the hallway. All the other rooms are empty. It's been slow lately. Slower every year she's been here. It was busiest in the mid-sixties when she first started. They used to book up full regularly, and back then the walls were a deep green. Six years ago, when the place was bought by a couple from the city who wanted a quieter life, everything was painted gold to spruce things up. A branding attempt to brighten the dull and drab feeling of the place. But the new colour didn't do the trick. Mostly because the painters didn't use a primer before they slopped it on and everything looks tarry now. When the sunlight slants in from the window at the end of the hall, you can see the paint rippling up from the surface where stray bristles from the brushes are curled and embedded in the paint. And the owners never did move to town. They hired a manager instead; no one's ever actually met them.

Lenore knocks again, the plates of Salisbury steak growing heavy in her arms.

"I'm coming." The woman opens the door, her hair fiery. Her temper is too. She grabs the tray from Lenore and carries it to the desk in the room. Lifts off the lids.

"Is there anything else I can get you?" Lenore waits. Sees the end of the bed and a pair of feet under the covers.

"This isn't what we ordered," the woman says, her voice clipped.

"Two Salisbury steak specials?"

"We asked for salads, not mashed potatoes."

"That wasn't on the order," Lenore says, not apologizing.

"I don't know why it wasn't because that's exactly what I said on the phone. How can you mix that up?" The woman's body is rigid, jaw clenched, like she's ready to box.

"I can eat the mashed potatoes." It's a boy's voice, from the bed.

"No, you need a salad. And drink up that water. All of it."

When she was younger, Lenore would put up with customers like this. She'd just take everything given to her. Then she'd spend the next few hours thinking about all the smart, stinging barbs she could have said in return. But with almost thirty years behind her, a sense of security has developed—she's outlasted five owners and eight managers, and she's lost track of how many co-workers. Lenore's outgrown the proper thing to do—remain polite and calm and provide the customer what they want. Instead, it's become a kind of game to her. She likes that little shot of adrenalin that shoots through her chest and arms at the threat of conflict.

Lenore puts on her faux-friendly voice. "I can take those back and get you the steaks with salads. Do you still want the carrots and peas?" Lenore steps into the room to take the plates.

"No." The woman puts her arm out to stop Lenore. "Leave them there. How long will the salads take?"

"A few minutes."

"Fine."

"Caesar or house?"

"House."

"Thousand Island, oil and vinegar, or ranch?"

"I don't care, just put it on the side."

Lenore sees the frustration in her pinched eyes and understands that there are other things in this woman's life that are pissing her off. But that's no reason to treat anyone else like shit. She leaves the room, shuts the door behind her and looks at her watch, marking the time. She'll bring the salads up in ten. Maybe fifteen.

—

SEAN DOWNS THE LAST of his coffee, swirling the final mouthful around his cheeks and teeth before swallowing. His habit for as long as Trish has known him. She notices his eyes, rings around each one. Faint, but there. Jase's need for her is hard on him too.

"You going to sleep on the couch again tonight?" Sean asks without making eye contact. He hasn't asked her about it all day. She hoped they'd ignore it like everything else but maybe things are piling up too high now.

"I couldn't wind down from the shift last night so I stayed up and watched TV. Stayed up too late, I guess. Don't even remember falling asleep."

Sean nods but still looks bothered.

Jase clutches a big green marker, twisting it in his hands as he eyes her and Sean, wary. A bug with long feelers, always attuned to any kind of tension.

"So, things are okay then?" Sean waits for her to respond.

She nods.

"It's not happening again?"

Trish is shocked that he's bringing it up in front of Jase but she doesn't show it. Doesn't even answer.

"Maybe we should talk this weekend?"

"Okay." But Trish has no idea what she'll say.

"Come on, Son, let's go." Sean taps him on the shoulder, but Jase continues to sit there. "Jase." The boy shakes his head roughly, his whole body swaying with the motion. Sean rises to grab Jase's coat, but when he reaches out to pick up his son, Jase launches out of the booth and bolts toward Trish. Suctions his body to hers.

There's a silent moment. Trish feels the heat from her son's skin through his cotton pyjamas. Smells it.

"Remember what we agreed on? I have to go back to work now, but I'll see you tomorrow before you leave for school."

He doesn't budge.

"Come on now, go with Dad."

Sean steps closer and holds out his hand. Jase twists away from him and wraps his arms around Trish's neck. A snake coiling around a tree. Trish pulls at his arms to loosen the grip. It alarms her, this unrestrained display of need.

"Let go, please."

"No," he shouts.

She stands up, hoping he'll slide off, but instead, he comes with her, his legs pinching her hips. She smiles for the benefit of the few customers who've turned to watch.

"Enough, Jase." Sean grabs him under the arms and pulls him off.

"I'm not going, I'm not going," he says, his voice fast and panicked. As he's separated from Trish, his legs and arms flail.

42

"No!" he screeches, and the sound startles Sean, who places him on the floor. As soon as he's free, Jase gravitates back to Trish.

Sean huffs. "Can you take a few minutes to drive him back home? Put him back into bed?"

"I can't just ditch Lenore." Though she knows Lenore wouldn't mind.

Sean looks like he might crack. "I don't know what to do here, Trish. I really don't."

"He can stay here. I'll bring him home when my shift is done."

"He has school in the morning."

"I know."

"And I work tomorrow so I can't watch him if he needs to come home again."

"I will."

Sean watches her, weighing the options. He's hurt. "Isn't he gonna get in the way?"

"I'll be fine. You go get some sleep."

He's reluctant and stands there for a moment. "What's happening here, Trish?"

Jase leans into her, his head down and pressed against her stomach, each vertebra on his neck visible and sharp, like they could cut.

Across the room, Roger enters and takes a seat at his usual corner table, hiking up his pants before sliding into his chair. Then, as is his habit, he moves the coffee cup to the other side of his placemat and pulls the salt and pepper closer. Everything's always the same.

—

NADINE FLICKS THE CHANNELS all the way from two to sixteen, then starts again.

"There must be something," Aaron says. He folds his pillow to prop his head up higher.

"Nothing but shit." She passes him the remote and moves to the window, pushes the heavy drapes open a crack. Town's dead and she can't decide whether the quiet is a relief or not. Then movement to the right catches her eye. Maybe a cat or a dog crossing the street. But when she turns her head, nothing's there. It pisses her off.

Everything pisses her off. Al pissed her off tonight when he wouldn't take her money. She handed over two hundred bucks in cash and he just pushed the money right back at her like it wasn't good enough. Like they were to be pitied or something. Nobody does anything for free in this world, she knows that much. If they do, it's only because they want something in return. Nice people use their niceness to build up guilt in you so you feel obligated to do things for them down the road. It's all manipulation. But at least she can afford that goddamn speeding ticket now.

Aaron's plate on the nightstand is still full. "You haven't eaten anything."

"I had some mashed potatoes." He's landed on *Northern Exposure.*

The whole thing is over and now he's just lying there in bed like it's a sick day from school. She scoops up some of the potatoes from Aaron's plate and eats them. Even though she

44

ploughed though everything that was on hers, she couldn't stop. She cuts off a piece of steak from her son's plate and puts it in her mouth. Then another. But there's no fucking way she can still be hungry, and she can't eat her son's meal.

"Here." She puts the plate down beside Aaron on the bed and sits. He winces when the bed moves and her own stomach flips. "You okay?"

"I'm fine. Not hungry, though."

"One piece of meat, that's all." Nadine slices it up into pieces and stabs a chunk with a fork. She holds it up to Aaron's mouth, but he won't open it. "Just one bite." She's feeding him like a fucking baby.

He shakes his head, but she won't back down. He finally opens his mouth and she puts it in. She throws the fork on the plate and rises, a surge of anger flaring.

"Mom?" he says, voice muffled with the meat still in his mouth.

She locks herself in the bathroom, balances on the edge of the bathtub and waits for the plug in her chest to loosen. It was the right thing to do. It was. Even when Aaron was a tiny guy, he was different. It wasn't because he was more interested in dolls than dump trucks, or because he'd beg her to put gloss on his lips and shadow on his eyes when she was getting ready to go out. Or the way he'd swish his hips to Madonna's videos while standing on the couch. He was different in a way that she couldn't explain to anyone back then, and still can't.

It was under his skin. It pulsed through him in every spot she touched. His toes, the whorl of his ears, the tender crook of his elbows. Quiet and loud at the same time. A kind of energy,

45

one that hummed at a different frequency. It was beautiful and powerful and full of pain. A scream inches its way up her throat. She wants to pound on something—kick the tub, the walls, break the mirror. She grits her teeth and cranks the bathtub taps on instead. She can't let Aaron hear her sobbing like an idiot.

These last few weeks, she'd only been focusing on how to get here, to Saltus, to this room. How to make this happen. She'd been running on autopilot and tonight was the only end goal. She'd only vaguely thought about what comes after. But there will be more to come. More doctors, more explaining.

If Aaron was normal, and she knows she shouldn't use those terms after all those fucking counselling sessions, but if he was normal, about this time in her life she would be thinking about pushing him to focus on his homework and to graduate. She'd even encourage him to find a part-time job while still in school to build that independence. If he didn't move out after high school, she'd charge him rent like any other adult. That's how she would have done it. That's where she could have been in her life.

The bathtub fills quickly, the water gushing out of the faucets. It's almost halfway up the sides, steam rising and fogging the room. She peels off her sweatshirt and jeans, yanks off her socks and sinks into the water. When her ass hits the bottom, she realizes her panties are still on. The loose cotton blossoms like a cloud around her, but she doesn't move. It's the warmest she's been in a while.

—

ROGER FEELS A PANG of guilt as he waits to be served. He already had dinner at home before his shift. Two fried-egg sandwiches with a small tub of coleslaw from the deli section at the grocery. They've teased him at the station that he's becoming obsessed with food, implying that he's losing control or something. But he's not. Yes, his belly has grown over the past few months, maybe it's been a year or so, but he's still in decent shape. There's still definition around his arm and leg muscles, and his face hasn't changed. He'd never let that happen, there's nothing worse than a fat face.

"Menu tonight?" Lenore brings him his glass of water and carries the coffee carafe. "Or is it today's special?" She points to the chalkboard above the kitchen window.

"Sure, special's good."

She leans her hip against the edge of his table, reaching past him to flip over his coffee cup and fill it, smiling as she does. She always flirts with him. She flirts with everyone, but he likes it just the same. When she was younger and the town was livelier, guys were always coming in to hit on her, but she was never his type back then. Loud, too much makeup, and she dressed provocatively. Maybe it was for the tips, but she also encouraged the attention. She's different now, though. Calmer. When she looks down to pour him some coffee, the skin on her neck crinkles like paper and he feels a little hopeful.

"So, only a few days left for you," she says. "Feeling good?"

"Suppose."

The bell that sits in the pass-through window dings and she starts to move off. "You should see what they've got planned

47

back there." She motions to the banquet room in the back. "Looks good."

The room's double doors are closed. It's usually only booked for weddings or birthdays, sometimes meetings or small conferences. It's a stark and narrow room, a stretch of windows along one wall, mottled navy and grey carpeting, and chairs with straight, stiff backs. Even with streamers and balloons it's not a festive room. It's fitting his retirement will be held there.

Across the restaurant, Sean walks away from his family and out the door. Why does it seem sadder when a young couple finds itself in trouble? Roger pours some sugar in his mug while watching Trish try to separate herself from her boy. Roger's adept at observing without being noticed. A quick glance here and there and the whole story unfolds. A skill that's sometimes hard to turn off. It can create a barrier between him and everyone else, but it's a hazard of his job he's learned to accept.

Logically, it should be sadder when an older couple finds itself in trouble. A couple that's been together for years and will have a harder time finding other partners. When you're young, you should be able to pick up the pieces more quickly and move on. That's how most people think. But when young people discover how painful love can be, it affects all their relationships that come after.

Kind of like Coda, that damn mini schnauzer his dad got him when he was ten. He loved that stupid thing, but when Roger was eighteen Coda signalled something was wrong—she wouldn't stop trying to go the bathroom, even in the house. Nothing ever came out, but she kept straining. Bowel cancer. She was trying to shit out the tumours. Roger had to put her down within a few days.

Months later Roger's parents suggested he get another dog, and at first it seemed like a good idea. He drove around and visited a few kennels. Even went to a pound across the border in Montana a few times to see what they had. But it didn't matter because just one look at any potential new dog and Roger knew what was in store for him at the end. You're blissfully unaware the first time around, and after that there's a permanent hard rock inside you that reminds you what's coming. He wonders if Trish is developing her own hard rock.

Of course, Roger only suspects the two situations are comparable. He's never lived with a woman. He dated one when he was in training at the depot and was going to ask her to move with him as soon as he knew where he was going to be posted, but it didn't last that long. He wishes now he had tried harder when he was younger. Wishes he wasn't such a chicken shit.

Lenore brings a set of utensils and his favourite hot sauce. She winks at him as she sets them down.

"Are you coming?" It trips out of him and she's confused. "To the retirement party." He points to the banquet room.

"Oh." She pauses. "I didn't know I was invited."

"Anyone can come." It's not true, invitations were sent out weeks ago.

"I may be working, I'll have to check. But hey, who am I going to bitch to now when the dinner rush is over?"

"I'll still come by."

"I won't tolerate anything less than three nights a week."

He laughs politely, and she reaches out and pats his shoulder.

"I could swing by your place and get you. For the party. It's no trouble." The mood shifts between them, and sweat breaks on his forehead when he sees her struggling to answer. "Unless you're working."

"I'm pretty sure I am. Sorry." She pats his shoulder again, but this time it's forced, and she quickly moves off to another table and stacks a load of dirty dishes in the crook of her arm. Rounds up several glasses with her free hand like it's a race.

Roger looks back at Trish to see if she witnessed his blunder but she's no longer there, just her son, who's focused on his drawing. He should be relieved no one saw what just happened, but it's not relief that flames up inside him.

—

"SORRY HON, BE RIGHT WITH YOU." Lenore bumps into Al, who's just arrived. A butter knife falls from her stack and grazes Al's foot, but even though her arms are piled, he doesn't bend down to pick it up for her. He continues on and takes a seat. Lenore leaves the knife where it is and keeps moving. She pushes through the kitchen's swinging doors where Trish is rolling clean cutlery into napkin tubes and Reggie's already prepping the counter in the back for the morning breakfast shift.

"Fuck." Lenore dumps the dirty dishes in the sink and starts running hot water over them for the dishwasher. "Roger aske me out."

"Really?"

"I lied and I think he could tell."

"Poor Roger." Trish sidles up to the pass-through and looks out. "He's a nice guy."

"I'm so used to assholes."

Trish continues to watch him. "I think he's leaving."

"What?"

"He's pulling on his jacket."

Lenore grabs one of the recently thawed pies and cuts a thick slice.

"A free slice of pie?"

"He likes pie."

"He might also like an honest answer."

Lenore shoves a fork onto the plate, accidentally stabbing the slice. "What would you know?" It comes out harsher than Lenore intended. She sees Trish glare at her as she uses her ass to push back through the door.

Roger's already passed the till by the time she gets there.

"Hey!" she calls out, but he's pushing out the door. She sets the pie down at his table with the intent of rushing after him, but her body locks up and freezes.

"Don't forget about those salads for 203," Trish says as she swishes past her, annoyed. Lenore looks at her watch. It's been over twenty minutes. "Shit," she whispers.

Upstairs in the hall, Lenore sees a slit of light under the door of room 203. She's waited too long and will have to eat some crow, but when she knocks, there's no answer.

"Room service." She knocks louder.

"Come in." The voice is muffled from the other side of the door.

"I'm sorry for the wait." She stops when she nears the bed and sees the kid Trish mentioned, lying on his back, head and shoulders propped up on pillows, and tucked under a mountain

51

of blankets. A teenager, not a kid, but there is something about him that's childlike. He watches her with droopy eyes.

"You okay?"

He nods.

The water's running in the bathroom and the door is shut. It's just the two of them.

She steps closer. His clammy, pale skin almost glows under the light of the bedside lamp.

"No offence but you look like shit, kiddo."

"I'm getting better."

"Well, you can't get worse."

He laughs. "Just a touch of the flu."

"Yeah?" she says, watching him a moment. "My dad always said the best cure for any bug is a garlic sandwich and a glass of bourbon."

"A garlic sandwich?"

"He'd slice up raw garlic cloves and put them on some buttered bread, then he'd down a glass of bourbon, and like you, he'd crawl under layers of blankets and sweat it out. You wouldn't believe the smell that'd come off him. The whole house would stink for days."

"Gross."

"It was rank."

"I'll skip the sandwich but try the bourbon."

"'Course you would, but your mom already hates me."

"She does."

Now Lenore laughs. She should set the tray down and offer him something. More water, a hot towel for his forehead, Aspirin.

But his mother is here with him and Lenore knows better. She's been accused of crossing boundaries before.

She looks down and sees the plate on the bed beside him. The meal has barely been touched.

"You eat anything yet?"

"I'm not hungry right now."

"How about I bring up some broth?" She can't help herself. "Or some ice cream if your throat is sore?"

The bathroom door opens. "What are you doing here?" the woman says, wearing a sweatsuit and a towel on her head.

Lenore holds out the salads to explain. The woman takes the trays from her and plunks them on the desk, then rushes Lenore toward the door.

"If there's anything else you need—" but the door's already closing behind her, there's nothing but a crack left open between the two women.

"No." The woman eyes Lenore, her face severe and sour. Lenore heads back down the hall, feels the woman watching the whole way. Just before she descends, the door shuts and locks.

Back in the restaurant, Lenore approaches the booth where Al took his seat.

"You're in late tonight. Kitchen might be closed already." But she sees he's finishing off the last few bites of a slice of blueberry pie. She looks back at Roger's table and the slice of pie she brought out for him is missing.

"He didn't come back for it," Al explains, then shovels a heaping forkful into his mouth. "Figured it didn't need to go to waste," he says through the food. He wipes his mouth with the back of his hand. Pushes the plate toward her. "The crust was soggy."

He always says it as he sees it, no bullshit. She kind of likes that about him.

"Given the kitchen is closed, is there anything else I can get you? Coffee?"

He nods.

She's always thought Al was attractive, even though he's much older. Tall, bulky, floppy hair. The only unfortunate thing about him is his skin. On a good day, it looks like he has a mild, rose-coloured rash dotting his nose and cheeks. Small bumps rising here and there. But on a bad day, like it is right now, it's inflamed and puffy. A scarlet blaze, spreading up his forehead, down his neck, angry and insistent.

—

"Hey," trish taps jase's elbow. "You promised you wouldn't fall asleep."

"I wasn't." He rubs his eyes, trying to wake up.

"If you're tired, I could call Dad. He'll pick you up and put you in your own bed."

"I'm not tired." He looks down at the picture he drew and hands it to her. It's torn in places where he pressed too hard but it's still intact. There's a boy playing in a lake.

"Is this you?" she asks.

He nods. "And that's you." He points to the woman sunbathing on the shore.

"Where's Dad?"

"At work," he says. "You can fold it up and keep it in your pocket when you're not at home."

He's been doing things like this lately, leaving constant reminders of himself behind. A lone running shoe in her car, one of his Ninja Turtles in her purse so she'll find it when she gets to work. Sometimes she wonders, if he didn't do these things, if he ignored her and ran off to play with his friends instead of thinking about her and following her around, if she would feel differently.

"Would you like some ice cream?"

"No thank you."

"Is it because I told you no sugar after dinner?" He doesn't answer. "Because if it is, I think we could make an exception this time. I wouldn't be mad."

He watches her. "Okay." He starts to pick up all the crayons and clear a space.

In the kitchen, Trish grabs the ice cream from the freezer as Reggie pulls on his jacket.

"Can you leave the door open when you go?" She likes to air out the kitchen at the end of the day. "Night," she says to him as he heads out. He doesn't respond.

At the counter, Trish drops a curl of vanilla into a dish. Lenore skirts up beside her with the chocolate sauce and squirts some on top, making a lopsided happy face. Trish hooks her hip and nudges Lenore off balance so a line of sauce trickles across the counter. Apology, and apology accepted. They've been working together so long they don't need to talk to have a conversation.

55

Lenore stands in the open doorway and lights up a cigarette. Outside, the sky is black but bright with stars.

Trish turns back around and notices Al through the pass-through, fixing his coffee. He's several feet away but even so his burgundy blotches are visible. "That rash of his... You think that's why he's so grouchy all the time?"

Lenore shrugs, exhaling her smoke high into the night air. "Al? He'd be a prick anyway."

"Lenore," Trish scolds, but also laughs.

"Besides, he's got more than one condition."

Trish gives her a curious look.

"Oh, come on. You didn't know he was gay?"

"Al's not gay."

"I'm not sure he knows it, either, but he is. I've known a few girls over the years who've tried to get with him but he turned them all down."

"Doesn't mean he's gay."

Lenore shrugs. "Doesn't matter if he is or isn't, anyway. Not in this town." She stares out into the night.

The damp air wafts in. That dirt and gravel smell coming up from under melting snow. A small spark tingles in Trish then quickly fades. She carries the bowl of ice cream out to Jase, but when she arrives, he's sound asleep again.

"Jase, you can't sleep here. Come on." She wakes him up. "Let's put you to bed somewhere." He follows her to the front desk, groggy and stumbling. Trish unlocks a desk drawer and pulls out a key to one of the empty hotel rooms. Leads him up the stairs to room 201.

In the room, she lets the light from the hall guide her to the nightstand so she can flick on the lamp. She folds down the bedspread for Jase to climb in and then moves back to the doorway.

"Don't go yet."

"I've gotta work. But look, it's almost midnight already. That means just over an hour to go. You can sleep here until I'm done."

"Please, Mom."

"Are you scared?"

He doesn't answer.

"You shouldn't be scared." She closes the door and walks to the bed. "You help me clean and tidy these rooms." On the weekends when Trish takes extra shifts, Jase sometimes ditches his friends and makes his way to the hotel. If it's around checkout time, he helps her strip the beds and dust the tables. Switch the dirty coffee cups for clean ones. If the manager's around he gives Jase a couple of loonies.

"Plus, I'm the only one with a key and I'll keep it right here." She drops it into the pocket of her shirt. "No one else can get in. If you need me, all you have to do is pick up the phone and dial nine."

He turns his head to look at the phone.

"Lenore might answer, but either way I'll come right up."

"Will you stay until I fall asleep like Dad does?"

Trish looks at the clock again. "For a few minutes." She pulls up a chair.

Jase rolls onto his side so he faces her.

"I can't read you anything because there's nothing here."

"That's okay."

"And you know I don't sing."

"I know." He continues to watch her. She fiddles with the tiny hole in her slacks above her right knee. It's slightly frayed and she pulls at the loose ends, making it worse. It's not long, however, before he falls asleep. She leaves the lamp on in case he wakes up. She slips out of the room, locking the door behind her. Voices from the room next door are audible in the hall. She listens at her son's door for a second before heading back downstairs.

Rounding the corner by the front desk, she hears rattling at the entrance. It's Al, trying to force open the door that Lenore's already locked up.

"Hold on." Trish grabs the master key from the desk drawer and lets him out. "Drive safe."

He grunts and steps out into the night, thick and inky.

—

It's after midnight. Roger passes under a streetlamp and uses the extra light to reach into the glovebox for his antacids. His stomach hasn't been well all evening. He doesn't know how he'll return to the Gold next week. He'd prefer never to go back again. The minty tablets crunch satisfyingly between his teeth.

He drives down Keepness Avenue toward the school to scan the fields. Sometimes the kids hang out on the bleachers, or along the stretch of hedges that separates the school from the highway. At least the younger ones do, the ones without cars of their own to drive out to the cemetery. But the fields look empty, and he's already been to the cemetery twice.

He backs the car away from the school, but as he turns the headlights catch something white moving inside the vertical orange tube on the jungle gym. Roger parks and gets out. As he walks closer, he hears shushing and the rustling of movement. He pulls the flashlight from his belt and shines it on the tube.

"It's Melnyk. Who's in there?" Probably some kids with a stolen stash from their parents' liquor cabinet. It's nothing new. No matter how much the town talks of it getting worse, it's not. It's just people only remember what they want to.

"Come on now, crawl outta there." He steps closer, shines his light through one of the tube's footholds.

Tucked inside is Mike Duick and Kyla Goesen, the strange-looking girl with the brittle brown hair. Her white bunny hug is what he saw glowing from a distance. But even though Roger recognizes them, he stands there a moment taking it in. Kyla's bundled up in her sweater and a coat, but naked from the waist down. Her feet and hands are all stuck into footholds, balanced in mid-air like she's doing the spider crawl. And there's Mike, pinned between her legs, his own pants pooling around his ankles. She's not even fourteen and he just got his licence this year. There's so much skin, and the smell of beer. A second passes, but a second is all it takes.

"Stare much?" Mike says, and squints when the flashlight's trained on him. "Or maybe you like the show?" Mike's hands are clutched firmly on Kyla's ass, and there's drunken defiance all over his face. Then he does a small thrust. Roger feels a pebble of anger in his gut. Mike does another, this time more pronounced.

"Jesus Christ!" It comes out louder than he wanted. "Get the hell out of there now." He reaches a hand through one of the holes but they're designed for kids and he can't get past his forearm.

Mike stops, cursing under his breath, and Kyla puts her feet back on the ground.

"Get dressed and get out of there." Roger steps away from the tube, turns his back to it. Mike's parents are only two streets over from Roger's. Kyla's live across town and run the bakery. Goddamn kids. If parents would just do their jobs. They're outraged when they find out their kids are having sex, but they let them watch TV night and day. All those music video shows that are nothing if not pornographic. If Roger had kids, he'd never allow that.

The teens emerge from the orange tube. Mike ambles up to the tetherball pole and leans against it, his baggy pants hanging low and his stained baseball cap askew. Kyla tugs her miniskirt down as far as it will go, which is hardly anywhere. It looks like a giant elastic band. The thick makeup around her eyes catches the light and sparkles. That's another thing Roger wouldn't allow. Letting his kids dress beyond their years. Anyone who didn't know Kyla would think she's at least eighteen.

Mike lights up a cigarette and breathes out a rope of smoke. "What now?" He's trying to be cool but his hands are shaking. Could almost feel sorry for him.

"Please don't tell my parents," Kyla says, the fear obvious in her voice.

"Relax, he's not going to. He can't." Mike turns to Roger, a smirk on his face.

"Some kinda punk, hey? Let's go then, I'm hauling your asses down to the station."

"No!" Kyla steps forward. "Please."

"Kyla calm the fuck down, we're not going anywhere. If he takes us to the station, we just tell them our version."

"Your version?"

"I saw you," Mike says. "I saw you watching. You're a fucking perv."

The burn in Roger's chest spikes. He holds his breath and while he waits for it to pass, the moment he had with Lenore earlier tonight floods back to him. And as if he's standing outside of himself, he sees himself the way Lenore must have seen him, and the way this kid is seeing him now. Old and pathetic. Roger turns and heads back to his car.

"Told you," Mike says as Roger walks away.

In the car, Roger looks up at the streetlamp on the corner, shining brightly. A few insects that have already shuffled off the winter are snapping around it. Roger was never like this before. He's been flapping and snapping himself. Going nowhere for far too long.

—

EARLIER, NADINE INSISTED SHE'D SLEEP in the chair so Aaron could have the bed to himself. But once he fell asleep, she slipped in beside him. Now she can't sleep herself. She drifts now and then but each time she's shot back to consciousness by a tremor in her chest. She rolls on her side to face the wall, curling into a knot. Her hair, still damp from the bath, trails across the pillow like soggy snakes.

Does he feel any different right now? Is his body already changing? What will be the first sign of change that she sees? It will take weeks for his body to be free of testosterone, but maybe it's already transforming.

In grade three, Nadine and her classmates were encouraged to catch their own caterpillars and keep them in jars. They even went out one afternoon to hunt for them. Some of the students, Nadine included, were lucky enough to find some already in their cocoon stage. Nadine's was tucked into the deep groove of a tree's thick bark. The bark was loose and Nadine carefully peeled it off like a scab and placed it in the glass container. She screwed on the lid that she'd already poked holes in and sat and stared at it while the others continued their search. She carried the jar to and from school and on errands with her mother so she wouldn't miss a thing. But something went wrong because it never changed. It stayed looking like a rolled-up cotton ball for weeks and weeks until her parents threw it out.

Later, in a high school science class, they studied this process. She learned that moths and butterflies actually melt inside their protective casing. They release an enzyme that causes them to digest themselves, liquefying into a soupy ooze. An ooze that then reconstitutes itself into legs, antennae, eyes. The process requires an incredible amount of energy so that when the butterfly finally does emerge, it's about half the weight it was before. The process is complicated and intricate so it's easy to imagine things could go wrong. The cocoon she had as a child probably partially melted. Maybe both caterpillar and butterfly parts were suspended in its own fluid, helpless.

Nadine shivers. The warmth from the bath has left her already, and she's cold under the blankets. Especially her feet, even with her socks on. She pushes them up against Aaron to share some heat and feels a dampness.

—

TRISH HAS MADE CHOICES that have kept her here. If she'd made other choices, maybe she would be wearing a slinky dress in a bar in Texas right now. Right this very moment. Or even Tokyo. Or maybe she'd be in a shiny glass condo somewhere in Toronto with business suits in the closet. Or in a small cottage on the coast where she'd live with a dog and a boyfriend who hikes the mountain trails almost every day. Maybe those women could have been her. She'll never know and it doesn't really matter but the possibility still pricks at her.

"Why'd you stay here? In this town, I mean." Trish sits at a table, counting the money from the till, sorting it and filling in the tally sheet.

Lenore sprays a table nearby, pushes the rag in circles over it. She's pulled back into the moment from her own haze of thoughts. "I don't know. It's home."

"Did you ever think of leaving?"

"'Course. Still do. But those're just fantasies, thoughts drifting in my head. I think about the city. I think about the coast since so many seem to head out there." She pauses. "But you know how some things don't seem meant for you?" She doesn't stop wiping to turn and see if Trish really does.

They both continue at their tasks for a while.

"You and Sean ever think of leaving? Even just going to Regina?"

"Sean talks of it all the time but it's mostly pie in the sky. Like everything else with him."

"Why do you say that? He's a hard-working, committed guy. He's got a steady job at the garage. He's more interested in being a dad than most men."

Trish bundles up the cash into envelopes, as if she didn't hear. A few moments pass, then she looks up at Lenore. "How would we ever get to the city or wherever, anyway? Whatever little scraps we manage to save get sucked right up again by the house or Jase's dental bills. It's endless." She puts the envelopes in the cash box along with the tally sheets. "Sean's talked about going ahead first. He's more likely to find work quickly than I am. And he could get room and board for the first while until he can save up a little. Then we'd follow."

"So maybe not so pie in the sky?"

She shrugs. "We can't think about moving right now anyway."

Lenore waits for her to continue but she doesn't. "You guys working through some things?"

"You wouldn't understand."

"Try me."

Trish closes the lid of the metal cash box, but a little too hard. "You've been single your whole life, Lenore."

"So?"

"You've never lived with anyone and you have no kids."

"Again, so?"

"Do you ever wonder why?"

"All the fucking time."

Trish shakes her head. "Forget it."

"No, let's talk about this. I may not have been married or had kids of my own, but that only allows me to see what you're pissing away. A good man, a good son. And Jesus Christ, Trish, that poor boy. The hurt is dripping off him he needs you so bad and everyone can see it but you."

But Trish does see it, feels it too. Right under her own skin and she'd tear it out if she could. She picks up the cash box and heads back to the manager's office.

—

JASE HEARS VOICES. They woke him up. He can't make out the words, but there's lots of talking. They're coming from the room next door. He was tired, but now he's awake. Sometimes he gets a tingling feeling in his stomach. Not like he's going to throw up, but it buzzes. He can grow numb to it after a while. He could go back downstairs and wait until his mom is done, but he'd rather wait here for her. When she does come, he'll pretend to be asleep and she'll have to pick him up and carry him home. For now, he'll just lie here and stare at the ceiling. It's one of those ceilings with the white bumps all over it. He likes these ones because if he stares at the bumps long enough, he can make out shapes and pictures. It's a game. If he finds a few pictures, he'll try to place them in an order that makes sense. Like it's some kind of message that's being sent to him. A message from someone else who lives somewhere else and is watching out for him. The messages never make sense, but maybe he'll understand them one day.

Footsteps stomp next door. Voices get louder but it doesn't sound like they're fighting. Jase concentrates on the ceiling. He never sees what he hopes to—strange planets, a spaceship, a robot. Instead, he sees umbrellas, shoes, a leaf. Things that are so ordinary and boring they can't possibly mean anything. And yet, Jase is certain that if he places them in the proper order, he'll get it.

Tonight, the first thing he makes out is a letter. It's a *b* near the door. And then above the television, it could be a sun, but it could also be the letter *o*. Maybe tonight's message will be different. Maybe tonight it will all be letters and Jase will receive a full sentence. An order he must carry out or a path he must follow. Finally, he thinks, finally he's going to figure out whatever it is he's supposed to. The thing that's been bugging him for as long as he can remember. The thing that makes his stomach tingle.

—

TRISH UNLOCKS THE MANAGER'S OFFICE and puts the cash box and tally sheets into the filing cabinet drawer where they go every night. She looks at the framed photo on his desk. Five smiling faces. Two small girls in matching outfits, a boy in a checkered dress shirt, and his wife with a white, white smile and highlights in her hair. And Robert in a golf shirt, beaming. Is that happiness? she wonders. And if it is, why can't she allow that to be her happiness too? Why can't she go to the salon, buy Sean a new shirt, get Jase's hair cut and head to the strip mall for their own family photo? Frame it in a five by seven. Why can't she turn her fucking brain off long enough so she can experience the happiness that comes to others so easily?

—

ROGER'S SKIN IS PRICKLY, ENERGIZED. That kid's attitude has him jittery, upset. He turns onto Blondeau Avenue and follows it down toward the dam, where there aren't any houses, just a couple shops that have been closed and locked up for a while now. Years, even. He pulls over to the curb and idles. Takes a moment to stare out over the Nistowin River that twists through town, dark and glittery from the stars. The whole town is quiet, but he feels something under the surface of the water. It's large and deep. It could stop his breath. He stares out. The light flickers like that girl's white bunny hug in the jungle gym's orange tube. So young, so animal. He could hear them fucking from some ways away. Not just their voices and their breath, but the sounds of their bodies against one another. The suctioning of skin. The wetness of them. Sex is so easy when you're young.

His cock goes soft in his hand. Another familiar feeling. His problem is that he can't control his thoughts. He always comes around to this state, this moment where he's reminded of what a piece of shit he is. Even those kids know he's a piece of shit. And no matter what he does, he can't convince anyone he deserves better. Not even Lenore.

THERE'S A LOUD THUD from the next room. Jase jumps. Voices rise. He hears the woman, "Aaron! Oh my god, oh my god."

Jase's heart punches in his chest. Her voice continues but he can no longer make out the words. Something's wrong. His throat goes dry. He could pick up the phone and call his mom, but he doesn't want to. He wants her to finish as soon as possible so they can leave on time together. If he calls her, she'd only get upset and he knows she's already upset about something at home. He feels it.

The woman is crying now. That's what it sounds like. But he doesn't hear anything at all from the guy whose name is Aaron. If his dad was here, his dad would get up out of bed. His dad would go next door to help out, even if he was scared. Jase pushes down the blankets, his insides growing weak.

The hallway is bright. It shocks his eyes and he stops in the doorway to let them adjust.

After a moment, he steps toward the door with the numbers 203 in shiny gold. Light and shadows stretch out across the carpet from under the door. Jase steps closer.

"Hold it close. Keep it pressed tight. Tighter."

"I got it, Mom!"

"Fuck!"

What could Jase even do? He's just a boy and they're adults. He knocks anyway.

Footsteps scurry to the door. The latch unlocks and a woman with frizzy hair like a red balloon stares down at him. A moment passes. "I thought you were the ambulance."

"Do you need help?"

"I called for help already. What's taking so long?" The woman storms back into the room. But she doesn't push the door hard enough and the knob doesn't catch. Instead, it bounces back open, slowly, hitting the wall behind it.

Jase sees the man on the edge of the bed. His legs dangle to the floor, but he's lying back, holding a bundle of towels between his legs. Jase looks closer and sees that he's not a man at all, but an older boy.

"Don't lie down, Aaron. Sit up!"

"I'm tired, Mom."

"Come on," the woman says, crawling onto the bed and pushing Aaron up so he's leaning against her.

"Are you holding it tight?"

"Yes."

Jase looks at the bundle of towels Aaron's pressing against himself. They're splotched with blood. In fact, Jase notices now, there's blood all over the carpet, and the blankets. He's oddly calmed by this. There is nothing he can do. This is for adults only.

"They should be here soon. It's okay, Aaron. It's going to be okay."

Jase takes a deep breath. Relaxes.

—

FUCK HER, LENORE THINKS as she puffs on another cigarette. Deep drags calm her as she stands in the still air. No wind. Nothing's moving. Then a truck whizzes by on the highway. The sound is so loud for a second and then so astonishingly quiet, its lights fade down the road. She flicks her smoke away and heads to her car. Her shoes click on the pavement, disturbing the silence that settled in.

People never listen to her, never think she has anything of value to say about family and marriage because she's never had either. But what she said to Trish was true. She may have gone too far but she had to say something. Lenore sees things others don't because she's outside of it all. Trish is making a bad decision, it's that simple. She's ruining her life, and worse, that poor boy's. Trish can't see it because she's too close, her thoughts are warped by her emotions. Trish may be unhappy, but who isn't? Everyone has their share of disappointments, those things that weigh them down so heavily it's hard to get up in the morning. But if you look at the bigger picture and put things into perspective, you can get through it. The bigger picture in this instance is that there's a good man who needs his love returned, and there's a young boy who needs his mother. That's it. Trish needs to get over herself and smarten up. Truth is, if Lenore could take her place, she'd do it in a heartbeat.

She unlocks her car door but is interrupted by the flashing lights of an ambulance coming down the highway. She pulls open the door, gets behind the wheel, and puts the key in the ignition but holds it there and doesn't start the car. The ambulance has turned off the highway and heads down Taylor Avenue. Then it turns again, on the street that runs past the Gold. She watches as it pulls right into the parking lot, its headlights momentarily blinding her. It stops at the front door, and two attendants climb out, one carrying a hefty bag of supplies.

TRISH LOCKS THE DRAWERS of the front desk.

"Room 203, ma'am."

She turns to see two ambulance attendants standing in the entranceway.

"Pardon me?" Her mind races.

"Room 203. Up this way?" But they don't wait for an answer and begin climbing the stairs.

Her thoughts come fast, piecing together what happened earlier. Jase arrived. Sean came and took him home. No. Sean left. Jase stayed here. He's upstairs on the second floor. But, 203... Was that the room? No, it wasn't. It was next door. Did he get up and move? Trish heads toward the stairs. Up each one quick and smooth as if she's in control.

At the top of the stairs, the door to 203 is wide open and there's commotion from inside, voices she doesn't recognize. But the door to room 201 is also ajar. "Jase?" She quickens her pace. The room is empty. She steps to the next room.

In 203, she sees her son, small and still, shrunk against the wall just past the doorway. He stares at the bed in front of him.

"Jase, what are you doing?"

But he doesn't answer, he doesn't even look at her. She moves toward him and stands near, then looks at the bed where both the attendants are squatted. One of them opens a bag and begins grabbing equipment and supplies.

"What's your name?" the attendant with the blond hair asks the boy on the bed.

"Aaron," his mother answers.

"Thank you, ma'am." He looks straight into the boy's face. "Aaron, can you talk?"

Aaron nods.

"Can you tell me what happened?"

The other attendant checks Aaron's heart rate, then pulls out a blood pressure cuff.

Aaron just stares at the blond attendant, eyes like dinner plates.

"He's bleeding. Right there." His mother points.

"Yes, ma'am. I see that. Aaron, can you tell me what happened?"

Aaron struggles for words. He's weak and tired, like he might pass out at any second. He may be years older than Jase but he still reminds Trish of her son in a way, fragile and delicate. His mother continues to cradle him from behind, grasping him with everything she has. And that's the difference between that boy and hers. Trish puts her hand on Jase's bony shoulder.

"You shouldn't be in here," she tells her son.

Jase's eyes take everything in. She should grab him, pull him into her arms and take him away from all of this, whatever it is. But she doesn't. She remains rooted to the floor, her hand a clamp on her son.

—

LENORE STANDS IN THE DOORWAY, car keys clenched tight in her hand. "Is everything okay?" she asks, feeling compelled to speak.

No one answers her.

One of the attendants looks familiar to Lenore. That fine blond hair. He resembles Jessica's son, Corey. Jessica and Lenore tore through high school together in messy Bardot bouffants and miniskirts. But Corey is just a boy. Lenore quickly calculates the years in her head and realizes this man who's taken control of the room is the same boy she took to the park years ago. The same boy she bought chocolate bars for when Jessica partied too hard and couldn't get up to make breakfast. Lenore watches Corey. Remembers that one day they were walking along Main Street and someone they didn't know said her son was a cutie-pie. She agreed that he was and they continued on.

The teenager's voice breaks through the silence. "He said he's done it before. That it was easy. He's never had any complications."

Corey removes the bloody towels from between the boy's legs and Lenore gets a glimpse of what's brought them all here. Corey lifts the boy's penis to examine the wound. She's too far away to see exactly, but she understands.

"The stitches have come out," Corey says. "We'll have to take him to the hospital."

The woman who was so angry and bitchy earlier now nods her head in calm compliance. Lenore herself feels a little different too, watching something unfold that makes her skin shake, like it might come right off and leave her insides exposed.

—

JASE'S MOM'S BREATHING HAS GROWN loud beside him. Her hand is like a claw digging into his skin. The room is so hot, his forehead is sweaty like it gets when he's sick, but he's not sick now. He smells rusting metal on a sunny day, tastes it in his throat. He knows he shouldn't be seeing this but he can also sense the normal rules somehow do not apply anymore.

The guys from the ambulance ask them to leave the room so they can pull in a stretcher and get Aaron to the hospital. His mom loosens her grip but there'll be marks for sure. It's weird that his own mom has injured him without meaning to, without even knowing she has.

Outside in the hall, he stands between his mom and Lenore. One of the men brings up a stretcher and they both wheel out Aaron, who now has a mask on his face. Jase reaches for his mom's hand and she lets him have it.

—

"WAIT," LENORE CALLS OUT a little too loudly. Corey stops just before he reaches the stairs. She hopes for a sign of recognition when she steps toward him, but nothing registers. Too many years.

"Should we call the cops?" she whispers so no one else hears.

"We've already let dispatch know."

Lenore steps back as Corey and his partner fold up the legs of the stretcher to carry him down the stairs, but they hold off when the boy reaches out to Lenore. He touches her hand.

"I'm sorry."

"For what?"

74

His face as white as the hotel's bleached sheets.

"You have nothing to be sorry about, kiddo." Lenore squeezes his hand in both of hers, and she bends over, touches her lips to the top of his head.

Corey and his partner move off down the stairs with the boy, his mother following in a trance. Lenore regrets kissing him, the night is strange enough as it is.

—

THE SALTUS TRUCK STOP CAFÉ has a few customers occupying its booths at this hour. It's a brown and white shack that never closes, attached to the gas station. A home to the night owls in town and the truckers who pass through.

Roger swirls two creamers into his takeout coffee. He wonders what it'd be like to climb into one of the cabs in the parking lot and light out somewhere.

"Almost done, you lucky bastard."

Roger turns and sees Willard Talbot, the pharmacist from the drugstore.

"What are you going to do with all your time now?"

The same question day after day. Sometimes he tells people he wants to take up woodworking, sometimes it's starting a garden, or coaching kids' baseball. It's never a question he answers honestly. He never tells people that he doesn't know what the fuck he's going to do. He never says he's scared shitless.

"We'll see where the wind blows," he says, snapping a lid onto his cup.

"Living the dream now." Willard chucks Roger on the shoulder.

Roger nods his goodbye and shoves the door open. Across the lot, the semis gleam, bright and shiny like toys. His radio cuts in, piercing the night air.

—

THIS WHOLE VALLEY WAS ICE ONCE. Now an entire town and its people live in the hollow left behind. A chasm so large and gaping, a chunk of the earth gone missing. Along the rim of the valley at the top of a hill, Al kicks some snow off a boulder and sits to take it in. Cranes his neck to look at the edges of the cavity that spread out wide, far beyond the little spot of civilization in its centre.

Only something powerful and violent could have left a mark like this on the land. But it was only water. The most destructive force on earth, that's what Al's read. The same water that glosses over his calloused hands when he holds them under the faucet. That tumbles onto his roof in a kind of cadence that leads him into sleep. That his farm animals, when he had them, lapped up with their large, spongy tongues. It doesn't seem possible that water tore this flat land wide open, but maybe it's just as deceiving as most other things. Then again, what does he know?

When Al arrived home from the Gold, he couldn't enter the house. Couldn't even walk up to the front door. Instead, he walked around back and along the water trail that leads from the eastern edge of his property to the hills that circle the valley. The trail where he often spots deer following before they dip down into the basin and disappear into the bushes and spindly birch, heading for the river, the last of the water left.

It'll be hours before the sun rises but he'll be here to watch it. He'll watch the entire cavernous hole flood with light. It'll douse him first before spilling onto the town below. He shifts his weight on the cold rock and regrets not bringing a chair from the shed. He's got nothing but time now and he doesn't know what to do with it. Endless time. But this place, this valley, reminds him that there are beginnings and ends to time, and the time in between is never as long as you think.

It took hundreds of years, maybe thousands, for that glacier to melt. He imagines it in fast-forward. Water trickles into small fissures at first, compelling the ice to crack and split open, melting more ice as it flows through. Persistent and determined, it eventually forces large sections to buckle and collapse under the pressure of its own weight. The rush of the melt pushes forward, remorseless, gaining momentum as it dredges up rock and debris and tears it apart as it moves along culminating in one final, massive roar. He sees that liquid animal right now, charging across the valley floor, ripping it up and sculpting something new, something much different than before. He feels his own rush under his skin.

What's really strange is this is all happening today, this very moment that he sits here on the edge, the breeze light on his cheeks. Ice all over the world is melting faster than ever before. Just a year and a half ago, the ice on a mountain range in Europe retreated so far it exposed Ötzi the Iceman, a man who had lived over five thousand years ago. His body well preserved, naturally mummified. All limbs intact and facing downward, his vertebrae visible and curved as if in prayer. While water ravaged the earth before Al, it also held that man's body together for thousands of years as if in tender embrace.

Part 2

Part 4

THE RESTAURANT IS ODDLY QUIET NOW. Not all the lights have been turned back on, adding to the strange mood. Trish warmed up a glass of milk for Jase earlier but it sits untouched on the table between them. He's wide awake, buzzing about and drawing pictures with the crayons like nothing even happened. He talks aloud to himself, asking what colour things should be. Blue for the car? A red house? He gets in these animated moods sometimes and usually Trish has no idea what spawns them but tonight it's clear what brought it on. When these moods do come on, regardless of their origin, she never wants to interrupt them because these are the times when he seems like all boys should be—talkative, unselfconscious. Alive. These are the times when he doesn't seem to care about her at all.

She was alert herself but the energy is quickly seeping out of her. All of her joints are achy. Even her fingers feel weak.

"What's going on?" Sean strides through the door and she's relieved to see him. But Jase doesn't run out to greet him, doesn't even look up from the picture he's so focused on drawing. Sean pulls over a chair from the table next to them and sits along the edge in the aisle, looking even more dishevelled than he did earlier.

"There's been an incident here."

"Are you guys okay?" He leans forward, elbows on the table.

"It was one of the guests in the rooms." She doesn't want to say anything more, much less tell him that Jase was in the room.

"What happened?"

"The ambulance took him to the hospital." She swishes her hand in the air, waving it off as if it's over now. All done.

Jase white-knuckles his crayons with intention.

"Can you take him home?" she asks.

"Do you have to stay?"

"Roger's here and he needs to ask some questions."

"Was it a heart attack or something?"

"Can we talk when we get home?" She nods toward Jase as if protecting him, but Sean will find out eventually. Jase still hasn't said anything.

"You must be so tired, Son," Sean says. "Let's get you home and into bed."

"No."

Sean gives Trish a look: not this again.

"You said I could stay with Mom. You both did."

"Only until Mom was done her shift. She's done now." Sean takes a deep breath. Rubs his face, then picks the sleep from his eyes. He's the one who gives everything to his son, packs his lunch, puts him to bed, takes him fishing. He's there for him all the time and all Jase wants is her.

A bubble rises in Trish's chest, a mixture of sadness and disappointment in herself. She clamps it down and reaches a hand out to Sean's. His are stained black with grease and oil, calloused, and his fingernails are far too long, but the familiarity is comforting. The bubble pushes up again—she needs to try harder, to be better. Trish folds into Sean and the crayon stops scratching on the paper. The half-lit room tucks in around the three of them.

—

THE GRAVEL CRUNCHES under Lenore's feet as she paces all the way to the tree and then back to the open kitchen door. Her cigarette burns fast and she lights another, offers one to Roger, who stands against the wall, watching.

"I'm fine, thanks."

"You used to smoke, didn't you?" she asks.

"Almost twenty years."

"How'd you quit?"

"Cold turkey. I know it doesn't work for most. Just stuck for me. Can't explain why."

"Lucky. I've thought about it but would never do it. And it's not because I need them, it's because I want them. There's a difference."

"It's good to know where you stand on things."

It's a funny expression now when the whole world feels wobbly under her feet. Lenore starts back to the tree again. It's the early hours and there's a bite in the air. It almost stings and she enjoys it. It takes her out of her thoughts, which have been spinning for a while now. The images play like a video on repeat, like there's a screen inside her head. A boy, bleeding on the bed. He was in pain, that was clear, and he was scared, but it was his mother who was in agony. Terrified to the point of trembling. Lenore shakes her head, willing a different video to play.

83

"You all right?" His voice comes from the darkness. She's so far away she can barely see him. She touches the tree and takes a final deep drag. Flicks the butt out into the night and heads back to him.

"You can't tell me you've come across anything like this before in all your years?"

"Can't say I have." Roger shifts his weight but remains leaning against the wall.

"Did that really just happen up there?"

"Appears that way."

"Jesus Christ." She kicks at a pebble. "Is he going to be all right?"

"He lost a ton of blood."

"He told me he had the flu."

"You spoke with him?"

"Only for a second when I delivered their food."

"He say anything else?"

"Not then, but after, when we were all in the room, he said, 'He's done this before.'"

"What do you think he meant?"

"I assumed he was referring to the person who cut him open. It wasn't his mother who did that."

"Is there anything else you can tell me?"

"All I know is they came and rented a room, ordered some food and then a little while later the ambulance was here. There's really not much more I know. Aside from their names, which you already have, there's nothing else I can tell you. And maybe those aren't even their real names." She folds her arms across her chest, holding herself in.

84

"You want to go inside for a bit?"

"No." Then, "Maybe."

He holds the door open for her and she notices how calm he is about this, like it's not even fazing him.

Inside, Lenore starts to brew a pot of coffee. Through the pass-through, Sean and Trish are huddled together at a table, then Sean pulls Jase into the embrace. It's moments like these when you need a family around you. She wills Trish to never let go.

Lenore reaches for two cups. "Cream and sugar, right?"

"Please."

They sit in a couple of folding lawn chairs the day-shift staff brought in. She props the door open a bit to let in a bit of the night air, and to remind her that the rest of the world is still out there, beyond the Harvest Gold and room 203.

"I wonder why..." she thinks out loud.

"Not sure that matters at this point."

"What do you mean?"

"You can't do that to a person, never mind your own son, for any reason," he says matter-of-factly.

"What's going to happen to her?" she asks.

"Too early to know."

A drop of water pings in the sink, and Lenore waits for the next one but when it doesn't come it doesn't surprise her. Nothing makes sense.

"What time did they arrive?" he asks.

"Around nine, I think, but Trish checked them in. I only saw them when they ordered food, which was around eleven."

"What was she like? Her manner."

"She was bitchy and mean to me, Trish too, but I never got the impression from the boy that he was afraid, or that he didn't want to be there." She stares into the dark corner, not focusing on anything. "She seemed protective of him actually." Roger raises his eyebrows and she catches it. "What do you think? She's crazy?"

"Like I said, doesn't much matter the why of it."

"Is that part of your training?"

"What's that?"

"You don't seem bothered at all."

"Certainly am, something like that. But we have to remain objective in all investigations."

"But you're not objective at all. You're very clearly on a side." It shoots out of her before she has a chance to think. She suddenly doesn't want to be drinking coffee with him in the early morning hours when they shouldn't be. How can he be so calm, no unmoved by what just happened? She'd like to scratch her nails across his skin. How shocked he would be by that. She's glad she rejected him earlier. Almost. "Shit," she checks herself. "Sorry."

"It's okay. Must've been quite a shock up there."

She can't tell if he's being empathetic or dismissive but either way, she doesn't want to talk about it anymore. "Why did you become a cop, Roger?" It seems like a safe enough subject.

He gulps down the last in his cup. "Not sure I put too much thought into it when I was younger. Knew I didn't want to farm. Worked in a hardware store from when I was fifteen and wanted a change."

"How old were you?"

"Twenty-two when I first went to the depot for training." He spins his empty cup in the centre of his palm. "And you, why'd you want to waitress?"

Lenore scoffs, then realizes he's not joking. For a moment, she thought he was being mean because no one dreams of growing up to be a waitress in their forties. But now she sees he's just oblivious, doesn't have a clue that what he's asked only points out all her failures. She's not sure what's worse—being mean or being unaware. Either way, it pisses her off more and she gets up from her seat. She's already flying high on caffeine, nicotine and shock, but she pours herself another cup of coffee and doesn't offer any to Roger. He won't get up to get his own, and he's too polite to ask for a refill because she's not on shift. She returns to her chair. The small space in the corner is cramped. They're sitting so close together that she can smell his underarm deodorant, or a faint aftershave. She's never noticed it before.

—

EVERYTHING FEELS DIFFERENT NOW. Like he's in a different world. And because of that, he wants to draw something different too. Something special. Something he's never drawn before. Jase is tired of drawing the same things. Trees, horses, houses, dogs. They all seem simple now, but he can't think of anything else just yet. He picks up individual crayons and stares at them, thinking about what each one might be a good colour for. Sometimes he holds them up to his nose and sniffs. He likes the way they smell. As he reaches for a brown crayon, he sees his parents watching him as they talk to the cop. He turns back to his picture and pretends to be absorbed in it, making scratches on the corner of the paper as if testing. He knows how to pretend that nothing really gets in, that he's in his own space.

"He was," his mother says quietly.

A few moments later, his mom's work friend leaves after saying a few things to the cop and his mom. There's a sad feeling around everything, and another feeling that he can't quite name. It's in the walls and the chairs, in the carpet hairs. The feeling follows them as they climb into the car in the parking lot, as they drive back home, and it seems to be inside their very own house when they get there. Jase tries to ignore it by focusing on the picture he's going to draw. Ideas have started to come to him. Not the right ones, but he's getting closer.

Jase doesn't have to brush his teeth again, even though he had ice cream at the restaurant. He also gets to sleep with his parents. He climbs in as soon as his mom pulls back the covers. He scrunches up beside her but not too close. His dad gets in on the other side and puts his arm around both of them. Jase can't remember the last time the three of them slept together in the bed and he likes it. It's only happening tonight because of that boy and his mother. Because something bad happened. But he doesn't care. He puts one hand on his dad and one on his mom and forces himself to think about the new picture he's going to draw. He wants it to surprise people. He wants it to be something that no one will forget.

—

THERE'S BLOOD ON HER SOCKS. She slips her feet out of her runners and peels them off. There's more on the bottom of her left pant leg. A patch so dark it's turned her green sweats black. She rolls the elastic cuffs up and walks in her bare feet to the garbage bin against the wall. Drops the socks in.

The hospital is a single-level facility that was built in the fifties. She paces the makeshift waiting room, an empty section of a hallway that's been stuffed with four chairs and a chipped coffee table. The floor is tacky under her feet, her skin peeling off of it with each step. The lights at the very end of the hall are off, the entire section shut down.

Nadine's still shaky but she can't sit. Around the corner, a nurse is stationed behind a high-walled desk. Nadine approaches her. "Excuse me, can you tell me how he's doing?"

"You'll have to wait for the doctor." The nurse barely meets her eye; her lip gloss glints in the fluorescent light, just like her wedding band.

"It's been a long time."

"It's quite a serious injury." There's a sharpness in her voice, and her corkscrew curls bounce as she turns to face Nadine. All along one section of the wall behind the counter, several photos are thumbtacked haphazardly. Some are of this very woman alongside a man with greying hair and two teenage boys, older than Aaron, closer to graduation. Nadine imagines that these boys would have full reign of the basement. It's where they'd play video games and keep a set of free weights, and where they'd spend all their time in between classes and hockey practice.

"Is there something else?" the nurse asks.

"Do you have a lost and found?"

"Did you lose something?"

"No."

"Okaay," the nurse says, drawing the word out, confused.

"I need some socks."

"Did you lose them?"

"No."

"I'm sorry then."

Nadine pads back to the waiting area.

Through a window in a closed door across the hall, she sees the light of a microwave flashing 12:00. She tries the door and it opens. A kitchenette with an apartment-sized fridge in the corner, a few cupboards and a sink, and a coffee maker on the countertop. She searches the drawers and finds coffee grounds and paper filters. She fills the carafe and uses enough grounds for two pots. The room's light flicks on, startling her.

"This is a staff-only area." The nurse stands in the door frame. "There's a coffee and snack machine near the entrance."

Nadine knows what she must look like to this woman, what kind of mother she adds up to in her mind. "I didn't see a sign."

"I'm asking you to leave," the nurse says.

Nadine hits the off button on the machine. "Could you just tell me if he's all right?"

"Ma'am, I cannot, and you must leave this room. Do you want me to call security?"

Nadine pushes past her, feet slapping the laminate. Balancing on the edge of the coffee table in the waiting area, she pulls her high-tops back on, tying the laces so tight they're snug. So tight they hurt.

LENORE IS BACK IN HER CAR for the second time tonight. Driver's side window rolled all the way down, keys still in her lap. Normally, there's nothing she wants to do more after a shift than head home, but tonight is different. Minutes pass. She lights up a cigarette and the smoke sits in a haze around her, trapped in the still, heavy air.

"You all right?"

Roger's voice startles her and she chokes on the smoke, then waves it away to see him approaching. "I'm fine."

"I was about to pull away but saw you sitting here."

She nods, uncomfortably, like he caught her doing something wrong. Indecent, even. He stands outside her door now, and Lenore looks up at him. Lit only by the parking lot lamps, he towers over her, still looking unfazed and in control.

"Could you give me a ride home?" It falls out of her, surprising them both.

In his patrol car, she stares at each house as they pass. This town is small and she's lived here almost her entire life, yet she's never been inside most of the houses. They pass an entire block of homes with interiors that are unfamiliar to her. It's silly but it saddens her. In this moment, she doesn't care at all about what she witnessed earlier. Those people staying in room 203 are strangers. She knows almost every single person in this town, but how well does she really, if she doesn't even know the colour of their kitchen?

Up ahead is a chocolate-brown house with tan trim. The Wickenheisers'. They come into the Harvest Gold every Sunday.

When Edith was in the hospital in the city for weeks for cancer treatment, Jon came in without her. One of their sons lives across town with his own family, the other is in the States somewhere and doesn't keep in touch. Lenore knows so much about them, but not if they have carpeting or hardwood, or if their basement is finished.

"Have you been inside that house?"

"The Wickenheisers'? I have."

"What's it like?"

Roger shrugs. "Big. Lots of space for just the two of them. I don't think she can manage stairs now so they just use the main floor."

"But what does it look like?"

There's an awkward pause. "Tidy, I guess."

Lenore waits for him to continue, but he seems confused by the question. "Is it painted white or different colours? Is there wallpaper? Do they have matching furniture or odds and ends?" The questions are strange but she doesn't care.

"All white inside, I think. I was only there a couple of times and it was a while ago. They have a homemade kitchen table and chairs. I remember that because it was a friend of his that made them. Anniversary gift. They had a lot of pottery, coffee mugs and plates. Those didn't match."

"Photos on the walls?"

"Some. Not many. A lot of plants, though. In every room, hanging from the ceiling and all over. But it was still tidy."

It doesn't tell Lenore anything new about this couple but it calms her somehow. She glances at Roger. He'd have been inside more houses in town than she has, and he'd know some things about them that even she might not know. Does Roger ever share those secrets with anyone? He's not a talker, doesn't blab about shit the way others do in town. He keeps everything to himself, even his feelings, as he proved tonight. She wonders if he's ever been shaken up, lost his shit. She'd like to see it happen if he did. He might be a different person afterward.

Roger pulls up to her house and gently presses the brakes until they come to a full stop.

Another question surfaces, but this time it's not a surprise. And this time she knows exactly what she's doing. "Would you like to come in?"

—

HE'S THRASHING. CRYING. He tries to yell out, but no sound will come. He kicks his legs and punches with his arms, fighting the monster that holds him.

"Jase." There's a voice from far off, but he can't see where it's coming from because the monster's grip is too tight.

There's a cool hand on his cheek, then his forehead, but Jase continues to kick because the monster's choking him now and pulling him away.

"Son, wake up."

Jase slowly opens his eyes and he's back in his own house, in his parents' bed. He's warm but shivering too.

"I'll get some dry pyjamas."

His mom heads down the hall to his room while his dad brushes his wet hair off his forehead.

"Shhh. You're okay now."

"Did he wet the bed?" his mom asks when she returns.

His dad pats the mattress. "No, it's just sweat on the pillow."

"Do you remember what it was about?" his mom asks while helping him change.

Jase shakes his head and they climb back in beside his dad.

"Well, it's over now and we can go back to sleep."

But Jase is determined not to fall asleep again. He lied to his mom. He does remember the dream. He was back in room 203 again. The boy on the bed was holding the ball of bloodied towels between his legs just like before but this time the boy looked right up at Jase. Looked straight at him and then his eyes turned red. They glowed like they were fire. Then the red towels started to twist and curl. They grew bigger and fatter and turned into long, oily tentacles. They reached out straight toward him.

Jase pushes the nightmare from his mind, but the real events from the night take its place. Part of him wishes it didn't happen, but from what he could sense, and from what the others were saying, the boy wanted that to happen. Or some of it anyway, so maybe it makes Jase a bad person for wishing it didn't. But if things are supposed to happen, why do they have to be so scary? It's not like in his comic books where there are forces of evil and forces of good and everything makes sense.

And then it comes to him. Jase knows what he's going to draw. A superhero. His very own. A rush of excitement rolls through him and he almost wants to tell his parents. But he won't. He's going to keep it a secret until it's all done.

He wonders if there are superheroes in the real world who are never recognized as superheroes. Maybe there are people out there who have special powers but don't want to use them. Who just want to be normal people and not have all the attention. He wonders how many there are and if, over time, they simply forget they have certain powers. Maybe someone he knows has superpowers. Who might it be?

If he had to choose someone, if he really had to guess, he'd pick his mom. She's so quiet all the time, it's like she's always hiding something. And if she is a superhero, she must've fought with everything she had not to do anything in room 203. She didn't turn back time so it would all be erased from his mind. She didn't teleport them somewhere else. She didn't step in to magically heal the boy on the bed and stop the woman from crying. She didn't do any of that, and it must have been very difficult for her not to.

His own superhero is going to be one that no one's ever thought of before. And he'll have his own special power that no one else has. Jase isn't worried about falling asleep anymore because he's wide awake. He has a lot more to figure out.

—

HE SHOULDN'T BE HERE but he's glad she invited him in. The coffee table is sticky and dust is already forming a fuzz on almost every surface. Dirty dishes are scattered around the room, and stray clothes are abandoned on the armchair, the television stand and the carpet. It's not what he expected of Lenore, the woman who serves everyone in town their food. Who's always wiping everything up with buckets of bleach and bottles of

Windex. He settles himself in the corner of the couch after wiping crumbs from the cushion and folding a T-shirt, laying it neatly on the end table by the lamp.

"Would you like a rye and ginger?" she shouts from the kitchen.

He glances at his watch. "Can't," he shouts back. Then, "Not yet."

She returns, having shed her uniform and now wearing a pair of stirrup pants under an oversized shirt. The neck is so wide one of her shoulders and its bra strap is visible. She carries two glasses and holds one out to him. "Are you sure? I won't tell."

He accepts the drink but only holds it. His shift won't be over for forty-three minutes. There's a clock above the television and one hanging on the wall near the front door. He eyes them both.

"What a way for your job to end." She curls into the other corner of the couch, folds both her legs underneath her and faces Roger straight on. Her bare shoulder catches the light. He shifts his position a little and the ice clinks in his glass, cold and sweaty in his hands. Still, he doesn't take a sip. And he doesn't want to talk about the incident, either. He doesn't know why, but he wants to be alone with the things that happened earlier. He wants his own time to mull things over, think about them, think about the people involved. There will be a lot more questioning tomorrow. Nobody has talked to the mother or her son yet. That will wait until the kid has proper medical attention and they're both calmer. This will be the last investigation he'll be involved in and it doesn't seem fair that he might not be able to see it through to the end. He hates not seeing things through.

"What about you?" he asks.

"Me?"

"You ever think about retirement yet?"

"Are you serious?"

He can't tell if she's mad or joking.

"How old do you think I am?"

He knows how old she is. Forty-seven, thirteen years younger than him. He assumes that everyone at that age would be thinking about their retirement, or at least should be. He feels a clench in his chest and he instinctively takes a large gulp from his drink, doesn't bother to look at either of the clocks.

"You're really rude, you know that?" she says, but then laughs.

"I didn't mean it that way, I know you're not that old. I was just wondering." He stares at the rug.

"I've fantasized about it, for sure. But that's all I can do. I'll be waitressing until my hips give out." She laughs again but this time it's forced and false. "Sometimes I wish I had made different choices, but you know, I did all right. Got my own house. Still paying it off but it's mine." She pauses. "Not everyone can have cushy jobs and not have to worry." It's cutting.

Roger sets his glass down. "I'm sorry, I should go now."

"Is that what you always do?"

He looks up at her, feels the edge in the air.

"Run when things get tough? That's what you did earlier after you asked me out. I said no and you ran away."

She's smiling like he shouldn't be offended but he deduces she's trying to pick a fight. It's familiar to him. It's what usually happens between him and women—he pisses them off.

97

Unintentionally, but repeatedly. "I didn't run off, I just didn't want to make you any more uncomfortable than I already had." It's the most honest thing he's ever said.

"It was to spare me, then. And now? You're leaving out of consideration for my feelings?"

Roger suspects that no matter what his answer is, it will end badly for him. It's one of those trick questions, the kind he always seems to walk into. All he wants is to sit quietly with this woman. That's all he ever wanted, to share the silence. But there's never any silence, it always becomes loud with regret and anger. He brings it out in women. If he knew why maybe he could fix it, but it seems to be innate, the way magnets repel one another.

He rises. "I didn't mean to upset you."

"So stop running away."

She stands up too and puts down her glass. She stares at him, confrontational. There's a long moment and he senses the mood changing but he's not sure in what direction.

"I don't know what to do here."

Still, she stares. Her face changes and the hardness disappears, almost melts away. Roger doesn't quite understand what's happening yet, but his gut tells him something. It's deep down but it's guiding him. He steps in closer, touches that bare shoulder. She closes her eyes and pushes out a breath, like she's giving in. He knows he should leave. As an officer, he knows she's experienced a trauma tonight and that's why he's here right now. That's why she's invited him in, given him a drink. Trauma makes people do things they normally wouldn't. It's a kind of craving. They crave control and that's what this is all about, and she's chosen him because he's easy bait.

She puts her hand on his waist, the part of him he least wants her to touch, but it feels good anyway. She pushes herself up onto her toes and kisses him. Lightly, and not at all what he expected. Then she lowers back down, picks her glass back up and walks away. Doesn't say a word as she disappears down the hall. He remains standing there, his cock stiff. He looks at both clocks. His shift is still not over and it's like it never will be. He picks up his drink, downs it all in one go, and heads down the hall toward a faint light that just flickered on.

—

"HE WAS IN SHOCK when he came in. His whole system." It's the nurse's voice.

"I can't even imagine."

Nadine stirs. She fell asleep in the chair without meaning to. Her head fell so far to the side the muscles in her neck are locked. The clock on the wall says it's four a.m. on the nose.

"Where is the mother?"

"Waiting area," the nurse says with a huff.

The voices from the nurses' station carry down the hall and around the corner. There's also a rustling of coats and bags. A shift change.

"Wait until you see her."

"Was she intentionally trying to hurt him?"

"Says he wanted it done, but still, my kids wanted to be Spider-Man and the Hulk. Like I was going to do anything about that." There's a long silence. "If anyone needs help, it's her, but this kid now has to pay for it."

Hypocrites. Feigning pity for him now when they'd be just like everyone else and raise their eyebrows if they passed him in the grocery aisle. Worse, if Aaron was a student in their child's class, they'd do the same things as all the others in her town. They'd keep their own kids from hanging around and even from talking to Aaron. And when Aaron would come home with scrapes and bruises and vacant eyes, they'd say it was his own fault. They'd convince the principal that it was in everyone's best interests for Aaron to be isolated and do his studies by correspondence.

"Did you call Social Services?"

"They're sending someone out today."

Nadine rises too quickly, a head rush blurs her vision. It grows splotchy with black and red fuzz, but she continues down the hall until it clears. "Where is the doctor?"

"Ms. Gourlay, the doctor will come and see you when he can. He's still with your son right now." The nurses exchange a look.

"It's been so long."

"Please just take a seat and the doctor will see you when he can."

But Nadine walks past their desk and to the hallway marked *Staff Only*.

"Excuse me, you can't go down there!" The nurse who's getting off shift marches after her. "Page Lyle," she tells the other one. "He's on his rounds and was just here moments ago."

Nadine pushes through the doors and they swish open easily despite their size. There are four doors to choose from but only one with any lights on behind it. The nurse runs in front of her and blocks her way.

"Stop!"

"Why won't you tell me anything?"

"You can't be in this area."

"I have to know how he is."

The doors behind them swish again. Footsteps race up behind them and then a twenty-something kid has his hands on her arm.

"You have to come back this way, miss," he says. He has a wiry moustache and far too much gel in his spiky hair. "Miss. Right now. Come with me, or I will restrain you if I have to."

His piercing eyes are waiting for her to disobey. It's obvious these are the moments he lives for. Nadine yanks her arm from his grip but complies.

They place her in an empty room in the abandoned end of the waiting room hallway. Lyle's stationed just outside the door, back straight and chest puffed. A little while later the other nurse offers her a sedative, but Nadine leaves it sitting in its paper cup on the desk nearby. The last thing she wants to do is rest.

—

TRISH STARES AT THE STAINS on the end of the bed in room 203. They spread down the sheets and blankets into a large oval on the carpet, still tacky and damp. It's hard to believe the body contains so much. Jase came home from school last fall and asked her if it was true that humans are mostly made of water. She said it was but couldn't explain why. It's a fact that doesn't seem possible. She pushes her gloved fingers into the carpet braids and watches the tips darken.

She was surprised when Roger told her they would have to clean the room themselves. They've had to clean up blood before—drops around the sinks and in the toilet bowls, even blood on the sheets. But this is different. It didn't seem fair to leave it for someone else. Besides, she couldn't stay in bed any longer. Last night, after it happened, she wanted nothing more than to be at home with Sean and Jase, and at first it was fine. Jase twitching and pawing at her back, Sean snoring lightly. It was almost enough to make her think all was normal again. But then the image of that woman would flood in. That mother. Her thin, wiry body, nothing but a bit of muscle on her bones. Her face twisted and tight while she held her son's weight in her arms, as if she was in more agony than the boy. Trish couldn't shake it from her mind and lying still in bed only made it worse.

Trish dunks the scrub brush into the bucket of soapy water beside her. No one knows much about the incident yet but the whole thing seemed to have been arranged. The boy had talked with the man who did that to him. "He's done it before," the boy said, as if he wanted the surgery, if you can call it that. There are people who don't feel their physical bodies match who they really are. She wonders how many. There must be more than most people would think if one of them could somehow end up in this town. Nature gets things wrong sometimes. She stops scrubbing at the stain while a thought grips around her, flattening her into nothing. Mothers should never be made so that they are indifferent to their own children.

The birds have begun their morning chirping. Trish rises and opens the curtains, letting the blue, hazy light seep in. She's been working here over ten years, longer than Jase has been alive. She was in her last year of high school then. Was going to save up money and head into the city, look for work and then think about college. She graduated, then stayed on through the summer because she knew she didn't have enough money to last her very long. The summer turned into fall and then the first snow hit. It was easier to wait until the next summer. But it was during that particularly cold and icy winter that she met Sean. She didn't really know him because he was two years behind her in school. When he asked her out, she had just turned nineteen and she thought it was silly to go out on a date with a seventeen-year-old, but he was so earnest about it and she had nothing to lose.

Their dates were awkward at first because Sean was so talkative, he left no room for her to get a word in. She thought he was nervous or trying really hard to make a good impression. But after several weeks she realized it was neither of those things—Sean just always talked even though he didn't have much to say. She thought it was odd that he could be so noisy and loud when his mind was quiet. Different than hers. His wasn't bursting with thoughts that twisted and battled in his head, unable to get out because there were too many vying for attention. When Trish realized this about Sean, and understood that they were so different, she wanted to be more like him. She wanted him, period. For a while, she found she was calmer around him, he settled her. He didn't want to dive around in her head. Didn't try to coax things out of her and press her to talk or share her internal struggles. He didn't even know they were there. And because he didn't know, it was easier for her to ignore them.

The first time they had sex was the first time Trish ever felt love. It leached out of her unexpectedly. It lasted while they lay on the pullout couch in his parents' basement. He stroked her arms and back gently with his fingertips as she was draped over top of him, covering his body with hers. After, they made popcorn and watched a cheesy late-night horror movie on TV, and everything was back to normal. The feeling was gone. She thought it'd come back, which was why she said yes to marriage when he asked just a few short weeks later. It was also what she wanted at the time, or thought she did. But that feeling has never been back.

The bloodstain grows bigger as the soapy water soaks in. That boy's blood. But he's not really a boy anymore. And in a sudden aching flash she wants to know if he still thinks it was a good idea. If he's okay. And did he get what he wanted? Is he lying in bed at the hospital a changed person, changed in all the ways he wanted? Is he now the person he wanted to be?

She scrubs harder so that her arms burn. The suds, candy-floss pink, gather on her yellow dish gloves, the colours suggesting the moment should be a happier one.

—

LENORE'S BODY ACHES FROM LYING as still as she can, knowing that any movement could disturb the man beside her. People are the lightest of sleepers when sharing a bed for the first time. Though it's unclear how much either of them really slept. It's also unclear how many hours have passed like this, in this strained fake restfulness. Roger shifts beside her. He takes a deep breath and lets it out slowly. She feels his body heat next to hers under the sheet. The sex wasn't so great. She wanted to be surprised and there was a part of her that thought Roger would do that. Ordinary and predictable in every other way. She was hopeful this might be an area where he would unexpectedly amaze. At least she did have an orgasm.

There was one moment. After the sex was over and they were both out of breath and trying to hide it, she rolled onto her side and reached for the last in her glass. It was mostly melted ice cubes but it felt good going down. She rested on her side for a moment and was thinking of what to say when his large hand cupped her shoulder. Warm and sure. His breath slowed and he didn't make any other move closer. Didn't try to hold her or pull her back to him. It was just a hand. She relaxed, and decided not to say anything at all.

Now, he lies facing away from her, turned on his side. He shifts under the sheets, his big chest inflates and empties. What would it have been like to wake up to that every day for years and years? To a body so close, sharing the same blankets and the same air. It seems too much to her. How would you know where one person ended and the other began? And yet, if that was the case, if she had lived her life alongside someone else's, would she have ever felt alone?

Lenore reaches out and runs her fingers along the back of his neck. He stirs, bends his head to make it easier for her. She moves them down his back, lightly. A sigh pushes out of him. She's turned on at being able to turn him on. The birds have grown louder outside the window and morning light peaks through the edge of the curtains. Lenore slides over and tugs him onto his back. Kisses him as she climbs on top.

—

WITH THE SUN UP and the valley filling with gold light, Al is caught in a weird state—it's the start of a new day, a new beginning, but the sense of an ending also judders through him.

He heads back to the house and scrambles some eggs in a pan, but when they're done, he leaves them on the stove because he has no appetite. He grabs his gloves instead, and some tools from the barn, and drives out to the north end of the property where a few days ago he saw a line post falling over. It's leaning so far toward one of its neighbours that the top length of barbed wire had already snapped. The other two lower lengths were taut and tense, ready to break.

Al pulls the post back into alignment and tamps the soil back down around its base. Given that there are no cattle roaming the land anymore he could leave it at that, but he has energy to burn and there's no point in doing a half-assed job. He pulls a couple pieces of lumber from the truck bed and uses them as braces for the straying post. He digs two holes at an angle for the ends of the braces, and hammers the top ends tight against the post, bolstering it as best as he can.

With that section of fence straightened, Al tightens the barbed wire on both sides, and fetches the extra coil from his truck to fix the broken length. Now, with the fence stretcher in hand, he creates tension in the new line. It's all taken much longer than he anticipated but he's glad to be busy.

He misses the cattle. Sometimes he used to hear them from the house calling out to one another, or to no one at all. He liked the way the earth would tremor with their weight when he'd corral them. The massiveness of them would sometimes make him immobile with awe. Everyone said he had a calming effect on the cattle and that explained why he was so good at castrating them, but the truth is the cattle calmed Al.

He regrets selling them and the land off so soon. Maybe he could've pushed through the arthritis. Maybe he underestimated the number of productive years he still had left. Maybe now all he has to do is wait.

He mended the Nielsens' fence that one summer. His father hired him out on the weekends because the Nielsens' oldest son, Douglas, enlisted the year before and was still overseas, and their younger son, Raymond, had asthma so severe he couldn't do any work on the farm.

The first weekend that Al rode his bike out to their property, Mr. Nielsen seemed reluctant to put him to work, as if he felt guilty for needing help outside the family. Initially, he asked Al to sweep out the barn, but when Al was given no further instruction, he took it upon himself to do anything he thought needed doing. The rest of that Saturday he cleaned and organized the whole barn, and ensured the animals had water and shelter from the heat throughout the day. And on the Sunday, he began repairing the fence that had been badly neglected. It was then Mr. Nielsen seemed to take him seriously. At the end of the day, he told Al he looked forward to the following weekend, then sent him up to the house for some refreshments.

When Al reached the house and leaned his bike against the porch, Raymond was already coming out of the screen door with a pitcher of lemonade and a plate of cookies.

Raymond poured out two glasses and sat in one of the Adirondacks. Al joined him, feeling awkward. It was odd to see Raymond outside of school. He was only a year older than Al but he'd skipped a year in elementary so was two grades ahead. And this fall, he'd be entering his final year of high school. He was practically an adult.

"I hope my dad's not working you too hard."

Al shook his head. "I like to help out."

"Wish I could."

Al reached for a cookie and took a bite. Peanut butter, his favourite.

"I wish I could join up like Douglas even more, though." He paused. "Don't you?"

"Yeah." It was a lie. Al took a gulp of his lemonade and regretted it, it was tart and sour after the sweetness of the cookie. He reached for another cookie to get the taste out of his mouth.

"Do you like them?"

Al nodded.

"You can take the rest of them home."

When Al rode back home that evening, he thought about the war. He had never considered joining up. The war seemed so far away, like it was happening in another world, so disconnected from his own that it didn't seem like a possibility. But, as Al discovered that summer, it was all that Raymond ever thought about.

AL PULLS UP TO HIS HOUSE, feeling the soreness of fence repairing setting in his shoulders and wrists. His eggs are still sitting on the stove but now he's too tired to eat. He heads straight up the stairs and falls into bed without washing up or even changing out of his clothes.

—

TRISH CLOSES THE DOOR to room 203 behind her and checks to make sure it's locked. She carries the suitcase that the mother and son brought with them, having packed all their things from the room back in it. Some of the day staff have already arrived for their shifts and wonder why she's here. She puts the suitcase in the storage area behind the front desk and only tells them that room 203 is closed until further notice. It's Robert's job to tell the staff what happened here, even though they'll find out from others much sooner.

She returns the room key to the locked drawer in the desk next to its duplicate, but then decides against it and places both keys in her purse as if barring others from the room will somehow help. As if locking it up tight makes it easier to deal with.

The cold air on the walk home wakes her. It's still the early part of morning when people are inside and the day hasn't really begun yet. Limbo. It's like being at the edges where time doesn't count. Like she could do anything and it wouldn't matter. She's the most alive in these moments. Right now she wants to run, race so fast her lungs would burn, but she doesn't want to get home too quickly and spoil the moment.

In the kitchen, she finds Sean putting on his boots. "Where have you been?" he asks, grabbing his jacket from the hook.

"Cleaning the room." She smells fresh coffee and her stomach grumbles. "You starting early today?"

"No. While you were out, I fought with Jase to get him washed and dressed for school. He refused to eat breakfast, threw his cereal on the floor. And now the school just called and said he's sick." He buttons up his jacket and pulls a toque on. "He shouldn't even be in school today, but I can't afford to take any more time off as it is. And you—" He stops himself.

"What?"

"You don't even try with him anymore, Trish."

"What do you mean?"

But Sean just shakes his head at her.

"What do you want? Should I plan birthday parties and bake cupcakes?"

"A little of that might help."

She scoffs. Pours herself a mug of coffee.

"You always keep him at a distance. Like you've been doing to me lately, and I've been pussyfooting around you because I don't want to push you, but he's your son, Trish."

The image of that mother and her boy on the bed flares up. Trish yanks her jacket back on.

"What are you doing?"

"I'll get him."

"Are you staying home with him too then?" He waits. "Trish?"

"Yes." She slams the door behind her.

—

ROGER'S STILL ON HIS BACK, his throat sore and dry from snoring. He hopes he didn't disturb Lenore too much during the night. The bedside clock says it's after nine a.m. Down the hall, a door opens and footsteps pad farther away. The faucet in the kitchen rushes on. In all his years on the force, he's always used an alarm clock, even on his days off, because he never wanted to get off track. But this morning, being stirred by the subtle sounds of someone nearby is unpredictably pleasant.

He finds her in the kitchen, lost in thought, watching the coffee maker gurgle and spit into the carafe. He says her name quietly, then a little louder.

"Shit," she says, startled, then smiles when she sees him.

There's an awkwardness in the air but that's to be expected. He won't let it bother him.

"Coffee's almost done. I could whip us up something." She starts to dig for food but there's not much to find.

"I should get going. I still have several things to wrap up over the next couple of days at the station." He's ravenous and his stomach is about to protest but he won't overstay his welcome. Lenore is independent, he senses that quite strongly, admires it, even, but it means they need to take things slow.

"Right, tomorrow's the big night." She pauses, and he wonders if they'll mention the night before. "If the invitation still stands, I'd like to come."

He clears his throat, it's phlegmier than he anticipated. "Of course. I'll pick you up at six." He heads to door. It's abrupt, but he wants to get out before anything changes. If they go slow enough, she'll eventually get used to him being around. Even when she needs her alone time, he'll be in her thoughts somewhere, a habit. He walks down the choppy walkway through her front yard, last year's weeds and decaying leaves visible through the patches of melting snow.

In the patrol car on his way home to shower and change, he stops in at the bakery to grab breakfast to go. It's not until he walks in the place and sees Ned Goesen sliding fresh muffins and doughnuts into the display case that he remembers his encounter with Ned's daughter Kyla last night. She was terrified and he's glad because that will set her straight. For a while at least. It stings a bit that he let that little punk-ass go, but Mike's just going to get even cockier after last night and that's going to lead him into more trouble. Trouble with very different results. That kid'll be in jail before he hits twenty, Roger'd bet his pension on it. Besides, he'd take a hundred smart-mouthed underage kids over a single mother who abuses her own kid. He cringes at the thought of the life that lies ahead of that poor boy. Aaron, was that his name?

The girl at the counter takes his order for an English muffin sandwich with extra cheese and sausage. Once this case is settled and he's done his job, he'll focus on eating better and getting in shape. It'll be easier then, especially if things progress with Lenore. But the immediate priority is this case.

The door opens behind him and Elliot Matkowski and his crew walk in, Gerry and Dennis. Retired men that gather at the bakery every morning to chew the cud. Most afternoons too.

"Rough night, eh?" Elliot asks. "What the hell happened at the hotel?"

Word's already gotten out and they want details. Roger fixes his takeout coffee and wonders who was talking out of turn. Wasn't Lenore. He's known Trish since she was a child and she's not a talker. Can't imagine it'd be Sean, either. It has to be someone from the station. It usually is but it's hardly ever the civilian staff and that's what upsets him the most. A colleague, bound by the same codes as he is, is generally the rat. Last night that new recruit from Ontario was in. Trevor Ryan. Nice enough guy, but officers from other provinces hate being assigned to rural Saskatchewan. Trevor dreams of being stationed someplace like Toronto or Montreal, of working the international cases like drug busts or child porn. Roger can smell it on him.

"Did you take the call?" Elliot asks. All the old-timers are looking at him.

"Of course he took it. It was his shift last night," Gerry says. "Besides, look at him." They all chuckle.

"What a way to finish up your career." Elliot shakes his head.

Instead of moving to their regular booth in the back, the group of them take the stools that line the front window so Roger's trapped with them until his order arrives.

"So?" Elliot starts in again.

"You guys know the drill." Roger forces a smile as he says it.

"We heard some guy tried to turn another guy into a woman. That true, at least?"

Roger just shakes his head, not giving them anything.

"He didn't deny it," Gerry says to Elliot.

"Holy shit, things just get crazier." Elliot picks at something in his dentures.

"I heard that whoever was cut up is not from here, though. Alberta or BC?" Gerry waits for Roger to answer.

"I can't confirm anything."

"Not from Saltus anyway. Can you imagine?" says Gerry.

"Never did think I'd live to hear such a thing." Elliot tsks. The waitress brings over a tray of coffee mugs for the men. "You're almost off the clock now anyway so you don't have to worry about it." Elliot grabs a steaming cup. "My folks always taught me that when we leave this world, we need to leave behind a better one for those that come after. Don't think that's possible nowadays with all this nonsense. People are just too damn crazy now."

"Ain't that the truth," says Gerry.

"Say, you're welcome to join us next week when you've shed your uniform."

"Might do." Roger nods goodbye and exits the bakery. But he won't. The last thing he wants is to sit on a stool and gossip like a brood of hens. Outside, he pulls the walkie from his shoulder strap and radios in to the station. He gets Glen, the sergeant in charge, on the other end and asks for any new developments.

"Nothing much. Kid's still dicey. We advised the doctor not to update the mother. Figured we should talk to her first. I'm sending Trevor as soon as he gets in."

"I'll interview the mother myself."

"You're not on until this evening."

"No matter."

"Trevor's on his way in."

"Trevor's too green for something like this. I'm heading to the hospital now." Roger unwraps his breakfast sandwich and finishes it in four bites, before he even reaches the car.

—

SHE ASSUMED JASE WOULD SLEEP through most of the day given everything that's happened, but as soon as they get home from school and Trish tries to put him down, he refuses. His eyelids droop but he will not go to bed. He follows her around the house instead, dazed and foggy. From the living room to the kitchen while she washes up the breakfast dishes. Around the bedrooms and bathroom while she collects dirty laundry, and even down to the basement to return the mop that Sean used to wipe up the milk and Cheerios. Velcro she can't tear off.

"I could read you a story. That might help."

He shakes his head.

"We could watch *Home Alone.* Or didn't Dad just buy *Mighty Ducks?*" A movie would surely help to conk him out.

"No."

"You're going to make yourself even more sick if you don't try to sleep." But he doesn't budge.

Trish folds the last towel and carries the stack to the hall closet. Stepping back to close the door, she trips on him and he falls back, knocking his head on the wall. A loud thud that startles her. His face scrunches and then the crying starts. Big, ear-splitting jags.

"Let's see." She inspects his skull. "There's a tiny bump but it's not bleeding. You're okay." She holds him on the floor until he calms. "Up you get. I'll make you some hot chocolate in just a minute, okay?" He nods. She imagines what Sean will say if he comes home to find Jase in worse shape than this morning.

Trish steps into the washroom. Sitting on the toilet, she sinks her head into her hands, focuses on pulling air in and letting it ease out. She reaches for the roll of toilet paper and sees him standing at the sink, watching her.

"What are you doing?" He turns his back but doesn't leave. "Jase, get out right now."

He walks out into the hall, leaving the door ajar behind him.

She closes the door while she washes her hands and braces herself before opening it again. "Come on." She picks him up and carries him to his room, but when he realizes where she's taking him, he starts fussing.

"No, no!"

"Jase, you need to sleep. Period."

"I won't!"

"Are you worried about having another nightmare?"

He doesn't answer.

"I'll stay with you until you fall asleep."

"But then you'll leave."

"I'll just be in another room. I'm home all day until Dad's done work." Jase settles a little and she pulls the covers up over him. "Please, just try." He doesn't fight her and in less than a minute his head is already bobbing. She helps to scoot him down and scrunches a pillow under his head.

She closes the door behind her and is two steps away when he yells out, "Mom!" She hears him scramble out of bed and run to the door, and without even thinking she grabs the doorknob and holds it.

"I won't sleep, I won't!" He fights with the knob from the inside.

"You'll feel so much better after a nap, I promise."

"Let me out! Mom!"

Is she really doing this? Is she this type of mother? She lets go of the knob and he yanks it open. He's out of breath and more alert than ever.

"Okay, I'm sorry. You don't have to sleep, but I do." She takes his hand and leads him to the living room. "You can do whatever you like, watch TV, play Lego, anything, but I just need to sleep for a bit, okay?"

He nods and collects his box of crayons, but as Trish reaches for a blanket, he says, "Mom, do you hate me?"

"What? No, Jase, please don't think that." But he's crying. She pulls him to her and holds him. You're my son, is what she wants to say next, but it doesn't come out.

When he eventually settles and turns back to his crayons, Trish lies back on the couch. A pressure under her ribs so big it might tear them open.

—

"You can't smoke in here."

Nadine turns the crank on the casement window and the glass stretches out from the frame at the bottom, an uneven triangle. "I don't smoke."

The cold air puffs into the room, cooling her cheeks and forehead. A policeman stands in the doorway, the same one who gave her a speeding ticket yesterday, ages ago now. Behind him, a tiny woman who looks barely of age skitters into the room hugging a notebook to her chest. The officer closes the door behind them. The room is a generic office but was once a patient room—there's a handwashing sink on one wall and exposed pipes where a toilet must have been.

"Ms. Gourlay," he says. "Hello, again." He doesn't sit behind the desk like Nadine expects, but perches on a stool against the wall adjacent to her. "Constable Melnyk," he introduces himself.

Nadine stands at the window, shifting her weight from foot to foot. The officer hasn't shaved, and his underarms are pungent.

"This is Claire Schroeder. She's with the Department of Social Services." The young woman hesitates before sitting on the far end of a short couch. "We're here to ask some questions and sort through the events of last night."

Claire opens her notebook and uncaps her pen, writes the date on a fresh page.

"The nurses here have told us a little bit about what happened in your room at the Harvest Gold, but we'd like to hear from you," he says.

A shock of cold hits Nadine from behind and she turns toward it, bending her neck to catch it on the forehead.

"Could you tell us what happened there? What happened to your son?" the constable asks. "Nadine? It's better if you talk to us now."

Claire continues to write and the scratching of the pen is sharp, almost shrill in the room.

"You know what happened if you're here," Nadine says.

"Who was with you in the room last night?"

"Does it matter?"

"Your son is still in intensive care right now, so I think it does matter. Don't you think the person who was involved in what happened should also be questioned?"

The folded piece of paper with Al's phone number is still in her purse.

"Do you love your son, Nadine?"

She looks up at him but swallows the words that want to spew forth.

"Why won't you talk to us?"

"Why is she here?" Nadine motions to Claire and the constable lets her answer.

"Our main role is to ensure the safety of children and their families."

"What does that mean?"

"I'm just here to listen to you. We have the same goal—to ensure Aaron's safe," Claire says.

"I don't know if he's safe because no one will tell me anything." Nadine's frustration is evident.

"Did you arrange for that surgery to happen, Ms. Gourlay?" Claire's voice comes out in a whisper.

Nadine nods. "He didn't want to be in pain anymore."

"What do you mean by that?" Constable Melnyk asks.

"Months and months we spent trying to get people like you, like her, to listen and no one would."

"We're here to listen now," Claire says.

Nadine falls silent again.

"I'm going to be honest with you right here," Constable Melnyk says. "This is a serious situation and there could be serious consequences. But those consequences don't have to be so harsh if you help us sort through this." He pauses. "Did Aaron know what was happening?"

"Of course he did."

"So, he agreed to it?"

"He didn't *agree* to it—he needed it."

"Needed it?" The disbelief is apparent in his voice.

"There is no point in talking because you won't understand." Nadine turns back to the window.

"If you're not going to cooperate with us here, we can go to the station."

"I'm not going anywhere until I speak to the doctor."

"That's not how this works."

"I'm not saying anything more."

"Okay, let's go." He rises and motions for her to follow. "Nadine, you're coming with me."

"Are you arresting me?"

"I don't want to go that route but I can."

"I didn't do anything wrong."

"Then you have nothing to be worried about."

"What are you charging me with?"

"We could start with child endangerment."

"I didn't harm my child."

"He's fighting for his life right now, Nadine."

The words knock the air from her lungs, and she teeters on her feet looking for balance. Claire rises to reach out to her, but Constable Melnyk puts his hand up, stopping her. After Nadine steadies herself, she rummages in her purse. "Here then." She pulls the piece of paper from her purse and hands it to the constable. "That's who was there. That's who I arranged things with." Then she sits on the couch beside Claire.

He looks at the paper. "I'll be right back," he says to Claire and steps into the hallway while unclipping his walkie from his shoulder. His voice is audible beyond the door but the words themselves are muffled. Long moments pass before he returns.

"Nadine, I think we should go to the station now."

"I gave you what you asked for."

"I know, but I have some more questions for you and the doctor says you're not going to be able to see Aaron for a while yet."

"You spoke with the doctor?"

He gives a slight nod. "There's no point in staying here."

Nadine's vision blurs. She rises but her footing is unsure and she clutches her purse to her chest in hopes it will help.

"You can meet us there," the constable says to Claire as he guides Nadine from the room.

—

Trish pushes through the doors to the station, Jase in tow.

"Morning," she says to Bev at the reception desk. "I was just called to come in and answer some questions about—"

"Follow me," Bev cuts her off, always more concerned with getting things done than with pleasantries. She leads them into an interview room. "Coffee or tea? Or juice for the boy?"

"We're fine, thank you."

"Officer Ryan will be right with you." Bev closes the door behind her.

Trish scoops Jase's crayons out of her bag as he carries his drawing that he rolled into a perfect cylinder to a chair. He spreads it out on the table before him. He's used one of the larger sheets of paper that he brought home from school, the ones his teacher gave him because he said Jase was a budding artist. It's a superhero, though Trish doesn't know which one. She can't keep track of all the characters from the comics and movies. This superhero is just an outline, but Jase has filled in some of the background. Birds and the tops of tall buildings below the flying figure. A city. Jase has never been to a city that large.

Trish dusts some assorted dry crumbs off an orange plastic chair at the other end of the table then takes a seat.

"Thanks for coming in," says Officer Ryan, the new kid who's fresh from the depot in Regina, as he enters.

He looks both eager and nervous as he asks questions. Trish recounts what she can from the previous night. She tells him she checked the mother and her son in and took their order on the phone when they called down. She tells him what she saw in the room after the ambulance arrived.

The officer looks at Jase, who's working on a giant sun in the upper corner of his picture behind the superhero. "How's he doing?" he asks, his voice low, gentle.

"It's upset him for sure," she says. "But," turning to Jase, "you're okay, right?"

Jase nods his head, not looking up from his drawing.

The officer turns back to her, his voice still quiet. "Did anyone else come to rent a room for the night?"

"No."

"Was it a busy night in the restaurant?"

"Earlier in the evening it was, like usual. But at around that time it was after the dinner rush and there were only a few customers."

"Did you know them all?"

Trish senses that he's looking for something. "I think so, yes." She thinks back. "Roger was there." The officer nods.

"Sean, my husband, came by for a while because our son was there too." Again, the officer nods. "Some other regulars."

"Like who?"

"Renée and Dorie Mitchell. Melissa Troupe and her two kids. Came in after dance class in the city. Daryl Pelletier and a couple of his cousins who're visiting. Al Klassen was there, and—"

"Did you wait on him?" he interrupts her. A flicker crosses his face, almost a spark. Trish catches it.

"No, he was at one of Lenore's tables."

"So, you didn't speak with him?"

She shakes her head. "Wait," she stops, "I did. Barely. Lenore had already locked the doors by the time he tried to leave. I let him out."

"Why was he there so late?"

"It happens. We sometimes have stragglers."

"So, it wasn't out of the ordinary?"

"No." Though, it was unusual for Al to be there so late. A wave of shock rolls through her. Trish answers a few more questions before the officer leads them out of the room. He follows her out into the bright light of the day, and Jase races ahead to climb the giant boulder on the front lawn.

"Thanks again for coming in. We may call you again."

As she turns away, Roger is approaching her straight on, and just to the side and half a foot in front of him is the mother from last night. He's leading her into the station. Trish moves off quickly to collect Jase. The woman doesn't seem to notice Trish, her eyes empty and unfocused.

On the drive home, Trish takes the long route. Was Al involved? How did he know the boy? Lenore said Al was gay, but that doesn't explain anything. Maybe there are other secrets he's been hiding? Secrets can be buried deep. Trish fights the urge to glance at Jase in the back seat. She stares straight ahead instead, squinting her eyes against the flaring sun.

—

THE KNOCK ON THE FRONT DOOR wakes him. Nadine and Aaron don't know where he lives, they've only had his post office box number, but it wouldn't be hard for them to find out. Al checks his skin in the mirror, to see how patchy it is, but it's surprisingly calm despite the stress he's been feeling lately, only a couple of flakes here and there. He opens the door. It's Roger. He's in uniform and his shades are on. Two big mirrors over his eyes so that when Al looks at Roger, he only sees himself.

"Afternoon, Al."

He nods back. Stomach sinking.

"Could I come in for a minute?"

Al leads him to the living room and knows they will be more than a minute.

"Can I get you a coffee?"

"Please."

In the kitchen, Al sets everything on the tray his mother had used to serve tea. He's not going to lie; he's going to be honest about everything. At this point, it doesn't make a difference, it's all over and done with.

"Thought you were finished your job now," Al says as he enters the living room.

"Pretty much. Just some paperwork left and..." He pauses. "This."

Al stirs his coffee, the spoon clanks. "I think I know why you're here."

Roger takes a sip, and then another.

"How did you find out about it?"

"Sutures broke. They called an ambulance."

Al's chest hums to life. He should have checked in on them when he went back to the Gold. He thought about it the whole time he was in the restaurant. It's why he went back and why he stayed so long, but he couldn't muster up the courage. Really, he shouldn't have left them at all. "Is he okay?"

"We don't know yet."

There's a long pause as Roger lets Al absorb this.

"I have some questions I need to ask you."

"Go ahead."

"How do you know this woman and her son?"

"I met them when I was helping out on a farm near their hometown."

"Was it their farm?"

"No. And sorry, it was just her I met then. We were both working on the farm."

"Whose farm?"

"Sherman Demchuk's." Al pauses, and Roger scratches in his notebook. "I didn't meet Aaron until yesterday..." His voice trails off.

"What were you doing at this farm?"

"Castrating calves." Al swallows loudly, though his mouth is dry.

"What was she doing?"

"Just odd jobs. She doesn't have farm experience, but Sherman hired her on as a favour to her brother-in-law. Something like that."

"When was this?"

"Last spring."

"When exactly?"

"Mid-June. Don't remember the dates but it was during a weekend."

His questions are endless but they're matter-of-fact, straightforward questions that Al answers in a matter-of-fact, straightforward way. He tells Roger about all the letters.

"Do you still have them?" Roger asks.

Al heads upstairs to his closet and pulls them from the box on the shelf. He hands them all to Roger. Twelve in total. As he watches Roger hold them in his fist, he wishes he'd lied about them. Wishes he'd said that he didn't keep them.

Long after their coffees are done and silence has stuffed itself into the room, Roger looks at Al. "I have to take you to the station now."

"I know."

"I'll need your tools too," Roger says.

Al leads him out to the barn and to the metal chest on the work table at the back. It's rusted and full of dents. It's where he stores the tools and what he uses to transport them to other farms. But he didn't use it the other night because he thought it too soiled and grimy for the hotel room. Disrespectful in a way he couldn't quite explain. He opens the lid and the hinges squeak. He reaches in and hands them to Roger.

"I'll take the whole box."

But Roger already has the letters in one hand so Al carries the chest for him.

"Can you do one thing for me?" Al asks. "Can you call the hospital and find out if he's going to be okay? I just need to know that."

"I can't do that." Roger's voice is quiet. He leads Al to the car and guides him into the back seat. The humming that was in Al's chest revs up, and stronger. So strong, his arms feel weak.

—

LENORE HOLDS THE SHEETS to her face and smells Roger's deodorant before placing them in the washing machine. He's a good man, maybe too good for her. Her mind and heart are always at odds. Her mind knows what's sensible and her heart doesn't. That's why she's knocking on fifty and still alone. She's never been able to trust her own taste in men. Daniel is the perfect example.

She was twenty-five the summer he came to town. Just a few months before, Lenore had found out that her biological parents were both Métis from the north. It explained her dark hair and darker eyes. So different from her adoptive family's. Her mother had died shortly after her birth, and her father only three years before Lenore began her search. She did learn that an older couple, Louise and Leonard Isnana from the Tipiskiskum community near Saltus, had also lived for several years in the same community up north and knew her biological family. She visited with them and had tea a couple of times to look at photos and hear stories. They introduced her to Daniel.

He was a master's student in Native studies from North Dakota and had come to town to do some research on Tipiskiskum. Daniel was excited for Lenore to learn more about her heritage and culture. He confessed he was a little envious. He'd grown up with the understanding that his family had links to the Otoe tribe around the area now known as Nebraska, but while completing his undergrad he couldn't make the connections.

Lenore was also excited, but nervous. She was raised by a family who loved her very much, and though they supported her in her search, she didn't want to betray them. And while she wanted to know everything about her parents, she didn't feel

Métis, if there was such a thing. It was strange to think that she was an entirely different person than she knew, like she was a stranger to herself. She needed to take things slow.

Daniel helped to track down some of her living relatives. An aunt, two uncles and several cousins living way up in the northeastern corner of the province near Pine Cree Point. He wanted to drive up there with her and record the reunion, so that he might use it in his thesis or another project, but Lenore wanted time to process everything and exchange a letter or two with her relatives before meeting them. She planned to drive up later in the fall, before winter set in.

In the meantime, Daniel took her under his wing and taught her a few things. She learned how to make bannock, how to speak a little Cree and how to bead simple designs. He taught her other things too that she wished she never learned. Like how to prepare a syringe.

Roger is nothing like Daniel. Daniel let her float free and unsecured, but she senses Roger would keep her tethered to the earth.

That's what he did last night. Even though his calm, robot-like demeanour pricked at her at times, it was exactly what she needed. It's funny how the night ended up. If that ordeal in room 203 hadn't happened, she might have missed her chance with Roger entirely. But it took that ordeal for her realize what's important. That her whole life since Daniel has been spent running from things she felt she didn't deserve. But she does deserve Roger. She does.

She has the next two days off but she wishes she was on shift tonight because she could talk about this with Trish. She could call her. It'd be a bit weird but it's been nothing but weird lately. Lenore grabs her purse instead.

Trish answers the door, tired and worn.

"Hey," Lenore says, like nothing's strange. Behind Trish, Jase leans against the wall in the hallway. "Hi, Jase. No school today?"

He shakes his head, always quiet and shy. He treats her like a stranger every time she sees him. Once, two years ago, she babysat him for a whole weekend while Trish and Sean went to the city for a romantic getaway, hoping to get things back on track. The biggest favour that Trish had ever asked of her and it made her feel good. She enjoyed the weekend too. She had Jase giggling so hard because of the gas she'd worked up from all the junk food. He even fell into her, held onto her so tight and begged her to stop because his stomach was sore. The next week she ran into him and Trish at the grocery store and he stood behind his mom, almost hiding. It broke her heart.

Right now, she wishes she had a fart ready to rip. She'd love to see his reaction. Would he remember or would it push him farther away?

"I'm just running a bath for Jase. Do you want to come in?"

The place hasn't changed at all in the two years since Lenore's been here. And hasn't since they first bought the place from that elderly couple who moved out to the coast to be with their kids. The couple left all their furniture behind and Trish and Sean never replaced it. Lace curtains. Gold-framed oil paintings of forests and streams. Velvet couch and loveseat with a matching floral pattern. The kind with the little covers on the arms and headrests. You'd half expect the elderly couple to walk in the front door right now.

Down the hall, Trish tells Jase to put on clean underwear and pyjamas. There were times when Lenore fantasized about Trish and Sean both passing—a car accident, or illness—and being asked to become Jase's guardian. She'd raise him to come out of his shell, to speak up, to laugh out loud in public. She'd teach him to never hold back.

Trish comes in with coffee and puts a mug down on the table for Lenore.

"How are you doing?" Lenore asks.

Trish takes a moment. "That was really fucked up."

"So fucked up."

"You get called to the station today?"

"No. You?"

"Went down for questioning. I thought they'd call you too."

"I told Roger everything I knew last night." She pauses. "He drove me home."

"I wondered... Your car was still in the lot when we left."

"Didn't feel like I could drive. That shook me up."

"Me too. I asked Tamara to take my shift tonight."

"How's Jase?"

Trish looks down the hall, toward the splashing sounds in the tub. "We haven't talked about it. He's having nightmares, though. He's too afraid to sleep now."

"Poor guy."

Quiet descends. The cuckoo clock on the wall, which doesn't cuckoo anymore but still keeps the time, tocks. This is new territory for them, sitting together and chatting like girlfriends who go for brunch. Maybe this wasn't a good idea. "He stayed over." It spills out.

"What?"

"It just happened."

"Wait. He asked you out and you said no, but that same night you sleep with him?"

"I think it just shocked me when he asked." That may be true.

"Holy shit." Trish leans back in her chair, staring at her. After a moment, a smile forms.

"What?"

"I'm happy for you."

"Me too," she says slyly.

"I don't need the details about Roger's abilities, please," Trish teases and they laugh. "Weird timing, though."

Lenore tenses, sensing the squabble they had last night surfacing at the edges but she doesn't care. She doesn't need anyone's approval.

"Did Roger tell you who was in the hotel room last night? Who did that to the boy?" Trish changes the subject and Lenore's glad for it.

"No, I haven't seen him since early this morning."

"I can't believe it." Trish pauses. "It was Al."

Lenore processes.

"Al Klassen," Trish clarifies since Lenore doesn't react.

A stone starts to grow in Lenore's stomach. "What do you mean?"

"He was the one in the hotel room who did that to the kid. It's awful. And so weird given what we talked about last night."

"You mean about him being gay?"

Trish nods.

"What does that have to do with what happened to that kid?" She feels defensive but isn't sure why.

"Maybe it doesn't, but how do you think they know each other?"

"He's just a boy, though," Lenore's stone continues to grow, heavy and full, like it will come right up and out of her throat. "I can't imagine..." But she doesn't continue.

"I don't know what to think about anything anymore."

Trish tells her she's already cleaned up the hotel room as best she could and put their suitcase of things in the closet behind the desk. They try to keep the conversation going but without plates of food to carry and orders to take, their rhythm is off. When Jase hollers that he's done, Lenore downs what's in her cup and makes her exit.

—

AT THE STATION, THE SAME QUESTIONS were repeated, and Al gave the same answers. He's been waiting hours now. The new officer has been checking in on him, bringing coffee and water, and as he comes and goes, the other officers' voices bounce down the hallway and into the room, snippets of conversations and ringing phones. He finishes four small Styrofoam cups of coffee with powdered cream.

Roger knocks once on the door before entering. He's carrying all the letters that were sent to Al, the sheets of paper all opened and stacked in his hands. The envelopes are missing. Roger sits and leafs through the letters a moment.

When the first one arrived, it came by general delivery. Al was confused and was sure someone got the name wrong or was mistaking him for someone else. Even when he read the first paragraph where she introduced herself as the woman he'd met at the Demchuk farm near Beauville, it took him a while to put the pieces together. The letter didn't say why she was writing. She only wrote a bit about what she'd been up to workwise since they met, and asked him how he was doing. It was as if they'd been close friends that had lost touch over time.

Al didn't respond right away. Not because he was ignoring it, but because he was carefully thinking about what to say. And while he was thinking, two more arrived in less than two weeks. At first, they were short and from Nadine only. She wrote about everyday stuff. It was odd at first, but it was nice to think of other ways in which his life might have played out. It was in the third letter that she mentioned her son. She said Aaron wished he could have met Al too. In a way, Al was touched by the notion.

A whole week went by without any more letters, and it was then that Al finally sat down and wrote back. He wrote about his farm and what it had been like when it was still operational, and how he could barely get everything done he needed to in a day. He also wrote about the cooler nights and the shorter days that were starting to set in. He signed it off *yours truly*. It didn't sit right but he couldn't come up with anything else.

"I've read through these all," Roger says, bouncing the end of his pen on the table so its nib clicks in and out, "but there's one thing I still don't understand."

Al waits.

"How'd she get you to do it?"

"Her son needed help."

"You believed her?"

"You don't think he did?"

"I've known you thirty-odd years now."

"'Bout that."

"You're a stand-up guy. Honest, work hard."

Al senses this is going somewhere.

"I read those letters and I think, here's a woman who needs some serious help herself. Who, if you'll excuse the expression, is off her rocker. But you didn't. Why?"

"I didn't think she was."

"Did you fancy her?"

"What?"

"It's understandable. Living alone for years."

After he sent his first letter back, more letters from Nadine and Aaron arrived, and more frequently. Sometimes Nadine and Aaron would write together, sometimes separately. In December just before Christmas, Al received three letters in one week. They were like presents.

Early on, Aaron only referenced his situation indirectly. *I haven't gotten out of bed since Tuesday*, or, *Today was a really hard day*. But in the new year, he started to share more details. He wrote about travelling to Winnipeg and Calgary, his visits with doctors and psychologists. How they just wanted to medicate him rather than help him. Aaron wrote that no one understood or believed him. It was difficult for Al, because he didn't really understand, either, but he never told Aaron that, he never questioned the boy. He also never asked about his condition. It was easier not to.

But maybe there was something about the kid's situation that Al did understand. Something about the kind of torture Aaron felt. About being different and not knowing why or how to fix it. But he'd never talked with anyone about it before and he certainly wasn't going to start by writing to a fifteen-year-old boy. It wouldn't be fair. Besides, Al wouldn't know what to say.

"I didn't fancy her," Al says.

"No?"

"Not like that." Al immediately regrets saying it because Roger smiles, gathers up all the letters and taps their edges on the table, like he's figured it all out. He rises and leaves the room, a smug air about him.

Sometime in the deep of winter, when the cold was so severe it was hard to breathe the air, Al started to daydream. Just fantasies, really. He didn't know why this family of two had picked him out of everyone else in the world to write to, but there it was. He was beginning to understand just how shitty life was for them in that town in Manitoba because of Aaron's condition. He thought if Aaron wanted to live as a girl, he should move to another place where no one knew. If he moved to Saltus, no one would need to know the truth, and it wouldn't bother Al. Not one bit. If it made the kid happier, then why not? It's none of his business, really, and it shouldn't be anyone else's. People might wonder if Nadine and him were a couple, but let them wonder. Let them believe it if they need to. Besides, over time, it would be like they were a family of sorts.

That was what he wanted to ask them when he saw them in person. He wanted to tell them they could move in with him.

Sometimes he'd hint at it in his responses to them. He'd write about how quiet his life was in Saltus, about how much room he had in the house, and about how distant he was from the other folks in town. But he never came right out with the offer in his letters. It was something he needed to ask in person.

He can't remember when his idea changed from a daydream, from a way to pass the time when doing chores around the house, to a real possibility. It likely didn't happen in a single moment. It likely happened slowly, over time. But he wishes he could pinpoint it to a week, to a particular day. To the exact second.

Almost an hour goes by before Roger returns, bringing other paperwork with him. He hands Al an appearance notice and tells him he must be in court on the day and time indicated in the document, two days from now. He tells him that he's being charged with practising medicine without a licence, and if he doesn't have a lawyer, one will be appointed to him.

"Also," Roger says, "you should know that the media from the city have gotten wind. I'll be giving a statement shortly. I won't provide any personal details, but a crew is coming to town. You need a ride home?"

Al nods. "Can I have my letters back?"

"Those are part of the investigation now."

It's the new officer who drives him. The kid who's not from around here. He lets Al ride in the front and he avoids Main Street, though there's hardly anybody out because it's past suppertime. It's still light out but the day's turned cloudy and cool, like they've skipped a whole season and fall is moving in again, like time is speeding up, racing past him.

"Do you know how the boy's doing?" Al breaks the silence.

The officer's confused at first, like it could be any boy Al's referring to.

"At the hospital..." Al trails off.

After a moment, "Oh. No, I don't." The kid leans against the driver's side door as he drives, putting the biggest possible distance between them.

People must think horrible things of him, worse than after that summer with Raymond. He decides not to say anything else the rest of the way, just stares out the window.

Raymond had his own letters but he didn't keep them private. He carried them everywhere and would read them out loud to anyone who would listen. Letters from his brother in the war. Raymond shared the first letter with Al that second Sunday afternoon after he'd finished helping Mr. Nielsen. Once again, he was sent up to the house for a snack and this time it was banana loaf, and the lemonade was just as tart as before.

There wasn't much in the letter, it wasn't even a page long, more like a postcard. All Douglas's letters were like that. Brief, almost perfunctory. But Raymond read into them like novels. He'd picture whole scenes from one sentence. In that first letter Raymond shared with Al, Douglas wrote about a soldier he met from Scotland. He only provided the soldier's name and hometown, but Raymond imagined his fiancée, the type of house they'd have when he returned, the number of kids in their future. Al liked his animated musings, and sometimes he stayed so late that by the time he rode home his parents had already finished dinner.

Al thought they'd become friends over those summer months but when he returned to school, Raymond ignored him and shared his brother's letters with the older students in his grade. Sometimes he'd wave to Al in the hallway but only when no one was around, almost apologetically, but that was it. Al worried he'd said or done something wrong but he was too intimidated to ask him. It wasn't until the end of September when they spoke again.

Al wonders if the young officer beside him has ever been told the story of what happened that weekend or if that rumour has long since died. No matter, the kid has no idea who Al really is, even if he's already formed his opinions.

They reach the outskirts of town and the highway that leads up through the hills and out to his place. When the snow has all melted and the weather is hot and dry, the hills will be covered in sage and brush. From a distance they'll look draped in green velvet.

—

IT'S A STALE GREY DAY. The trees still naked but looking hopeful. After leaving Trish's, Lenore takes a long, circuitous walk through town to the Harvest Gold to get her car. The whole way there she thinks about Al. If there's anything she's learned from her job, it's that there are always things about people you never expect. But she learned that off the job too.

The day before she first found out about Daniel's drug use, they had spent time at Tipiskiskum visiting and listening to some of the kokums and mushums tell stories about the past. She was happy Daniel invited her and allowed her to share that with him. It was intimate. The next day they stayed in bed all day, and only got up to eat leftovers from the fridge and make love. They had nowhere to be, and even if they did, it didn't matter. Then just before the sun went down, Lenore said she was hungry again. He smiled at her and said he had something she might like.

She laughed when she saw his kit. She thought it was a joke. It was wrapped up in a leather satchel traditionally decorated with beads. But he didn't laugh and she couldn't believe that for the two months they were dating, she never knew.

She resisted at first, said she wasn't interested, but he told her it was the most spiritual thing she could experience. It was similar to peyote, he told her, a sacred medicine. He was smarter than her, smart enough to know just how ignorant and fool-ish she was. He reached out and caressed her arm, squeezed it. "Kiskinwahamâtowin," he said, "kiskinwahamâtowin." He said it each and every time after.

Lenore quickens her pace to her car in the Gold's parking lot and works up a sweat. The engine catches at first and eventually starts, but instead of heading home, she remembers what Trish said about the suitcase and she drives right up to the restaurant doors. Leaving the car running and her driver's side door open while she heads inside, Lenore grabs the suitcase from the closet behind the desk and puts it in her trunk.

In the hospital parking lot, before pulling it back out, she stops and looks at the case. It's grass green with a plastic handle and two metal clasps. She tells herself not to, but she pushes on the clasps and opens it. She's glad she did because Trish hasn't folded anything properly, and the tubes and bottles of lotions and such are just thrown in willy-nilly, with no protective casing. Lenore digs for a plastic grocery bag in her back seat and puts all the bottles and other containers in it. Ties a knot at the top. She folds a sweatshirt, two pairs of jeans, and then, underneath everything else, she finds a pretty yellow dress with white flowers. She folds the dress carefully and places it on top.

AT THE NURSES' STATION INSIDE, she waits for assistance.

"You're here to see who again?"

"The Gourlays." The nurse eyes her. "They came in last night." Though it's clear the nurse knows who she's referring to. "I have some of their personal things." She holds up the case. "I work at the Gold and just want to return them."

"The mother's not here."

"Is the boy? Can I leave this with him?"

"You can leave it here with me but we don't guarantee the safety of personal belongings."

"How is he doing?"

"We can only disclose personal information to family."

"Of course."

"Do you want me to take that?" The nurse points to the case.

"You can't lock it up anywhere?"

"We can't, no."

Despite having just gone through the case herself, Lenore doesn't want anyone else to do so except the boy and his mother.

Strangely, she has an urge to protect their privacy. "I'll hold on to it."

In the parking lot, she puts the suitcase back in her trunk. Heading back home, she has to cross the highway again to get to her house in the north end, but following another urge, she turns west on number 53.

Years ago, she once tried to escape on this same highway. It was three months after the first time she shot up and the first few snows had already fallen. Her plan to take a trip up north long forgotten. It was just before morning and Daniel was still in bed. She walked into the kitchen to get some water and saw his car keys on the counter in between the dirty dishes. The decision was made before she even thought about it. By the time she reached the outskirts of town the sun was starting to rise, and a part of her that she'd been silencing was too. She turned the music off. The air rushing through the open windows was all the noise she needed.

She had no plans, no clothes and hardly any money in the bank but it didn't matter, she'd figure it out. Without Daniel. Without his satchel. Step by step, she told herself. Don't think about next week, next month, next year, just think about the next second. That worked for half an hour, and then the seconds grew longer. Each one pulled her thoughts back to that beaded bag.

SHE TURNS OFF THE HIGHWAY and onto a grid road, second-guessing herself the whole way. In less than fifteen minutes, she arrives at the Klassen property.

When she was a kid, Al worked at the grocery store. She always stopped in there on Saturdays with her friends to fill bags of candy from the bulk bins before heading out to the gravel pit to play. He was much older than her, a young man already, with floppy hair that was out of step with the buzz cuts all the other guys had. She would stare at it and think about sticking her fingers in it, scrunching it. She didn't tell anyone.

She slows as she approaches his driveway. His truck is there and she could pull in, go knock on the door. But she's already knocked on one door today and regretted it. She drives right past the house and heads farther down the grid road, feeling stupid. Once she's far enough away, she slows to a stop.

Out here beyond the town limits the land looks different. It's up above the valley. She can see where the land dips down to the socket that holds Saltus. Up here there are no buildings, no streets with houses, no hills to block her view. Up here there's just sky. So much of it, it's dizzying. All those years ago, when she first drove herself outside of town, that moment was thrilling because it felt like a new beginning of some kind. A change for the better, for all the things she wanted. Now, here she is, in this moment, still in the same spot.

She grips the steering wheel, then turns the car around. Foot heavy on the gas.

Driving back to town, Lenore thinks about Roger's hair. It's thinning and not floppy at all, but maybe she will still be able to scrunch it.

—

HE MADE A MISTAKE. The boots shouldn't be so red. Jase was going to do them brown but picked up the red crayon at the last second and now they're too bright. His superhero looks more like a clown. He might have to go over them in black, but he'll have to be very careful not to colour over the red lines too far and make the boots look larger. It'll be tricky. He doesn't want to start all over because he likes how he drew the body flying in the sky, and he won't be able to draw it again and make it look as good.

His mom's watching a show about lawyers on TV, and his dad's out back in the garage, tinkering on things for other people. Sometimes it's motorbikes, sometimes lawn mowers. Jase wants them all to be back in the bed like they were last night. They were a family again, if only for a short time. They only shared the bed again because of that boy and his mother. He hears that woman's voice yelling, sees the blood in a pool on the bed and floor.

Today, everything's gone back to normal. Except it's even worse because his parents are fighting, even though there's no yelling or shouting.

"It's time for bed," his mom says. "Did you hear me?"

"Yes." Jase doesn't want to cause any more trouble tonight so rises and takes his juice glass to the kitchen. As he places it in the sink, the wooden block full of the sharp knives catches his eye, the ones he's not supposed to touch. They remind him again of the hotel room. When his dad took him to pick up the bucket of chicken he'd ordered for dinner, Jase went inside with him and he heard his dad talking to the woman who worked there.

144

They said the boy in the hotel room had asked someone to cut him like that.

Jase takes one of the knives out of the block, his reflection visible in the shiny blade. Why did that boy want to do that to himself? He must've wanted it real bad to go through that much pain. Jase doesn't think he'd be strong enough to do something like that. He presses the knife against his thumb but it hurts too much before he breaks any skin.

"Jase?" His father steps into the room from the back door. "What are you doing?"

Jase slides the knife into its slot. "It was in the wrong spot." He walks past his dad. "Good night."

In bed, he examines his thumb. He could never be as strong as that boy was.

—

THE SUN NOW DOWN, Roger sits on his back deck with a cold Scotch in his hand, finally able to debrief himself on everything in his own head. The entire day slipped away from him because he had been going non-stop straight through until now, and on a lack of sleep from the night before. But it had reminded him how important his job is. That boy, still in the hospital with part of his manhood gone. Things are in motion with the mother, though. Roger sips at his Scotch.

In between all that and trying to close out his other files and wrap things up, he'd get a little flutter in his stomach once in a while. Out of the blue, like a little wave of nausea. It'd take him a moment to realize what it was. Lenore.

He's not sure when his attraction to her first took hold. They've chatted regularly over the years at the Harvest Gold but it's only been in the last couple years that he thought about the possibility. It took almost a full year of him thinking about it, and then another to work up the guts to ask her out. When she first said no last night, he wasn't sure how he could go back there, which is the fear that had kept him from asking for so long. If that incident hadn't taken place, things might not have ended up the way they did. Maybe Lenore would've come around later? Sometimes people get so stuck in their ways they just need a little push. Same goes for him. He doesn't believe in fate but maybe sometimes things do happen for a reason.

He takes another pull on his drink, stares at the stars growing clear in the sky. It's not until she's already standing in front of him that he realizes he heard footsteps along the side of the house.

"I rang the bell but there was no answer."

"Doorbell hasn't worked in a while." He straightens himself in his chair. "Never been a handyman."

"I was about to leave when I saw the light out back." She holds up a bottle of rye. "Retirement present."

"Please, join me." He'd like to share a nightcap. "Scotch okay, or should I open this?"

"Scotch is fine." She steps by him to an empty chair and he can see she's careful with her footing. She's already been drinking and he feels a pang of sadness. He doesn't want to be a late-night call.

Inside, he checks himself in a mirror, pours her a single finger. When he hands it to her, she holds it out and they clink glasses before she takes a sip and puts it down on the table, which wobbles with its weight. Another thing Roger will have to figure out how to fix.

"I heard Al was taken to the station today."

Roger nods.

"Did you see him?"

"I brought him in."

"Can't wrap my head around it." She shakes her head. "Did he say how he knew that boy and his mother?"

"The investigation's still going on so I can't really get into the specifics."

"Of course."

"It's not that I don't trust you." He's not sure that he does, though. Working down at the Harvest Gold, it'd be hard for her not to say anything, but that doesn't make her any different from anyone else in town.

"I understand." She sinks back and stares off into the yard. It may be the bit of light from the kitchen window above, the way it slants down across her, or maybe it's the stars way up high, but Lenore is prettier than he realized. Her black hair is darker in the night, it slurps up the light, and her eyes are black too but they shine the light right back.

"When I was standing there watching that kid," she says, her tone softer, different, "I thought there'd been an accident at first, like he'd fallen or something. I never thought that it was on purpose."

Somewhere down the street a car door slams. A chilly breeze wafts through a couple of times.

"You knew I was adopted, right?"

He nods, glad for the change in topic.

"My parents were Métis."

He figured there was some Native background in her but it wasn't something he'd ever bring up.

"Could've met some of my family years ago but didn't."

"May be just as well." Roger uses his foot to nudge a twig within arm's reach. "The Schills were good people."

"They were, but I often wonder what would've happened if I met or was raised by my real family. Where would I be and, I guess, who would I be?"

"But being Native or Métis or whatever, that's just where you came from," he says, tossing the twig off the deck. "It's not who you are."

"But that's exactly what I'm saying," she says. "What if it is who I am? Who I'm supposed to be?"

"The Schills raised you right, though."

"What do you mean by 'right'?" There's an edge there.

"I mean, like one of their own. Didn't they?"

"I'm not saying they didn't, and I'm not saying I wish they hadn't." Her jaw clenches.

"Then I don't think I'm following."

"What I'm trying to say is, I have no idea what that kid in the hospital is going through, but sometimes I wonder if there was another person I was meant to be."

He doesn't see the connection at all. Plus, pining and longing doesn't get anyone anywhere. He finishes what's in his glass.

"Does that make sense?"

"Are you comparing your being adopted with that kid?"

"No, not exactly. I've just heard the rumours in town that the boy wanted that done to him because he wants to be a girl, and I can't imagine how terrible things must have—"

"You believe that story?"

"You don't?"

"You think he's a girl trapped in a boy's body?"

"Why wouldn't I?"

Roger scoffs.

"What do you think?"

"Doesn't make a lick of sense. What's next in this world? Someone's a rabbit born in a human body?"

"Sex change operations do happen nowadays."

"Doesn't mean they should."

"You don't believe people can be born with the wrong body parts?"

"I think that woman brought up her son to believe that."

Lenore stares at him a moment, lost for words. She downs her drink and then opens the bottle she brought over. It's definitely not going the way he wanted, though he doesn't decline when she also fills his glass.

"But why would she do that?"

"Attention."

"No one was supposed to find out about it."

It's like she came here to pick a fight, but he really doesn't need to be grilled after the day he had today. "You can't make sense of crazy."

"I thought she was bitchy, but not crazy." She takes a swig. "There's a difference, believe me." It's meant as a joke and Roger forces out a laugh.

"You didn't see her today, but I can tell you she was something. She was glib and unapologetic about all of it, even with her son still fighting for his life. A night in a cold cell will make her come to her senses. Tends to do that."

"She's at the station?"

"Had to haul her in. She was uncooperative." He's letting her stew overnight.

"So that kid's all alone at the hospital?"

"Best to keep them separated. Doctors don't know how this'll all play out for him."

The night settles in around them. An owl hoots in the distance.

"It's getting late," he says.

Lenore gets up right away and his stomach sinks because he assumes she's about to stalk off, but before he takes a step, Lenore's against him. Her face stern, serious. And maybe there's a tinge of anger too, but she kisses him, roughly. Nips his bottom lip and he tastes the alcohol on her but he doesn't want the night to go that way again. Last night was different, last night things were already heading that way before they poured anything. But if they do it again, it might just make the whole thing about sex. He pulls back and sees her hurt immediately.

"Maybe we should wait."

"For what?"

"I don't want to screw this up."

"By being together?"

"By moving too fast."

"Too fast?" She laughs. "We're old, Roger. Fast is for when you're young and not sure about things. But we're old and I

don't know about you, but I don't want to waste any more time."
She brushes her fingers lightly down his forearm. Gooseflesh
rises, and he leads her inside.

—

THE CELL IS SMALLER than she expected. Cleaner, too, though
she's never been inside a cell before. She's never even visited
anyone in jail. A few people she's known have done time. Her
own father for one. That was one of the first things the officer
who dragged her down here wanted to discuss. He dug up info
on her parents, then called the detachment in their hometown,
where Nadine grew up. When she was a kid, her father spent
a night now and then drying out in the tank. Mostly he'd be
picked up when out at the bar or partying with his friends, but
a couple of times the cops came to the house and took him in.
Neighbours had called.

The officer didn't stop there. He seemed to have found
everyone who was willing to spill shit about her. He even found
out about the time her own neighbours called the cops on her.
She wasn't even nineteen at the time and was living in a trailer
outside Beauville with that asshole. It wasn't unusual for there
to be yelling and screaming, maybe a hole punched in the wall
or a broken stool, but after one particularly bad night, he tossed
her out the front door and locked it. She was practically naked
and the kids next door watched her through their bedroom window as she trudged through the pathway between their trailers
to the back door, her feet squishing in cold mud. That was after

she left home, when she hated her parents but was still heading down the same road as them. It was also before Aaron, before she changed direction.

"You've had some difficult men in your life," the constable said, as if pitying her. As if his mock sympathy was going to win her over. Like all the therapists and psychologists who tried to use her past to make sense of the present. They always seemed to distill it down to the same explanation: she hated all men, including her son, and therefore, wanted him to be a daughter. It was mind-numbingly stupid for such highly educated people.

She's not cold but she pulls the brown woollen blanket around her anyway. It's sometime in the middle of the night, but the light in the hall is bright enough to keep the inside of her cell well illuminated.

It's been around twenty-four hours since Aaron was taken to the hospital and she has still not heard a word. She consoles herself that surely she would have if things went really wrong, though that's hardly comforting.

She doesn't want to think about it, but if things were to go badly, she'd rather just stay in a cell. Sitting here now, there is something appealing about it. She wouldn't have to make any more decisions and worry about whether they were right or wrong. There'd be a set of regimented rules to follow. The cell is small. Tiny, even. But it would contain her. Hold her in.

—

"YOU STAYING UP?" Sean pokes his head into the living room before heading to bed.

"Just for a bit." She points to the television. A *M*A*S*H* rerun is on, but she's really waiting for the news. During a commercial break there was a clip announcing an "unbelievable" story from the town of Saltus. She could've told Sean, he would've stayed up with her to watch it, but she'd rather watch it alone.

The brash *Nightly News* theme song plays and Trish turns the volume down a couple notches. First, there's a story about a fire in a retirement home in the city, followed by one about a snowmobile accident that killed two people. Then it's on.

"Last night in the town of Saltus," the anchorman says, "there was a horrific incident in the local hotel." He flips over a paper in front of him while continuing to stare into the camera. "We have reporter Stacey Zerr out in Saltus now to give us the details."

The broadcast turns to a young woman standing in the parking lot of the Gold. A bright light shining on her and the hotel sign in the background. "Thank you, Sterling. Down in the idyllic Nistowin Valley, surrounded by rolling hills and the sparkling Nistowin River, the residents of this sleepy town have been jolted awake."

The screen cuts to an image recorded earlier in the day, around sunset. From the top of a hill, the camera scans the valley, an aberration on the landscape, then zooms in on the town, enclosed on all sides by brown hills patched with snow.

"A local farmer is alleged to have performed what is sometimes referred to as 'back-alley surgery' in a room here at the Harvest Gold Inn and Restaurant."

153

They cut to a close-up on the door of room 203. There's no police tape on the door, no sign or anything to indicate that something has happened inside. Stacey Zerr gives very little detail on the event itself but explains what "back-alley surgery" means and mentions some other high-profile examples, mostly in the States.

"We tried speaking with Sergeant Glen Boehmer about the incident."

On screen, Trish sees Glen inside the detachment, standing awkwardly beside a desk. Roger is just behind him next to a large potted plant, its fronds brushing his shoulder. There's a sheen of sweat glistening on Roger's upper lip, catching the light of the camera crew. An odd sense of sympathy for him sneaks up on her.

"We are concerned for everyone who was involved," Glen tells the reporter, "but to protect the integrity of the investigation, we are unable to speak to the specifics of the case."

"But haven't charges already been laid? There's been a confession, hasn't there?"

"I can't discuss the details."

Roger shifts on his feet, back and forth, as if he has something to say, but Glen ignores him.

"Who's confessed?" Stacey asks. "Is it someone from Saltus?"

"Again, I'm sorry, we are unable to comment on an investigation that's still in progress," Glen says.

They cut back to Stacey in the parking lot. "As you can see, Sterling, there is still a lot of information that we don't have, but we will continue to follow up and will have more for you tomorrow."

Trish flicks the TV off and sits in the dark. The reporter called it an idyllic valley but it's not. It's an open wound that never heals.

THEY'LL BOTH BE UP SOON. Sean for work, Jase for school. Trish rose early after a fitful night on the couch. She'd drift off occasionally into sleep, brief and shallow, until being jolted awake by thoughts she couldn't control. Sean won't be happy again.

The coffee she made is too strong but it'll keep her going this morning. Doing what, she doesn't know. Yesterday, she thought all she wanted was some time alone to think about things, but that may have been misguided because last night her thoughts only kept her awake. It's not time away from people she needs, it's time away from herself. That image of the woman on the bed, holding her son, her red hair falling forward like a veil over both of them. It's locked in her brain like a ghost. A warning.

The first time Trish held Jase in her arms, she felt panic, blistering and sharp. She looked at his squashed, wrinkled head of black fuzz and wanted to give him away. Throughout the pregnancy she had been indifferent to the boy in her belly, but she told herself that she would fall in love as soon as she saw him. She was wrong. When he was out, it wasn't that she didn't like him, it was simply that she knew in that moment she shouldn't be a mother. She wasn't meant to look after something so gentle. So malleable. It wasn't a choice she was making. It was just fact. The panic's been there ever since, it's submerged now, but always there. A deep, moving current.

And now here they are. They both stood in that room, side by side. Like they were meant to be there, a curse finally fulfilled. Trish is both terrified and transfixed by Nadine. By the mother who would do anything for her son. It suddenly occurs to Trish what she will do today, and she sets about making sandwiches, a flicker of hope in her periphery.

—

THE STAIRS CREAK as Al makes his way to the kitchen to put the kettle on. He's been awake all night but doesn't feel tired. He grabs the milk from the fridge, which is bare aside from condiments and leftover stew from the week before last. He couldn't eat right now anyway. He's hasn't had much of an appetite for a while, but still, he'll have to get some things from the store soon.

He moves into the living room, switches on the lamp on the side table and slips into the well-worn dent on the end of the couch. Sips his tea and stares at the phone, a beige rotary that his parents bought in the seventies and he's never updated, much like everything else. He wants to pick it up and call the hospital to find out how Aaron's doing. All he knows is what Roger's told him and what's been on the news—the sutures broke, he lost a lot of blood. He must've been so scared.

He used to know some of the nurses who worked there. Like him, they grew up in Saltus, but they've long since retired and moved away. Most of the staff that work there now drive in from other towns or the city. He doesn't know any of them. And they all wear those scrubs that look like pyjamas. It wasn't that long ago when whey still wore that white dress uniform like they wore during the war.

During the last week of August that summer in 1944, Raymond received another letter from his brother overseas. It was Al's last weekend on the farm. He had offered to continue coming but Mr. Nielsen said school should take priority. When Al leaned his bike against the porch to join Raymond for a snack, he was a little sad that it was the last time but neither of them mentioned it. Instead, Raymond shared Douglas's letter with him.

It was dated nearly a month earlier and Douglas was in France, near a place called Caen. Like all of his other letters, it was just a few sentences. Douglas wrote that he was resting in an emergency hospital for a few days after catching some shrapnel in his left leg. He had eighteen stitches but was fine and would be heading to Belgium soon. He was being tended to by a nurse named Julia who didn't speak English. *She has a pretty smile*, he wrote before wishing his family well and signing off.

Raymond folded the letter and slipped it back into its envelope, and Al watched him, waiting for the stories to begin. Raymond was quiet at first, and drank down most of his lemonade, but then he started.

"I bet she never thought of being a nurse before the war. I bet she had other plans to go to school and study. Maybe become a teacher."

Al listened and nodded while Raymond created her whole life story. Her three younger siblings, her father, who was also fighting in the war, and her mother, who was run ragged trying to keep meals on the table and the house in order. He figured

Julia didn't have a steady boyfriend but many suitors, especially with all the soldiers in the area.

His story went on a long time and Al didn't want to interrupt because it was his last visit, but he knew dinner was about to be served at home so he thanked Raymond and stood up.

As Al headed down the porch stairs, Raymond asked, "Would you want to be a nurse if you could?"

Al assumed Raymond meant that if he was in a similar situation as Julia. If he was a woman living across the world in a place called Caen, France, and the world was being torn apart, would he become a nurse?

"I suppose, yeah." Al grabbed his bike and swung his leg over it. "See you at school tomorrow?" But Raymond didn't answer. Maybe he was already planning things then. And if he had talked to Al about what he was thinking, maybe Al would've been prepared. Maybe things could've turned out differently.

Al's tea is losing its heat. He cups both hands around it as if to keep it warm. How could the sutures have broken? They couldn't have broken from tension because he was careful, but was he too careful? Did he tie them too loosely so they simply unspooled?

After all those months and letters, he had started to believe that it really was the only way to help the boy. But it was stupid of him to think that he could be the one to do it.

—

JASE HOPS AROUND THE DIRTY PUDDLES trying not to get muddy. It's bright and hot, and if the sun stays out all the snow might be gone by the time he's out of school. He notices one of his shoelaces has come undone. He stops and holds his lunch bag between his teeth, not wanting to put it down on the wet ground. It's the first time his mom has made his lunch in a long while. He doesn't know what's inside because he's waiting for lunchtime to be surprised.

Jase grips his lunch bag tighter with his fingers. She even asked to look at his latest drawing of his superhero, but he didn't show her. He wants that to be a surprise too. She asked him what kind of superhero he is but Jase lied. He said she'd have to wait to find out, but the truth is he doesn't know yet. He's been thinking about it all the time. He wants the superpower to be different than the ones all the other superheroes have in the movies and comic books, but it hasn't come to him yet. Plus, he still hasn't figured out some of the colours on the costume, or the superhero's name. But the name will come when he figures out the superpower. The two will be connected, he knows that much.

The first bell of the morning rings and Jase still has almost two blocks to go. He starts to jog and as he reaches the stairs, he sees Isaac running toward them from the other direction. Isaac is always teased by the girls because he has a red birthmark across most of his face and he once used his mother's razor to shave off his eyebrows. Everyone called him Alien Isaac and they still do, but he still has lots of friends. He's two years older than Jase even though he's in the same grade, and he sometimes treats Jase like he should be happy Isaac even hangs around him.

The boys stop rushing when they meet up with each other at the bottom of the school's stairs.

"Dude, you're back." Isaac doesn't even wait for Jase to respond. "I heard you saw that guy's nuts being chopped off."

"No." Jase pauses. "Not really."

"But weren't you there?"

"Yeah..."

"Was there blood everywhere?"

Jase feels sad, like Isaac wants something from him that he doesn't want to give. The second bell rings and startles them both.

"I'll tell you at recess." Jase starts up the stairs, clutching his lunch bag so tight his fingernails tear the paper.

—

The smell of frying breakfast sausages wakes her. In the bathroom, he's left out a toothbrush for her on the shelf above the sink, still in its protective blister package. Lenore smiles at his thoughtfulness. Beside it is a half-empty tube of toothpaste, the top half folded over and secured with a binder clip so the paste is already oozing out the end when she removes the cap. It's for sensitive gums and reminds her of all the old people who come into the Harvest Gold who don't want ice in their glass or their soup too hot. It tastes like lotion and she only manages a cursory brush before spitting it out. She turns to the towel rack to wipe her mouth. A hand towel is folded into a crisp rectangle with a washcloth folded over it. A perfect square on a perfect rectangle. She wipes her mouth on some toilet paper instead and puts it in the trash.

His neatness surprises her. He doesn't come across that way with his belly and his too-small uniform. She pictures herself living here. With him retired, maybe they would have breakfast together every day, and dinner when she's not on shift. It could be the kind of easy life you'd think only existed on television but that some women do seem to find. Even in this town there are more than a handful of women who live in neat houses like this with neat men who take care of them. It's the kind of life she never thought would exist for her, but now here she is.

In the kitchen, the table is already set and several pans are warming on the stove with their lids on. A full pot of coffee waits to be poured, but Roger isn't there. She heads back down the hallway and hears his voice behind a closed a door. She puts her hand up to knock on the door but pauses a moment when she hears him speak the mother's name. Nadine Gourlay. Then Roger introduces himself to whoever's on the other line. She steps closer, leaning in, but then there's the click of the phone being hung up and a chair rolling back on the floor. She knocks on the door just before he opens it.

"Morning."

"Good morning," he says. "Just getting started on the day but wanted to let you sleep."

Lenore scans the room before following him to the kitchen. He's converted a spare bedroom into a home office. A large desk and shelves stacked with binders and files. Even though there are mountains of paper and notepads, everything is still in its place.

"Isn't today your last day?"

"Which is why I started early."

"What is it you're working on?" she asks, treading lightly.

"Doing some digging into that mother's background. From the hotel."

"Really? Does she have a history or something?"

"It's what we're looking into."

"Any word on how the kid is doing?"

"I'll get an update this morning."

"How long will you keep the mother at the station?" she asks. She keeps her tone light, feeling Roger's growing distance.

"Depends on what we find out. Any charges will depend on what that turns up, and on whether the kid makes it."

"God, I hope he's okay."

"If it was up to me, even if he does pull through, I'd keep her in there." He shovels some scrambled eggs into his mouth, his upper lip catching a dollop of ketchup that he doesn't notice. Lenore slices her breakfast sausage but pushes the pieces around on her plate. The ache in her stomach isn't for food. She thinks of the soft yellow dress that's still in her trunk. She can't tell Roger she has it.

"You okay?" he asks, motioning to her food.

"I know we already talked about this last night but, Roger..." She pauses. "Do you really think she should be punished for only trying to help her son, even if you don't agree with her definition of help?" She knows she's pushing too far.

"Intentions don't matter. There's right and there's wrong, and I wouldn't be doing my job if I just turned a blind eye." There's a sharpness in his voice. "Not every murder that happens is because someone intended to do it, but they still gotta pay the price. Even when they are mothers with good intentions." He pauses. "I'd say even especially then. Kids don't know any better than to trust their parents. Besides, I just got hold of someone in Brandon who doesn't seem to think that woman was helping at all."

"What do you mean?"

"A therapist who doesn't believe that the kid should really be a girl. And when the therapist said so, the mother stopped their sessions. He's calling back when he's done with a client." Roger spikes a sausage with his fork. "But I do have to get going." He puts the entire thing in his mouth and pushes his plate away.

"Don't let me hold you up."

"You won't mind if I hop in the shower real quick?"

"Not at all. I'll clean up."

When he's in the shower, his office phone rings and Lenore answers it. It's the therapist in Brandon returning Roger's call. Lenore says she'll take a message, but when Roger gets out of the shower she doesn't pass it on. She regrets it when he leaves for work. Maybe Roger is right. Maybe the mother is crazy and the kid's at risk. Maybe he's been led to believe things he shouldn't. It's possible. Nothing about that boy made Lenore feel that was a possibility, but her instincts have led her astray before.

—

THE SUN BURNS IN THE SKY, as if the day might actually get hot. Trish rolls down the car window, letting a cool breeze waft in. At

163

a stop sign, she closes her eyes a moment to take it in. Spring, as muddy and filthy as it is, also brings an energy.

She pulls into the hospital parking lot and takes the first available visitor's spot. Climbing out, she's sorry she wore her tattered jeans and one of Sean's old plaid flannel shirts, even though no one will be thinking about clothes. Still, she wishes she looked nicer, even for a woman she doesn't know.

Approaching the nurses' station inside, Trish sees a small group of people gathered at the desk. One is Stacey Zerr from the *Nightly News*, in a pastel pantsuit with shoulder pads. Her cameraman hovers around her, equipment slung over his shoulder, ready to capture anything at a second's notice. There are two other people holding notebooks and tape recorders, likely from the city paper or another town.

"Can you please just ask her if she's interested in speaking with us," Stacey asks one of the nurses.

"We can't."

"What's the harm in just asking her?"

"We can't because she's not here, okay?" Another nurse chimes in, while the other nurse throws Stacey a reproachful look.

"Where is she?" Stacey asks.

"That's not information we can provide. Now, please move on."

"Will she be coming back?"

The nurses ignore the news crew and go about their business. Trish heads back to the car and drives to the last place she saw the mother.

The reception desk at the station is unoccupied so she takes a seat and waits. Beyond the entrance and in the main area, there's a large open room connected to the offices and other rooms, including the room where she was interviewed yesterday. Glen's in his office in the corner on the phone. The reception phone rings and rings.

"I'll be with you in a moment, Trish." Bev rushes out from one of the rooms to answer it. While she's on the phone, Glen hangs up and jots some notes down before he exits his office and descends a set of stairs near the back. Bev is still on the phone when he reappears, escorting the mother up from below. Trish straightens in her seat and questions her decision to come here.

Bev twists the mouthpiece away from her. "Judge is on the line!" she says to Glen, who nods and then leads Nadine into one of the side rooms before returning to his office. "He'll be with you in a sec," Bev says into the phone, then hangs up.

"Everything's gone to hell in a handbasket," she tells Trish. "I'm all alone today juggling double the work."

"The Harvest Gold is always hiring," Trish teases.

"No, thank you." Bev laughs.

"I was here yesterday with Jase and I think he left some crayons and maybe a toy behind. Do you mind if I just take a quick look?" Bev considers this, and when the phone rings again, she waves her consent.

Trish treads quickly through the open area, watching to see if Glen will spot her. She makes it to the side room and pauses with her hand on the doorknob. Through the small window in the door, she sees Nadine in a chair facing the window that overlooks the marshy area leading to the river. Her tangle of red frizz is brassy under the fluorescents and puffs out like a helmet. Trish enters and the door clicks shut behind her, but Nadine doesn't move.

"Excuse me," Trish says.

Nadine turns, takes her in. "What are you doing here?"

"Do you mind if I sit a moment?"

She doesn't answer. Trish pulls a chair around from the other side of the table and sits perpendicular to her. Despite all that happened in that hotel room, this is the closest Trish has ever been to her, and she's surprised to see a quarter inch of silver roots along the part in her hair, almost sparkling.

She hasn't planned what she's going to say, but just followed her instincts all the way there. But now sitting here, she's at a total loss for words.

"You gonna lecture me too? Call me names?" Nadine asks. "Save your breath because I've heard it all before."

"That's not why I'm here."

Nadine watches her, sizing her up. "Why then?"

"I have a son."

"Hey, it wasn't my fault he saw that," she snaps. "What was he doing there anyway?"

"He couldn't sleep..." But this isn't what Trish wanted. She didn't come here to criticize anyone's parenting choices or hear criticism of hers. If anything, she came for the opposite. "He's fine. I mean, he's not fine but that has more to do with things unrelated to the night at the hotel." She's saying more to this stranger than she has to anyone else.

166

Nadine's shoulders relax, as if her guard is coming down.

"Is he okay? Your son?" Trish asks.

"They won't tell me a fucking thing."

"I'm sorry."

Out the open window, birds flit and chirp in the marsh, though they are almost drowned out by the traffic from the highway just beyond it and the river. The roar of engines bounces off the hills and sounds much louder than it should.

"You think I'm a horrible mom," Nadine says. It's a statement, not a question.

"No, that's not it at all. I just don't understand."

"You want to know why?"

But Trish isn't sure that's the right question, either.

"Every day of his life, he struggles so goddamn hard. No one believes him because they don't want to. Because it's easier not to. But I know what he says is true. Fuck the doctors and therapists. I'd do anything I can to give him the life he wants." She pauses, looks right at Trish. "I did it because I love my son." Her voice doesn't rise but the anger is palpable.

Trish looks away.

"But fuck..." Nadine smacks her hand on the table, fear and pain in one single strike. "We're not a circus sideshow anyway." She rises and paces the floor. "Where is the sergeant anyway?" She moves to the door and Trish panics.

"I don't love him." It drops out of her like a rock, hard and jagged. And then, with a kind of clarity, "Not like I'm supposed to. Not the way mothers should."

It's odd, the feeling after. A weightlessness.

"Now who's the fucked-up one?"

But the only thing Trish hears is the semi truck that's starting its climb up the hill. It gears down, rumbling low, preparing for the ascent. She watches it crest, until it rises all the way to the top, and is up and out of the valley.

—

MAIN STREET IS FULL of parked cars, as usual for lunchtime on a weekday. Part of Al regrets coming but he wanted to get it over with. Facing everyone is like pulling a bandage off, it stings at first but then it's over. And maybe, if he's honest with himself, he's also punishing himself. If that kid is in pain, he should be too.

The bakery and the cafe on the other block are bursting with people, but there are very few on the street. There's no spot for him to park so he turns onto Saunders Street, which is an equal distance from each of his two errands—the post office and the grocery store.

He walks up to the corner and heads east toward the grocery. Renée and Dorie Mitchell are across the street, heading in the same direction, but don't notice him. A rush of heat tingles his skin. He pulls on the glass door and the bell above it rings. He nods at Shannon, who's standing behind the register, but he doesn't wait to see if she'll greet him back. He heads straight to the carts and pulls one from the line. Pushes it to the dairy section, where the aisle is empty.

Lingering over the cheese section, he reads the labels, calming himself. His lungs feel stuffed with cotton, like there's no room for oxygen. He picks up a cylinder of cheese encased in orange wax. There are so many kinds he's never even tried. Muenster, Manchego. He's tried Camembert but it was ages ago and he can't remember what it tasted like. He places four different kinds in his cart. In another aisle, he grabs cans of soup with names he's never pronounced, and boxes of flavoured crackers he's never tasted. When he winds back around to another aisle, he sees Shannon is not at her post and is slightly relieved. He will have to face her eventually. That's what he came to do.

He always gets his meats last and orders the same thing every time—three hundred grams each of bologna, turkey and roast beef. But today, the pimento loaf catches his eye, and the mortadella. He probably won't like either, but he might as well make everything he buys today a first.

He waits for Leon, Heath Chartrand's son. Leon's middle-aged now, it's hard to believe. He used to work at the meat processing plant outside of town until it closed down a few years back. The timing of the closure worked well for Leon because the store's butcher was planning to retire soon. He took Leon on as an apprentice and he's been here ever since. He knows Al's order by heart. Even prepares it for him as soon as he sees Al enter the store. The neat brown envelopes are usually waiting on the counter by the time Al gets there. When it's busy, like on Saturdays, there are lines and Al waits along with everyone else. But today, there's no one else in the store. He glances down the aisles to see if Leon's there—sometimes he helps stock the shelves. He's not. Neither is Shannon.

Back at the meat counter, Al leans against the glass, listens to the country music playing on the little black radio on the shelf. The song ends and another starts. Still no Leon and no

Shannon. He looks at the long curtain draped across the doorway to the back where the storage area is. A pair of running shoes peek out from the bottom edge of the curtain. His insides seize. A second pair in the other corner, and the twitch of a curtain as a set of eyes peeps through the slit.

He pushes his cart to the register, doesn't know whether to abandon it or to place all the items back where he got them. But his cupboards are bare at home. He estimates the amount the groceries would cost but he really has no idea because they're mostly things he's never bought before. He leaves sixty on the turntable, an overestimate for sure. He reaches over the counter and grabs a stack of plastic bags, shoves things in haphazardly, doesn't care if things break or leak. He leaves the cart at the till.

Up at the corner and gathered on the stairs of the old Hudson's Bay building, a small group of older teens from the high school are smoking. Used to be where kids gathered when Al was in school too, though he never hung out there himself. He quit school not long after his final visit to the Nielsen farm. The bullying died down after a few weeks, but things had changed too much for Al himself. Besides, he didn't need school to be a farmer.

Al hears snippets of the kids' conversations—a bullshit chem test, a trip to the city on the weekend. They're absorbed in their own worlds. He rounds the corner and drops his bags in the bed of his truck. Contemplates heading straight home right now, but steels himself instead.

Janice has been the postal clerk at the office for over twenty years, though she's still quite a bit younger than Al. Over these last few months she's commented on the number of stamps he's bought. She's likely taken notice of the return address on his personal mail too. And by now, she'll have heard the whole story.

His mailbox is empty aside from flyers and an electrical bill. He knew there couldn't be another letter from them because they're still in town. There may never be another letter. He'd like to write them again anyway, even if they never write back. He'd write about different things, maybe he'd tell them about the western movies he loves, some memories of the cattle he has. Maybe he'd even share with them some stories of his parents. But maybe they wouldn't want to hear from him after what's happened. Goddamn it, he wishes he knew the kid was okay. He locks up his mailbox and walks past the glass door to the office, avoiding Janice if she's there. He won't buy any stamps today.

Outside, he pulls his cap lower over his eyes. The sun has shifted from out behind the clouds and shimmers in the middle of the sky. It could almost be summer if the wind didn't carry a chill on it.

Back on Saunders, he sees it right away. Clearly visible from several feet away. Scratches so deep and thick in his truck's paint that the metal underneath almost glistens in the sun. Across the entire driver's side door. *Faggot.* The street is empty. Whoever did it, did it quick. He can't imagine what tool was used to make such a wide mark.

Inside the cab, Al throws his bill and flyers onto the passenger seat. He's left the windows rolled up and the sun has baked the inside. The steering wheel is scorching. He should roll the windows down but he drives off instead, trying to breathe the heat. His skin reacts and a tingle begins. He wants it to flare up, ignite. He wants the whole fucking truck to go up in flames.

"Didn't think i'd see you today," Bev says as she whizzes past Roger. "Shouldn't you be primping and preening for tonight?"

"You know me well."

"Bloody well should after all these years." She scoops up an armload of files.

"Where's the cart? Your back's gonna go again."

"I could use some time off work." She winks at him and heads into the filing room.

Roger taps on Glen's door.

"Man of the hour." The sergeant's sorting through files and papers and stacking some in his briefcase. "Still in your uniform?"

"Why wouldn't I be?"

"Figured if there was any day to slack off, this would be it. What do you have left to do anyway?"

"This morning I tracked down a therapist in Brandon—"

"Before I forget," Glen interrupts him. "Please clean your desk. Lemon Pledge, Windex, the whole nine yards. Bev doesn't need another excuse to play the martyr around here. With Caroline off again she's winding herself up for a full-fledged fit."

"Caroline's sick again?"

"Another MS flare-up. Looks like she'll be taking another leave, and as Bev has so delightfully informed me this morning, our casual pool is dried up now that Joyce moved and Chelsea had her baby."

This is exactly why Roger never wanted to advance up the ladder. At one time, he thought he wanted to and even wrote the exam, but he was glad when he didn't pass. The higher up you go, the more bullshit there is to deal with. You lose perspective on what's really important. Glen's a classic example. Just have to look at his walls and all the framed photos of him standing alongside politicians, sports celebrities and country music stars. The higher up you go the more show ponies there are. Workhorses stay on the ground.

"Listen, about that therapist in Brandon. He doesn't believe what the mother says."

Glen doesn't say anything, just pulls on his jacket.

Roger continues. "Says there's much more going on than just a boy confused about his gender. We're going to talk again later and I'll get more details." He glances at his pager to check for messages.

"That may be," Glen says, "but it's of no matter now." He rummages through a drawer.

"What do you mean?"

"Trevor's at the hospital—"

"What's he doing there?" Roger cuts him off. "I said I'd go in this morning."

"Roger, you're done, and Trevor's the only one I've got in the office since Blake's in training this week." He shoves the drawer closed, unsuccessful in his search. "Trevor spoke with the doctor earlier, and the kid's doing fine."

"Doing fine?" The news knocks Roger back.

"Medically, at least."

"How's that the case given what he's gone through?"

"Doctor says now that he has blood back in his veins and he's properly sutured, he's stabilized. He can go tomorrow."

"Go? Go where?"

"Home."

"You can't be serious."

"Trevor also spoke with the boy. He's fully conscious and wants to go home."

Roger's belly turns to lead and weighs him down. He sinks into a chair at Glen's small, round meeting table squished in between the desk and the bookshelf.

"Kid's confirmed everything the mother said."

"But that's just it—he's a *kid*. Of course he wants to go home, but that doesn't mean we let him. Isn't that our job, to protect him? Or what've I spent my life doing?"

"Your passion was always appreciated, Roger."

"Christ, don't patronize me, Glen—"

"Hey," the sergeant warns, "you may be retiring but you need to cool it."

"Let me speak to that therapist again. Hear him out."

"No point. The mother also gave us the number of a doctor in Winnipeg who's been seeing this kid for a couple of years and I spoke with him myself. Apparently, the kid was working his way toward surgery. Got impatient it seems."

"So that's it? The boy goes back home with that woman?"

"I've been back and forth with the judge this morning to discuss things, and with Social Services, who were in the room with Trevor." Glen zips up his case.

"And they all think slicing that boy up is just fine?"

"Listen, I don't know what's what in this situation. This whole boy-girl, or girl-boy thing... it's beyond me. But my

174

priority is the safety of this community, and the one person from this community who was involved is making his way through the system. He's up in court tomorrow, that correct?"

Roger nods.

"These other two, whether they're right and nature or God screwed something up, or the both of them are batshit crazy, doesn't make no difference to me because they're no risk to this community. Judge agrees." He pauses in the doorway. "You hear me?"

"I do." Roger shakes his head.

"Then will you drive that woman back to the hospital? I'm running late for my meetings. She's in the interview room but I haven't spoken with her yet." He waits. "Roger?"

"I will."

"She can stay there until he's discharged tomorrow." Glen stops in the doorway. "I won't make it back to the office today but I'll see you tonight. And clean your fucking desk, or I'm retiring instead of dealing with another tantrum."

Roger remains wedged in the chair. The table's edge cuts into his ribs but he still doesn't move. The thought of telling that woman she can just go free and then chauffeuring her back to the hospital is too much.

"I'm taking an early lunch," Bev says as she pops into the office. She pauses and takes him in. "You all right?"

"Yep." When she's gone he finally rises but heads to his own desk. The last stack of files waiting for final entries sits by his phone. Bev's already left him an empty box for his personal things but there's not much. Last year's calendar is still on the cubicle wall, stuck on December 1992. A few birthday mugs, received mostly from those in this office. A glass dish that he bought years ago because it reminded him of the one his grandmother had. He filled it up once with the same chalky mints she used to buy but it's been empty ever since. None of these things matter. He wonders if anything in his entire career has mattered if he's got nothing but this garage sale shit left to show for it. Maybe he can do something for this poor kid that matters. Hell, what does he have to lose? He tosses the box on the floor and kicks it against the cubicle wall. He never thought it'd end like this. He shoves the chair and it cracks against the desk.

—

TRISH WALKS IN THE FRONT DOOR and leaves the keys on the coffee table. She won't need them anymore. In the bedroom, she pulls a black gym bag from the floor of the closet. Dust bunnies stick to the Velcro handles. She stuffs clean clothes from folded piles on top of the dressers into the bag. She won't take much, she'll stay as light as possible.

In the living room, Jase's crayons are scattered across the coffee table, a few strays on the floor. She should write a note. But she doesn't have to leave any instructions for meals or Jase's activities' schedule because Sean cooks more than her and has all of Jase's information detailed in his head. There was never a need for her to remember. It's easy to leave a life when you're not really living in it.

Still, she has to leave something. Scraps of paper are stacked on one of the couch cushions. She flips one of the pieces over and reaches for a crayon, indigo, and scrawls the only thing that comes to mind. *I have to.*

Rising and reaching for the gym bag, the back door opens. School's not out yet.

"Jase?" But it's Sean who steps into the room.

"Hey, babe." He pauses. "It's my half day, remember?" he says. "My hours are cut back this week and next. I told you."

She doesn't respond.

"Trish?" He looks at the bag gripped in her fist. "Where are you going?" But she can see by the look on his face that he understands.

"I'm sorry," she says and pauses, though nothing else comes.

"Are you kidding me?"

"Sean." She sets the bag down. "You know this hasn't exactly been working lately..."

"Lately?"

"Neither of us have been happy."

"No, stop right there, Trish," he says. "Don't bring me into this, this is all you. It's all on you."

"You're telling me you have been happy?"

"I can tell you I was. With you, yes. And even more so when Jase came along. And no, things haven't been great for a long time because you checked on out us"—she opens her mouth to speak but he doesn't let her—"and I tried. I tried to bring you back to us but you wouldn't come."

"You're right, I haven't been here, and I'm sorry. I'm really sorry." He shakes his head at her. "I made choices I shouldn't have. I thought they were right at the time, but they weren't."

"I was a wrong choice?" he asks, then laughs. "Your son was a wrong choice?"

"I know that sounds—"

"No, I don't want to hear it, Trish." He puts up his hand and stops her. "I can't anymore. You can just walk out on me, that's fine, I can deal. But you can't do that to him."

She reaches for the bag again.

"Trish, you have to talk to him."

But that's always been her problem—she doesn't know how and never did.

"You can't let him come to the Gold anymore," she says and moves around the coffee table and the armchair, creating the widest possible distance between them. But he gets to the door first and holds it closed. "Sean."

"Mothers don't do this," he says through clenched teeth.

"I know." She pulls on the door but can't open it. "That's why I have to." She shoves him away and he yields.

The air outside smells of wet gravel and recess. She wonders how long it will be before she stops thinking about him.

—

"I've been waiting awhile," Nadine says, turning in her seat when the door opens.

"Sorry about that, Ms. Gourlay."

"You're not the sergeant."

"He had some other business to take care of." It's Constable Melnyk, and today he's wearing cologne. Cedar and something citrus. It fogs up the air in the tiny room.

"Ms. Gourlay—"

"Nadine."

"Nadine," he says, pulling the chair from the end of the table to sit opposite her, his back to the window.

"When are you taking me back to the hospital?"

"That's exactly why I'm here."

"To take me back?"

"Not yet."

"I just want to see my son."

"I understand that."

"I've answered all the questions you guys have asked. I told you everything."

"We appreciate that."

"And it's got to be twenty-four hours now, if not more. Don't you have to let me go?"

"Normally, that would be the case."

"Normally?" Her limbs go numb.

"We're entitled to hold persons of interest for up to forty-eight hours when the charges being considered are more serious."

"Serious?"

"I'm afraid so."

She waits for more but his face is blank. "What are you talking about?"

"Your son is not recovering well."

She opens her mouth but remains silent.

"As you know, there were some complications, and there have been a few more. His situation is tenuous." He pauses. "We know you were trying to help your son, Nadine. Unfortunately, your decisions have only put him at risk and we need to carefully consider our next steps. All of us do. Are you hearing me, Nadine?"

"But he's going to be all right?"

"We hope."

She stares at the coffee ring stains on the table. She ignored Aaron's behaviour in the beginning. She banned dolls from the house, threw out the catalogues and magazines so he couldn't make paper cut-outs. The My Little Ponies he said he traded for his Lego also went into the trash. He'd scream and rip at the garbage bag as she went around the house searching.

One morning when she woke him for school, she found him asleep, a stuffed Smurfette clutched in his arm. The one she threw out the day before. And in the middle of the living room floor was the torn garbage bag, its insides spread all over the rug. Eggshells, soup cans, bones from the pork chops they ate earlier that week. She had placed that bag of garbage in the bin in the back alley before they went to bed. After that night, Nadine would drive each haul to the town dump.

"Nadine. I can give you some time if you want to process."

She grounded him the first time she found him in one of her halter tops and a scarf that he tied around his waist like a skirt. He was eight. When he was ten, she found a dress in his closet that wasn't hers but she knew immediately where he got it.

The week before, they had gone to the Belhumeurs' for Josh's birthday party. After the cake had been sliced and passed around, Aaron turned to Josh's sister Kailey and told her she had really beautiful dresses. The kids laughed at him and it was the last party he was ever invited to. Nadine didn't call the Belhumeurs to return Kailey's dress. Instead, she took the scissors to it after Aaron had gone to bed.

"What's going to happen?" she asks.

"The charge being considered at this point is child endangerment."

"But—"

"I know what your intentions were, and I do understand you only did this because you thought it was the right thing. Unfortunately, there are laws that prohibit such acts. And now our next steps have to be about ensuring that Aaron will be okay. You understand that, don't you, Nadine?"

Then there was the Tuesday right after his twelfth birthday. She still had a job in town at the lumber yard and had some overtime to burn so took the afternoon off. She came home and found him in the washroom. The case of makeup that she had kept hidden in her closet was opened and spread out all over the counter. His face was all done up, the colours harsh but the lines perfect.

But it wasn't the makeup, or the matching olive-green panties and silky camisole he was wearing that made her cleave in half. It was all the other lines on his body. Narrow slices on his thighs and inner arms, a couple on his chest below his collar bone. A blade from her razor sat in between her tubes of mascara and plastic containers of eye shadow.

It was like an animal had clawed at him. There was a fresh gash on his stomach near his hip bone. He was pinching it tight so the blood beaded to the surface. But something hadn't clawed at him, he was letting something out. Without thinking, she snapped the cases closed, twisted the lids back onto the foundation and blush, and placed them in the vanity. She grabbed her terrycloth bathrobe from the back of the door and handed it to him, and with no hint of anything but control in her voice, she said, "There's no need for this now."

But did she change out of love or fear? Who was she really protecting? After all, she's never once called him her daughter.

She crunches forward to hold in a sob.

"Nadine?" He reaches out and pulls on her sleeve.

"Constable..." she trails off.

"Roger. Roger's fine," he says.

"I don't care what happens to me, I just want him to be all right."

"Of course. We're all working toward your son's safety and well-being." He rises. "Our immediate next steps include me taking you back to the cell, just for a little longer, until we know for sure what's next."

She follows him out the door and back down the stairs to the lower level. He opens the cell door.

"I meant it when I said that we all have to consider how things are going to move forward from here. That means you too."

"What can I do?"

"Let me make a few phone calls and I'll come and see you later. Just sit tight."

—

THEY'RE NOT SUPPOSED TO CLIMB the trees that line the back fence near the highway. Rumour has it a kid fell off a branch and broke his leg years ago. Another rumour, a darker one, says that a high school student tied a rope to one of them and hanged himself. But these are stories from long before Jase's time. And even if they are true, it doesn't matter because most of his teachers don't bother to walk all the way out to the fence anyway. They're rarely ever booted off. Jase finds a high crook in a knotted branch and curls into it until it's comfortable. His belly's full with a jelly sandwich that had hardly any peanut butter. But he won't tell his mom he didn't like it.

He came with George, who's digging with his foot at something in the dirt nearby. George always has white flakes in his hair, but no one cares because he brings candy to school a lot and always shares it. George is the only one who didn't bother him with questions during morning classes, but Jase can tell when he looks at him that the questions are there, sitting right in his pupils. Maybe he's too scared to ask. Jase thinks he would be too if he wasn't the one who had been there.

"Yo, nerds!"

Jase doesn't look to see who it is because he recognizes the voice.

"Reach for your weapons!" Isaac yells like some kind of beast. It's what they always say before a game of war or battle. Others follow behind Isaac, already carrying artillery. Normally, Jase would reach for the nearest dead branch, break it off and chase the others around, shoot them dead. And he knows he should do that now, but he's tired. He wants everything and everyone to be quiet. He doesn't move. Just watches as the others race around below, climb partway up the tree, then jump off onto one another. Sometimes these games are silly.

"What's your problem?" Isaac stands on a sideways trunk that runs near the ground before curving and stretching upward. He's watching Jase.

"I'm not feeling well."

"Should I get the teacher?" George asks.

Jase shakes his head. George moves up to Jase's tree. Leans against it. Jase didn't want to stop the game, he only wanted to disappear but that's what caught everyone's attention.

"Tell us about the blood," Isaac says, like he's taunting him.

"What blood?" another asks.

"Didn't you hear about the guy who had his nuts sliced off?" Isaac says.

The other boy shakes his head.

"Jase was there and saw it."

"Holy crap." Now the others sidle up to the tree, gathering around him. Jase feels the sandwich in his stomach, feels it all the way up to the back of his throat.

"My brother says the balls look like jelly when they come out," Isaac says. "He's done it before when he worked on a farm. Says they're soft and squishy."

"Gross."

"How'd he do it?"

"Some old man from here did it. Right, Jase?"

Jase wishes Isaac would stop talking.

"Did the guy die?"

"No."

"Where'd it happen?"

"At the hotel where my mom works."

"Why'd he do that?"

"I don't know."

"Did the cops come?"

"How much blood was there?"

"Did you see the knife?"

But Jase doesn't want to answer questions. They continue to pick at him at like a scab, scratching at the outside crust. He's going to bleed.

"My brother said he was a fag, that's why he wanted them off. Wants to be a woman."

"What?"

"No way!"

"What's going to happen to him?"

"My brother says they'll lock him up in a loony bin."

Something inside Jase breaks. He can't stop it. He doesn't think that guy on the bed needs to be locked up. He isn't going to hurt anyone. He can't. All he needs is help. Which is what Jase thinks he needs too but he doesn't know why or for what.

"He's crying."

"Shit."

"You okay?"

And it's coming harder now.

"He said he was sick."

"I'll go get the teacher."

The others run off, except George, who climbs partway up the tree closer to Jase, and Isaac, who doesn't move. Just watches Jase, like he's sizing him up. Jase doesn't care, the crying feels good. He feels calmer already and he knows it'll stop. But right now he's far from done.

HE LIES ON THE PRINCIPAL'S COUCH with a scratchy blanket over him. He doesn't know how much time has passed or what afternoon class he should be in.

Principal Olsen comes into the room. Squeaky shoes and mouldy breath. "I got hold of your dad. He's coming shortly."

Jase sits up. "My dad?"

"Yes."

Jase isn't disappointed, he just wants to get home, crawl into a cave of blankets. The principal keeps talking, but Jase only catches words here and there. "Difficult." "Need to talk." "Shocking." Jase wants him to shut up, but not in a mean way.

When his dad arrives he looks different somehow, but Jase slides off the couch and walks toward him. Lets his dad shoulder him as they head to the car. They're both silent all the way home. And it's exactly what Jase wants.

Inside the house, Jase notices his mom isn't there. Not in any of the rooms. He wonders if she was called in to cover a shift but he knows something's different. He can feel it. He's not going to cry, though. He's moved past crying, moved on to someplace else. A place that's unfamiliar. One that he has no time to explore or understand because sleep is pulling him under and he wants the darkness.

—

LENORE SIFTS THROUGH MAKEUP at Talbot's Drugstore. The eye shadows and blushes are mixed together in plastic bins. She's not sure what particular shade she's looking for but trusts that the right one will pop out. Her cases at home are all blues, or silvers and greys, but tonight she wants something softer. A little more feminine. She settles on a single pot of eye shadow called Amulet, and in the spinning display case of lipsticks, she picks Spiced Plum.

At the counter, Cynthia's in a lawn chair behind the counter watching *Shirley* on a tiny television with broken antennae and a turn-style knob, an open bag of Cheezies on the shelf beside her. Just behind her, a transistor radio is also on.

"That all for you, hon?" Cynthia says, punching the prices on the register, barely turning away from the TV.

Lenore's eye is caught by the headline on the newspapers stacked near the counter, *Saltus Man Charged with Illegal Surgery*.

"Can't hardly believe it," Cynthia says, noticing Lenore reading the paper. "Expect something like that in California or Florida, but here?" She puts the items in a small brown bag and crunches on a Cheezie. "And Al Klassen too. Thank goodness that kid came through."

"Came through?"

"That's what I heard." Cynthia returns to her chair, this time reaching for an opened pack of cigarettes.

"From who?"

"Janice was in here earlier, but don't know who she spoke to. Others are talking about it, though."

The clock in Lenore's car says it's 4:11, but it's always at least ten minutes behind. Roger's coming at six. Even with an hour to get ready, she'll have time. She crosses the highway and heads to the hospital. This time, she doesn't bother to stop at the nurses' station, but heads directly down the halls as if she knows where she's going, carrying the suitcase, looking through each of the narrow rectangular windows. She has no luck down the first hallway, so enters the staff only section and finds him right away. Lying on his side, turned away from her. She taps lightly on the glass but voices down the hall prompt her to push on the door and enter without waiting.

He rolls over but doesn't say anything when she nears. His hair is oily and matted to his scalp in places. A whitehead blooms in the crease of his nostril. He seems even thinner than before, but wide awake. She expected him to be groggy and listless.

"I thought you'd want your things." She holds up the case. He sits up, adjusting the hospital gown that's twisted around his torso, and makes room for it on the bed.

"Thank you," he says as he clicks it open. He sees the yellow dress on top, carefully folded, and glances at Lenore.

"It's pretty," she says.

He fingers it briefly, then leans back into his pillows.

She hovers at the foot of the bed, flattens out the blankets as if working a shift at the hotel.

"How are you?" she asks. Nothing else feels appropriate. The radiator lining the wall under the window starts to click, erratic and loud, and eventually fades.

"So, you're okay?" she tries again. The words come out staccato, and she worries she's prying where she shouldn't be.

"I just want to go home."

"I bet." Beside him, an IV bag hangs from a pole and she traces its line to his right arm. "Have they said when you'll be able to go?"

He shakes his head. "They won't even tell me where my mother is."

"She's not here?"

"No." Then he tucks his chin to his chest and covers his face.

"Oh, kiddo." She steps near and touches his arm.

"I spoke to a cop this morning and I asked if she was in trouble but he didn't answer. Said she was just at the station to answer some questions. Why wouldn't she be back?"

All day Lenore has thought about the phone call from the therapist in Brandon and her lie of omission to Roger.

"She wouldn't have left you, hon."

"But then where is she?"

Without hesitating, she sits on the bed and puts her arm around him. "I'll see what I can find out for you. How about that?"

"Would you?"

She looks at the clock, the station's closed now. "She could just be grabbing a meal somewhere before heading back here." He's so small in her arms. "But if she's not back soon, I'll ask around and come back to see you."

"Promise?"

"Of course." He doesn't move away from her but sinks in even farther. Moments pass and his breath smooths out, becomes slower and deeper as he drifts off. She continues to hold him.

She's been to the hospital since it was rebuilt in the seventies. When her parents needed tests and such. But she's still surprised by how unrecognizable it is compared to how it was when she was a patient here herself. After that final night with Daniel.

They had spent the day at a powwow at Tipiskiskum watching dance competitions. They were both struck by the dancer who won the women's jingle. Her regalia was stunning. Spring green with flashes of white and scarlet beadwork. White feathers stretching high from the band on her head. The silver cones dangled from her dress and caught the sunlight, scattering it across the field. She was blinding.

That night, Lenore lost track of Daniel at one of the gatherings and after searching for him around town, friends' places and the bar, she finally went to his place and let herself in to the apartment he was renting. He was there in the armchair, and the women's jingle winner was lying on the couch, eyes glassy, lazy smile.

"I haven't heard from you," she said, like nothing was out of the ordinary.

"Needed some quiet alone time." He leaned back in the chair and stretched, his shirt crumpled on the floor near his feet.

Lenore sat in one of the hard-back kitchen chairs in the corner, though she should have left right away. The beaded bag was open on the coffee table.

"You want some quiet time too?"

Everything inside her wanted to get up and walk out, but her body wouldn't move. The dancer just smiled, eyes not focused on anything in the room.

Daniel turned to the woman. "What do you think? Should we share?" The woman laughed, then nodded; Lenore's stomach turned. She watched as Daniel prepared the syringe. He spoke to the woman while he did so.

"Of course she wants our medicine. But the thing is"—he pauses, and reaches out to pat the woman's bare foot—"she's not pure like you." He turned back to the table and sucked the liquid into the needle. "She's a *Me-too*." He laughed and glanced at Lenore. "That's what the half-breeds are," he said. "Everything you have, they want. *Me-too*, me too."

Lenore had once seen Daniel act horribly with a friend from Tipiskiskum, berating him for something small and stupid, but his satchel was empty at the time so Lenore ignored it. This night was different. He was high and happy, and still nasty. She knew it was over between them but she didn't know why. Maybe that was just the way he operated. Still, she didn't leave. Daniel stood up and walked toward her, held out his hand and she gave him her arm. He grinned at her like he had won something. Maybe he had.

Two days after that, she woke up in this hospital. That was over twenty years ago.

"Aaron, you awake?" Lenore rests her cheek on the top of his head and closes her eyes too, falling asleep along with him.

When she wakes, it's almost twenty after five. There's just over half an hour before Roger will pick her up. Before slipping out of Aaron's room without disturbing him, she pulls the yellow dress from the case and hangs it in closet near the door. On her way back home, the SAAN store's sign still flashes *open* and she pops in with minutes to spare. She can't remember the last time she bought a new dress. She never wears them anymore but she wants one now. She wants one for tonight.

THE LIGHT FLICKS ON and Trish stirs.

"Jesus!" Lenore says, startled by her presence.

"Sorry." Trish sits up, pushing off a blanket.

Lenore steps into the room and her ankle grazes Trish's bag on the floor. She stops, doesn't say a word, but Trish reads the disapproval on her face.

"Shouldn't you be at the Gold?"

"What time is it?"

"Almost six."

"Fuck." Trish digs in her bag for her work clothes while Lenore heads down the hall. Trish is working the banquet tonight, but then she's off the next two weeks. She arranged it this afternoon. Tamara and the other girls were eager to take on more shifts, especially with all the extra attention and media. Trish has never been away from work that long before but she wants the break. And there'll be so much to sort out.

Trish scrambles to get ready and heads to the washroom, where she finds Lenore opening a bag from the drugstore. Newly bought makeup. Lenore makes room for her in the mirror and Trish pulls her hair into a ponytail. There's a tightness between them.

"If you don't want me to stay, just say so."

"And go where?" Lenore tears the plastic wrap from a pot of makeup.

"I just don't want this to be an issue."

"It's not. It hasn't been for the last five or six times this has happened."

"It's different this time." Trish pauses. "I'm not going back."

Lenore shakes her head, starts applying eye shadow.

"I don't expect you to understand."

"No? A good man, a good son, that's what life should be about, shouldn't it? Love and family?"

Trish doesn't respond.

"Is there someone else?"

"No. It's nothing like that."

"Then why?"

"Love and family. I don't know if I agree with that."

"Then tell me, Trish, what is life about? You're twenty-eight years old already. You can't still be acting like a teenager."

"You should talk. I've known you for over ten years now. There have been men who wanted to give you all that, but as soon as you got a whiff of the possibility, they were gone." It pours out of her and won't stop. "So don't you judge me for leaving something that you never had the guts to go after yourself." Turning to head out the door, she sees the new dress hanging on the hook of the bathroom door. It's so unlike Lenore. "Or maybe you think Roger's going to give you all that." She strides down the hall.

"Don't wait up for me," Lenore says just before slamming the bathroom door.

—

THE PHONE RINGS BUT HE IGNORES IT this time. Pranks. All afternoon. He figured they'd have died down by evening when parents were home from work but he was wrong. Besides, not all of the calls have been from kids. He can't place the voices, though; he's lived apart too long.

The answering machine picks up but the caller hangs up. Al sits at the kitchen table, wrapping a piece of sandpaper around a wooden block he found in the barn. Uses a staple gun to secure it in place. The phone starts up again.

He'd been answering throughout the day. Didn't want to hide from any of it. *Sad fuck. Sick monster. Fucking retard.* He's heard it all before. *Come near my kids and I'll chop* your *balls off.* He figured if they got their nonsense out on the phone directly with him, maybe it'd make everything die down just that much quicker. But he's got a task at hand now.

He fills a plastic bowl with water and carries it out to the driveway, along with the sandpaper block, a milk crate and a lantern.

It's overcast but there's still a little sunlight left. He dips the sandpaper into the water and then rubs it in circular motions across the side of his truck. At first he's gentle but he makes very little progress, so he presses harder, not caring if he's doing more damage than good. Besides, he doesn't really care what his truck looks like. It's splotched with rust, like his own skin on bad days.

His arm burns. A kink in his neck forms, tightening into a solid lump. He'll feel this in his shoulders for days, maybe weeks. He is allowed to increase the pain medication for his arthritis when it gets particularly bad but he never likes to do that when he's brought the pain on himself. Only the *-ot* left. He stops and rests a minute, lets his head fall slack to his chest, feeling the muscles stretch long as he rolls it side to side. He closes his eyes.

He was surprised to be called back to the Nielsens' at the end of September. He knew right away something was up when he rode his bike up to the farm and didn't see Mr. Nielsen out in the field or his truck in the front yard. And when Al reached the porch, Raymond was at the door and invited him inside. Even when it was pissing with rain on a Sunday, the two still sat on the porch, they just pulled their chairs farther under the veranda.

Raymond led Al to the kitchen. "Have a seat."

"Are your parents here?" The kitchen smelled warm and sweet. A plate of neatly stacked cookies was on the counter. Dishes were drying on the rack by the sink.

"They went to the city to run some errands." Raymond was heading down the hall.

"I thought I was supposed to come today," Al said, stepping back into the hall to follow Raymond, but Raymond was already scampering up the stairs.

"You were," he shouted as the hardwood creaked under his feet on the second floor.

Al returned to the kitchen and took a seat at the table as Raymond had instructed. He'd eaten breakfast not long before at home but the smell of the cookies made him hungry. After several moments had passed, Al got up and walked over to the plate. Chocolate chip. The chips on the top still drooping with warmth. Raymond had made them. Maybe he had made all the treats he ate out on the porch, but he never corrected Al when Al told him to thank his mom.

More time passed and Raymond still did not come back down. Al grabbed a cookie and ate it in two bites. He immediately felt guilty for not asking first, but everything was strange already, he was only reacting to the charge in the air.

"Raymond?" He headed into the hallway, and walking past a mirror on the wall near the front door, saw a streak of chocolate across the corner of his mouth, trailing to his cheek. He wiped it on the shoulder of his shirt. At the bottom of the stairs he called up again. "You okay?" There was a loud thud on the floor and more silence.

"Raymond?" Al put his hand on the banister and waited, but still, Raymond did not respond. Al started to climb the stairs, knowing he shouldn't, just like he knew he shouldn't steal the cookie.

Raymond was in his room, the second door on the right. The door was partly ajar and Al pushed it open. Raymond was waiting for him. He stood at the end of his bed, stock-still and eyes on the floor. He was wearing a dress. It was all white and came below his knees. It must have been one of his mother's but it looked too soft, too fine to be one of hers. His feet were scrunched into a pair of cream-coloured heels that were too small for his feet. His ankles trembled. And there was a cap on his head, a nurse's cap folded from sheets of newspaper. A big red cross drawn with crayon on the front. Raymond looked sad and terrified all at once.

Al stared at him, wondering if this was a game but knowing it wasn't. He sensed something was happening in the room but he couldn't grasp it. It was beyond him, like so much else seemed to be.

Raymond flattened the dress out along his waist and thighs, smoothing out the wrinkles. "What do you think?" His voice was a whisper, hardly there. He looked straight at Al.

Al's face flushed, the heat prickling. He knew that this was inspired by the nurse, Julia, in Douglas's letters, and he also knew this was about so much more.

Raymond's chin quivered. Al laughed. Then turned away and strode back down the hall to the stairs.

"Tell your dad I couldn't make it," he called over his shoulder and left.

THE SHARP SHRILL OF THE PHONE breaks the night air. It floats out easily through the windows Al opened earlier to circulate the fresh spring breeze through the stale house. He's thankful for the interruption. He sands off the last of the paint so the word is entirely erased. The dull metal still shines in the lamplight, a glossy lesion across the entire driver's side.

He drops the block into the bowl of water and heads inside, readying himself for another earful. Each one another notch in his belt, like he's earning toward a debt he owes.

—

TAMARA'S ALREADY SET UP the square silver chafing dishes. These events are always buffet style but there will still be lots of work, especially once the drinks flow. Trish sets the last couple of tables. Early birds have already started to arrive, half an hour before the event is supposed to start.

"Excuse me."

Trish turns. It's Stacey Zerr and her cameraman, edging their way around another couple that's just arrived.

"No one's out front." She points back to the restaurant, which is closed because there's not enough staff to run both places. "We were wondering if the room has been opened yet."

"I'm sorry?"

"We were wanting to film in the room where the incident took place, but the person we spoke to earlier said it was locked and we should ask again later today."

"It's still locked."

"Do you know who we could speak to about maybe unlocking it?"

"The manager's out of town." Trish continues laying napkins and cutlery.

"So we've been told, but isn't there someone here who can let us in?"

"Have you spoken with the police?"

"Yes, but they said to speak with the hotel."

"I'm sorry, but I don't know who has the keys."

Stacey let out a frustrated breath. "Can you ask around? We're staying in room 200 across the hall."

"Sure." She shouldn't lie but she knows they'll only get more things wrong.

—

LENORE OPENS THE DOOR and he's standing there in a navy suit jacket and tie. His dress pants are also navy, but a different material and a slightly different shade. Like his uniform, the shirt strains against his chest and the collar bites into his neck. Still, he looks good. In all the years she's known him she's never seen him dressed up. Everything about him looks like a schoolboy on a first date. She'd like to kiss him but feels weirdly shy herself. She invites him in out of the cold.

"Wow." He stands there, taking her in.

She reaches for her coat but before she can slide it on, he holds out a wrist corsage in a clear plastic box.

"I popped into the flower shop on a whim. I don't know if you like them. You don't need to wear it."

"Of course I will." She breaks open the box's sticker seal and pulls open the lid. It's a small cluster of daisies with some green spiky fronds, all of it made of satin.

"I thought white would be a safe bet."

"Would you help me?" She holds it out and he ties the ribbon for her. On the underside of the flowers the satin is faintly yellow, stained with age. She carefully pulls on her coat so it doesn't get scrunched. "Ready?"

"As I'll ever be." He opens the door and even though it's her house, he guides her out the door and to the car with a hand on her back, light and secure at the same time.

On the drive to the Harvest Gold, Lenore's knees peak out from her newly bought dress and she catches Roger glance at them once. She picked the right one.

The parking lot is already more than halfway full. Roger walks around to get her door for her and when she steps out, she notices the car with Manitoba plates still parked in the spot nearest the south side of the hotel. The look on her face must've changed because Roger asks her what's wrong.

"That car..." She pauses. "It's that woman's." She turns to Roger but he tightens and she lets it go. They're here to celebrate and she'll wait until tomorrow to talk about it. They enter the Harvest Gold.

—

ROGER'S KNIFE SCREECHES ACROSS THE PLATE and his tablemates, including Lenore, shudder.

"Sorry," he says, reaching over to pat her hand. It's dry and scaly but it's just another sign that she works hard. Her fingernails catch the light and sparkle. He's never seen her wear nail polish before. It's pretty. And her dress. It fits her in all the right places. Everything about her looks amazing tonight. He enjoyed the looks on people's faces when he walked in with her. When he introduced her, he didn't say she was his date but everyone knew. Of course, some people were judging, it was plain as day in their eyes, but he didn't care. Mostly people seemed happy for him.

He wonders if that kid is ever going to find someone that will make him feel the way Roger does right now. The thought makes him ache.

After he put Nadine back in the cell this afternoon, he wasn't entirely sure what the next steps were going to be. But he made a call to Claire Schroeder, the social worker, and asked her a few questions, and then he knew how to work it out. Glen won't care because it won't affect the budgets, and all the paper-work will be correct. There will be no issues. Lenore spotted Nadine's car but that'll be sorted soon too. Roger tops up both his and Lenore's glasses and passes the bottle around the table.

"You two have any travel plans coming up?" Roger asks Glen across the table.

"We were just in Hawaii in February," says Glen.

"I'd live there if I could," says his wife, who's right next to Roger. "You ever been?" she asks Lenore and leans over Roger, invading his personal space.

"No, I haven't."

"You must. Maybe your first post-work vacation?" She nudges Roger with her elbow.

"What about the summer? Heading out with the RV?" Roger asks Glen, trying again.

"It's in the calendar," Glen's wife jumps in again. "But it all depends on whether the new constable is trained up by then and who else is on board. And if Caroline's still off, well then Bev will blow a gasket if she's all by herself and the boss is away."

Roger spots Bev across the room. She's with her own hus-band, an electrician who retired years ago after a stroke. The stroke affected the whole left side of his face and every once in a while, Bev lifts her own napkin to his face and dabs at it. For the first time, Roger suspects he understands why Bev hasn't retired yet even though she can. Roger couldn't play nurse like that, even for someone he loved. There are many ways the age difference with Lenore works in his favour.

"Have you ever worked in an office?" he asks Lenore before the thought has even fully formed in his head.

"Never. Before here, I worked at the Ice Cream Shack at the beach during the summer when I was in school, then for a couple of years at MacLeod's."

"I remember that place," Glen's wife chimes in, voice loud and cheeks already red from the wine. "Bought my favourite purse there years ago." She turns to Glen. "That grey one with the black snaps." Glen nods as if he knows what she's talking about but Roger can tell Glen's tuned out. He gets like that at the station when he's tired. "Shame that place closed down."

"I'm going to introduce you to Bev before the night is over," Roger says to Lenore.

"I know Bev, I've known her for—" Lenore says.

"Oh, that's an excellent idea," Glen's wife cuts her off. "Bev needs someone who won't kowtow to her and you seem like just the person. Don't you think, hon?" Glen reacts as his wife's elbow digs into his side this time.

"That woman pretends it's rocket science," he agrees.

Lenore's face flushes as she finally catches on. Looking at her now, Roger imagines a raised table along the back wall of the room. Long and rectangular. Bottles of champagne and full glasses. She'd have baby's breath in her hair, and maybe her dress wouldn't be white but it'd still be lacy and classic. But he's getting ahead of himself. He swigs back half of the wine in his glass. "Dessert?"

She nods and they head to the buffet tables. Just a slice of the New York cheesecake would be enough, but he's never been able to resist peanut butter confetti cake, and his mouth waters just looking at the chocolate mousse in the shooter glasses. He caves, and grabs a Nanaimo bar as well. It's his night, why shouldn't he celebrate? And by tomorrow, everything will all be sorted.

Before they even get started on their desserts, Glen clinks a spoon on his glass and the room hushes.

"I promised Roger I wouldn't do this," he shouts into the room as he rises, "but I do have to say something. I won't say much because Roger himself is a man of few words." He pauses. "Except when it comes to his reports." The room laughs, and Glen motions with his thumb and forefinger to indicate about three inches. More laughter. "But that's just proof that this man here is thorough, and honestly, one of the hardest-working men I've had the pleasure to work with. I'm honoured to have had him in my detachment all these years. Roger," he raises his glass, "I want to sincerely thank you for all your years of dedicated service."

There's more tinkling of glasses and clapping. Roger nods his head but doesn't look up. He can't.

"I also promised Roger I wouldn't do this but I know he has a few drinks in him—I poured them myself—so I'd like to invite the man of the hour to say a few things himself."

Roger slides his chair back and stands, finally looking around the room. He's going to keep himself together. "I signed up for this job for one reason only: to serve people. I think it's why we all signed up. There's nothing more rewarding." There are a few nods at several tables. "But I discovered something in the process. I discovered that I got to work with some of the best people there are. Never been prouder of anything in my life." His voice catches. "I'm going to miss the hell out of it." He pauses to clear his throat and compose himself.

"But I'm also looking forward to the future and the new people there." He sits down quickly and tugs his chair in, a little closer to Lenore.

—

TRISH IS LOADED DOWN WITH dirty dishes, waiting for others to move out of her way when she sees his head, bobbing between chairs. He moves from one table to the next, searching. A woman in her eighties rises from her chair and approaches him, asks him who he's looking for. Trish hears him from all the way across the room: "My mom."

The woman offers her hand to help, but Jase ignores her. "Mom," he calls out, which is odd because he never likes to draw attention to himself.

Others in the room look around. She can see that a panic is rising in him, his back and neck rigid, his eyes narrowing. She looks for a place to put the dishes down so she can approach him quietly. Lenore's watching her but there's no judgment there this time.

"Mom?" Louder this time.

"Jase," she says. "I'm over here."

He turns and starts running toward her.

"No," she says, but it's too late. He grabs her waist, knocking her off balance and the dishes fall, clanging on the carpet. A glass hits a bowl on its way down and breaks, shards scatter like raindrops. Those nearby step away, others strain in their seats to get a better a look, but Jase holds on. Trish breathes through the arms wound tight around her, sees blueberry sauce from the cheesecake sink into the carpet.

"Jase, I have to clean this up." She waits. "People could hurt themselves." She sees Tamara come forward with a garbage bin, then feels a hand on her shoulder. It's Lenore. She nods Trish away.

"Go," she says.

Trish is torn. "This is your night off."

"Go on." Lenore gently pushes her. "But if I ruin my dress, you're paying for it." She smiles.

Trish picks Jase up and is surprised by his weight, she has to work to get him up. He's far too big to be carried. People slide their chairs closer to tables or step out of the way, creating space for them to exit the banquet room. She moves through the dimly lit restaurant, her feet hitting the floor hard, and heads to the manager's office.

Once the door is closed behind them, she sets Jase down, surprisingly without a fuss. He stands, watching her as she moves behind the desk to use the phone. After a moment, he takes a seat in the chair nearest the door. She calls Sean, and then waits in silence. Jase sits upright, alert the whole time.

After a while, Sean knocks lightly on the door and lets himself in. "Jase." He sits beside his son, puts his arm around him. "We had a deal. You will always tell me when you want to leave the house, remember?"

"I know." Jase falls into Sean and cries. It's loud and hard and she didn't see it coming.

"I'm sorry," she says to Sean. But he looks away and stands up, lifting Jase with him. The boy doesn't fight him this time but holds on tight and wails into the crook of his neck. When they're gone, Trish gets up and closes the office door, wishing there was a way to do this without causing so much damage.

—

THE ROOM IS THINNING and there are fewer jackets on the coat rack. A few tables have already been cleared and the buffet is empty. Lenore imagines the bickering that's occurring in the kitchen. Dishes aren't being washed fast enough, the garbage still needs to go out, the linens need to be collected for the laundry service that comes early in the morning. She's happy to be sitting beside Roger. She knew there'd be a lot of folks from town. Mostly old-timers who look forward to a restaurant meal and an excuse to get out of the house. But she's impressed by the number of people who drove in from other places, most of them with the force and who've already retired or are about to. When they come over to talk with Roger, she's surprised by the closeness between him and the other officers. It would be nice to have that strong sense of connection in your life. She's happy to be near it, even if just on the sidelines.

Aside from the incident with Trish and her son, the night has been a good one. She feels proud of Roger in a way she didn't expect to. At one point in the evening, she reached out and placed a hand on his shoulder, just held it there as if it's something she's done her whole life.

When the last stragglers are heading out the door, Roger turns to her. "You ready?"

She follows him to the coat racks. "That was a great turnout," she says, and it's obvious he was pleased with the night too.

"I'm going to make a pit stop before we drive back to my place," he says, pointing to the washroom.

She likes that there's no question between them about where they'll spend the night. "I'll meet you outside." She hasn't had a smoke in a few hours. She didn't seem to notice but now the itch is there.

She walks through the barely lit restaurant. Throughout the evening she was taken far away from her job, and even when she helped to clean up after Jase she didn't feel like an employee, she was just a guest doing the right thing. Some of them who came from out of town likely saw her that way too. But she'll be back on shift soon enough and the thought is sobering.

She welcomes the damp, crisp air of the night. Buttons her coat against the chill. Her heels click on the pavement and she likes the sound. She has a couple deep puffs before the doors open.

"I was hoping I'd catch you," Trish says.

"It's cold tonight." Lenore's legs suddenly feel it. Sheer nylons aren't much protection.

"I'm sorry for being bitchy earlier at the house. And thank you. For helping with Jase."

"Not a problem. How's he doing?"

"Not good." Trish folds her arms across her chest, hunches her shoulders.

It's nice to hear Trish acknowledging the impact of her decisions on her son. She won't say that, though. There's a different mood in the air tonight and she doesn't want to spoil it.

She looks at Trish, how young she is. Maybe there is a prettiness about her, you just have to be open to it. She's a good friend too. She'd like to be able to say that to her but they've never had that type of relationship. She digs in her purse for her pack of cigarettes and holds it out to her.

"No, I better get back in. Still have lots to do."

"A quick one?"

Trish caves. Lenore lights it and feels a rush of warmth for her friend. It must be the wine. There were two bottles on their table when they arrived and as soon as the bottles were emptied, they were replaced. It was a cash bar but as soon as someone saw Roger's glass was empty, they'd fill it up, and hers too.

"You coming back to the house tonight?" The smoke pours out of Trish like a snowstorm.

Lenore shakes her head. "You might as well have the bed. More room."

"Maybe I will. Thanks." Trish looks up at the hotel rooms above them, focuses on room 203. "A few people were talking about it over dinner. Wondering what's going to happen with the kid, and mostly with Al."

"They'll be talking about it for a long time," Lenore says.

"I know. But it was the way they were talking about it. Like it was years ago. But the blood is still on the fucking carpet."

"Did you hear Robert extended his vacation?"

"Fucker."

"Said his parents need him to stay a bit longer. But we all know that's bullshit. He's trying to avoid things here. Gonna drop it on our shoulders."

"Such an ass," Trish says.

The door opens and light floods out. Roger walks toward them, the button on his pants undone. No matter whether it was intentional or had popped open by accident, she won't point it out. For some reason, it makes her fonder of him.

"Can we give you a ride?" he asks Trish.

"Thanks but I'm still on the clock." She takes a big, final pull on her cigarette then grinds it out with her toe. "Congratulations, Roger."

He nods, almost shyly.

"Have a good night you two, and thanks again, Lenore." Trish looks at her briefly, but it's enough for Lenore to feel that flood again.

She reaches out and grasps Trish's hand. "You too." She holds it a little too tightly and a little too long, and a flash of confusion crosses Trish's eyes before she lets go.

Lenore walks to the car with Roger. His hand on her waist, warm and sure. The mood stays with her all the way home. And even when they're in the bedroom and he's removing her dress, then her nylons. They have sex quietly this time. It's not a big deal between them anymore. It doesn't have to be.

—

ROGER WAITS UNTIL HE HEARS LENORE lightly snoring before he climbs out of bed and dresses. He contemplates putting his uniform on but decides against it, reaching for jeans and a snap-button denim shirt instead. He leaves a note for her on the bedside table saying he's going to the station to wrap up some things at work and wouldn't be more than an hour or two. It is true, after all.

The night air is bracing. It knocks the fog of a few too many drinks right out of him. He couldn't be more awake. The slush has hardened in the cold and it crunches beneath his feet. The whole night is crisp and sharp.

On the drive to the station, he doesn't see anyone. Not a single person on the street, not even a car coming home late from a party somewhere, or from another town. The only sign of life is the flickering lights from the windows of a few houses. Late-night television keeping some folks company. Years he's spent going up and down the streets, making sure that everything and everyone in town was okay. But those who are sleeping, and even those who are awake, have probably never thought about that. Out of sight, out of mind. It's okay by him, but he wonders when his instinct to patrol and monitor wherever he goes will fade.

He lets himself into the back door of the station with the keys that he was supposed to leave with Bev earlier. She didn't say anything to him at the dinner but he'll drop them off tomorrow. The sound of the door to the cell area unlocking wakes Nadine. She sits up from the steel pan bed that's bolted to the concrete wall. She's using the thin mattress, even thinner pillow, and the wool blanket given to her when she was brought in.

"What's happened?" She pulls the blanket around her, a flash of terror in her eyes.

"He's okay," Roger says. "He's still in hospital and still critical, but the doctors are hopeful."

"What did they say? Is he awake?"

"That's all I can share on his status, but I'm here to discuss next steps with you. Remember what we talked about before?" She nods. "I think I've found a way to resolve things in the least harmful way." Nadine tugs the blanket even tighter around her.

"Come on, let's talk out here." He holds the cell door open for her and guides her to a small metal desk at the end of the hall. There's a stool and a few chairs. He lets Nadine have the padded chair and takes the metal stool for himself. He puts his elbows on his knees, leaning on them, and makes a point of taking a deep breath and exhaling slowly, as if this is tough for him too.

"Listen, I don't know if Aaron is going to pull through. Like I said, doctors are hopeful, but that's no guarantee."

He looks up at her, but her face is blank.

"I've been having conversations with several folks today and no one wants to press charges against you. I think you'll agree that enough damage has been done and there doesn't need to be any more."

Her eyes grow wet, catch the light.

"But we also can't just let things go. Laws were broken and a boy's life has been irreparably damaged. We need to ensure his safety. That's our only concern now." He pauses. "Do you hear me?"

"I do but I don't know what that means."

"What I'm saying is that we're willing to let the charges go. We don't want to see you have to face a judge in court. No one needs that. Look, Nadine, we understand that you thought you were doing the right thing, but it clearly wasn't. What we're willing to do here, right now, is to let you go, if you agree to allow Aaron to continue to have the care and attention he needs."

She squints her eyes, trying to understand.

"We think it's best if Aaron is allowed to continue healing in the proper environment, and we think that he can be provided that if he's placed in care."

Although still wrapped in the blanket, her body visibly stiffens.

"Listen carefully here, Nadine, because this can happen in two ways. One, we can apprehend him, which would mean hearings in court and a whole lot of mess. Or two, you can sign some papers and then it's done. And I can let you go right now."

There's a long silence.

"Can I see him first?"

"No, I'm sorry." He pauses. "And I didn't want to mention this because Aaron is still weak and traumatized, but he has indicated that he doesn't want to see you. That may change, but this offer I'm proposing to you right now won't." He can see she's gone somewhere else in her head. "A lot of people are riled up about this, Nadine. When kids are hurt, people get upset. So that's why I came down here right away in the middle of the night. As soon as I heard they were willing to consider this option, I wanted to present it to you right away before anyone changed their minds. Do you understand?"

She opens her mouth but nothing comes out.

"Let's think only about Aaron right now. What do you think is best for him? Right now."

"I just want him to be okay."

"So do we."

"What will happen to him if I sign?" she wipes her nose on the blanket.

"He'll continue to receive medical attention, and he'll be placed in a safe environment where his needs will continue to be met by professionals. There are homes that are experienced in caring for kids with unique needs. He will be safe, Nadine."

She covers her face with the blanket, its straying threads just as wiry and snarled as the strands of her hair. She says something but the wool muffles the words.

"I'm sorry?"

She repeats them, not any louder than before but Roger catches them. "I'll sign."

Roger reaches out and puts a hand on her shoulder. Holds it there for several moments before rising and heading to the car to collect the papers he got from Claire that afternoon.

After the papers are signed, he drives her to the Harvest Gold to collect her car. He was prepared to pressure her into leaving that very night, but he didn't need to. In the car beside him, she seems relieved to be heading back home. She was quiet before, but there is something calm about it now. It settled in after she handed him back the pen. At the hotel, she tells Roger she doesn't need any of the stuff she left in the hotel room but asks him to make sure that Aaron gets his things.

Roger follows behind her now as she leaves the town limits in her own vehicle. He continues on farther just to make sure. In Wakamon, she pulls in to the gas station to fill up, and then walks to his car. He rolls the window down.

"I just want to call my sister in Brandon. I'd like to go stay with her for a bit."

He waits and watches her walk to the pay phone, and soon after he's watching her car turn back on the highway heading east. He drives back to Saltus and as he dips back down into the valley, the sight of the streetlights all lit up and glowing makes him think of sparklers, and candles on a birthday cake.

At home, the bedside lamp is on and Lenore's awake, thumbing through one of his Louis L'Amour paperbacks.

"Did I wake you when I left?"

"No, I only woke up a few minutes ago but couldn't sleep so thought I'd wait up."

He undresses and climbs in beside her. "You didn't have to do that."

"I know."

"You can continue to read, the light won't bother me."

For the first time, he's not worried about not going back to work. He slides up close to her so their bodies touch.

—

THE HIGH-PITCHED TRILL OF THE PHONE wakes Al. He thought the calls were all over for the night. He checks the clock. It's after two a.m. He stumbles downstairs to the kitchen. Two floors and two phones in the house but both phones are on the main floor.

"Hello?" He eases himself into a chair at the kitchen table. No one answers. "Hello," he says again. "Anyone there?" He hears someone breathing, and the sound of an occasional vehicle in the distance.

"You got something to say, just say it."

But still nothing.

"I've heard just about everything there is, so don't hold back."

This time there's a sharp intake of breath, but not the kind that happens before someone's about to speak. It's a breath that's taken when someone's upset.

Al's chest locks up. "Aaron?" he says, his own voice gone quiet. "Is that you?"

More shallow breaths of someone hurting, someone crying. A woman. And then the dial tone howls in his ear. He listens to it, letting it burrow in.

Part 3

Part 2

THE ALARM PEELS THROUGH THE HOUSE and Roger, a bit hung-over from the retirement party, races down the hall. "You okay?"

"There's no fire," Lenore shouts over the alarm. "It's just smoke!" She waves a tea towel through the air and opens the window as Roger drags a chair into the hall to disconnect it.

"I was going to surprise you," she says, motioning to the burnt sliced ham in the pan. "But your stove is different than mine, and I only turned my back for a second to get the coffee going. I'm sorry."

Roger inspects the meat. "We can just cut around the edges."

It's kind of him, and when she places the toasted breakfast sandwiches on the table, he doesn't point out how terrible they taste, but dunks each bite into a puddle of ketchup first. She did want to surprise him, and she is a good cook. Always has been. But over the years she's gotten used to eating at the Gold, stealing whatever doesn't make it to the plates. The kitchen staff always make extra and everyone's grocery bills benefit. On her days off, she's so wiped out from work that it's easier to open a can. She misses cooking proper meals, though, and is disappointed she messed this one up.

"What are you going to do with your day?" she asks, pushing her barely touched plate aside.

"Nothing at all, and I feel damn good about it."

"Well, I don't start until five."

"No?" he looks at her slyly.

She shakes her head.

"I wonder what we could get up to?"

"I wonder too."

He leans in and kisses her.

"I like that idea," she says.

"Do you need to run home for anything?"

"I don't think so."

"'Cause you could bring some stuff over here if you want."

"Yeah?"

"I'd like you to."

He was reluctant to move so quickly before, but she likes that he's changed his pace. She mentally packs up a bag while he turns on a country station, and they both clear the dishes. He steps around her as if square dancing, even twirling her until she laughs.

After, they settle in the living room, Roger with the newspaper, and her with the book she started last night.

"Anything in there about that boy and his mother today?"

"Could be," he says without interest.

"I heard he's recovered."

He flips the pages but doesn't react.

"It's strange her car is still at the Gold."

He looks up at her briefly but doesn't say anything.

"I wonder where she is." She waits. "Do you have any updates?"

"Glen mentioned something about it yesterday. He's got Trevor on it."

"Is she still at the station?"

"I don't think so, but I was closing up files yesterday."

"You don't know what's going on then?"

"Why are you concerned?" He flips a page, roughly.

"Because the kid's still at the hospital but I don't think she's there with him." She treads carefully. "That's what I heard in town."

"I'm sure it's all being sorted. Besides, I'm done with work now." He folds the paper closed. "Are you going to put in an application at the station?"

"Are you serious?"

"Of course."

"I have no office experience."

"Doesn't matter. Bev'll train you."

"But it's casual, right? That wouldn't work with me at the hotel."

"You'd get full time over the summer for sure. And Caroline's leaves in the past have been at least six months. She's also very close to retirement."

"I'm not sure." Lenore taps the book on her thigh. "I can't see them being interested in hiring me."

"You're dependable, you work hard, you'd be great at it. Plus, it pays well and there are better benefits, I'm sure."

"I'm sure, too," she says, laughing.

"I could drive you over."

"Today?"

"Word's going to get out, better not to waste time." He walks over to her. "Didn't someone say that to me once?" He sinks in beside her for a kiss.

It was obvious that he changed the subject on her but they don't have to see eye to eye on everything.

—

JASE SITS IN A CIRCLE with Isaac and Liana near the coat racks at the back of the classroom. There's a large piece of bristol board between them. The other groups have scattered to other corners, or the hallway. Jase holds the card they picked blindly from the box—*Victoria, British Columbia.*

"What are we supposed to do?" Isaac asks. He never pays attention.

"We have to create a poster for the city," Jase explains. Each group has a different capital city.

"And we got Victoria?" Isaac says. "That place sucks."

"My grandparents live there," Liana says. "We go every summer. Have you ever been?"

"No," Isaac says, "but I've had aunts and uncles and cousins who've gone and they say it rains all the time and they hate it."

"It does rain a lot, but they hardly ever get any snow. I think it's really nice. My parents even got married there."

"Good. Then you can do the project since you know so much about it."

"That's not fair," Liana says.

Jase takes a marker from the small pile they were given and starts writing the name of the city in the middle of the poster.

"What are you doing?" Isaac leans over to look.

"Getting started."

"Shouldn't you tell us before because we might not like your idea?"

"I'm just writing the name of the city."

"That makes sense," Liana smiles at him. "Maybe Jase should do most of the drawing anyway because he's good at it."

For a moment, Jase feels a bit happy. He didn't know Liana had noticed his drawings. His teacher's said nice things about his pictures, but teachers are supposed to do that.

"Whatever," Isaac says.

"Victoria is near the ocean," Liana says to Jase. "Can you draw an ocean?"

"Yeah," Jase says, thinking of all the squiggly lines he recently drew for the picture of him and his mom at the beach.

"Are you guys, like, boyfriend and girlfriend now?" Isaac asks, a sneer in his voice.

Jase doesn't dare look up because he starts to flush. The moment of happiness is gone.

"Should I leave you two alone?" Isaac says, then laughs.

Jase ignores him and continues to copy the city's name from their card onto the poster, his stomach turning to lava. Liana falls silent too.

Isaac taps Jase on the shoulder with a marker. Jase tries to focus on the curve of the letter *O* but it turns out crooked. He's messing up because of Isaac.

"But Jase might not like you," Isaac says to Liana. "Not now anyway." Isaac waits for one of them to respond, but they don't. "Ever since that night at the hotel. Right, Jase?"

"Can we just do the poster?" Jase asks.

"'Cause all you can think about since that night is balls." He flicks the marker at Jase's shoulder again, harder this time. "Isn't that right?"

"I don't."

"Balls, balls, balls, balls." Isaac mocks him.

"No..."

"Crazy for balls." He laughs again. Another flick.

"It's not funny."

"My brother says you're going to be crazy for the rest of your life because you saw that." Isaac pauses. "Crazy just like that guy." Flick, flick.

"He's not crazy."

"Yes, he is. And you're already crazy if you don't think so." Flick.

"You're wrong." He shouldn't go against Isaac, he should just keep his mouth shut, but he hates it when people say bad things about that guy. People think they understand, but no one does, not even Jase.

Flick-flick-flick.

The lava's bubbling now. Jase glances at Liana but she's hunched so far forward she looks round like a circle.

"Balls-balls-balls—"

Jase lunges. He leaps out and knocks Isaac onto his back before he even knows what's happening. The marker is still in his hand but he's punching Isaac. He should drop it but his body's working faster than his mind, and it feels good to let it out.

—

THE FOOD STAINS ARE MORE NOTICEABLE under the hissing fluorescent lights. A tomato sauce stain near her left cuff, a few drops of gravy or coffee on her shirt pocket, and a streak of grease on her pants above the knee. They're normal at the restaurant but here at the station they stand out. Lenore sits in a grey chair in the corner of a hallway, waiting.

She's never really had a job interview before. At the Gold, her parents knew the manager at the time and she just walked in and asked. That was it. Roger coached her for this, though. He told her some of the questions that would be asked and the type of answers they were looking for. It felt like cheating.

After, she called Trish and Trish said it was a great opportunity and offered to help her with her resume. They used Robert's computer at the Gold.

"Lenore." Glen comes out of his office and waves her in. "Thanks for coming in this morning. We really need the help around here." He gathers some stray papers on this desk and places them in a file. "Orientation is a three-week program, and then we can offer you full time for four months, which will likely be extended." Glen waits for her response.

"I'm sorry?"

"Caroline's formally requested a leave of absence, but they're generally extended. And both her and Bev are close to retirement so there may be a permanent opportunity fairly soon. Are you able to start orientation now, or do you want to wait until tomorrow?"

"I thought this was just an interview." She hasn't even given him her resume.

Glen reaches across his desk for a couple more files and makes a small stack. "It is, but if you want the job you can start right away." He pauses. "Roger's a dependable guy. I figure anyone he recommends would be dependable too."

Lenore nods, looks away. She got the job at the Gold because of her parents, she shouldn't feel bad about this.

"Do you want to work here?"

She nods again.

"Good." He smiles at her. "Then if you want to take these files to Bev out front, she'll show you around and give you an application form that you'll need to fill out for our files. She'll also go over all the details regarding pay and benefits."

Lenore takes the stack of files from him. "Thank you," she says, though she doesn't exactly feel grateful. "Do you want my resume?"

"The application is fine."

Bev is pleased to finally have some help. Apparently, Caroline's MS had been flaring up for weeks and she wasn't able to do much even before she finally went on leave.

"I'll set you here at this empty desk for now, and then we'll look at moving you up front." Bev points to Caroline's desk, covered with knick-knacks and photos of her family. Bev hands her an application form. "You can fill that out any time, but for now, I'll put you straight to work if you don't mind."

"Sure." Lenore puts down the stack of folders she's been carrying ever since Glen handed them to her.

"Bring those with you."

Lenore picks them up again and follows Bev to the middle of the station. The large, open space is lined with cabinets. They're stacked against every wall, and there's an island of them in the centre of the room, backs touching.

Beverly steps into an office and emerges pushing a cart that's overloaded with files. "All of these need to go into all of those."

She motions to the cabinets. "There's another cart in there too." Bev smiles at her. "I know it seems like a trivial task but it's not. Everything runs smoothly when the files are in order."

Lenore starts filing the folders she's already carrying, sliding each one into its proper place in the drawers. At the Gold, the cooks like the orders to be dropped off in the same place, and the dishes and food all have their specific shelf space. It's familiar, and for the first time this morning, Lenore feels calm.

After almost two hours, she finishes the first cart. Even though a monkey can put files away in their proper order, she's proud of herself. She makes herself a coffee from the machine, then heads to her empty desk in the corner. The blank application form lays there, and a pang of guilt hits her and she picks up the phone and calls Trish.

"You got it?"

"I'm already working my first day."

"That's great."

"But I've got a shift at the Gold tonight too."

"Someone will take it."

"Probably. But what about the rest of the week? And how do I give notice?"

"Don't."

Lenore laughs it off.

"I'm serious. You can't work twenty-four seven, and they'll manage at the restaurant until someone else is hired."

"Just walk away?"

"Fuck Robert. This opportunity is too good to give up."

It's true. Even adding in her tips, which are usually good, the Gold can't compare to this job.

"I'll make sure you get your final paycheque," Trish promises.

Trish congratulates her before they hang up and Lenore realizes she won't see much of Trish anymore, or Jase. She looks at the application form but sets it aside and gets back to work.

She glances at the clock. It'll be the lunchtime soon and she thinks about the rush at the Gold. Hears it. The controlled chaos in the kitchen. Someone yelling for their tuna melt that another person stole. Reggie swearing under his breath as he wipes sweat from his forehead with the towel that's draped over his shoulder. The din of voices seeping into the kitchen each time a waitress leaves or enters. Sometimes, the rush hours would be so loud that Lenore could still hear the noise when she got home at the end of the day.

She slips another folder into a drawer. It swishes like a whisper.

—

"DON'T TOUCH ME!" Candice wails from inside the house. Nadine sits on her sister's front porch and hears her niece and nephew scrapping in the living room. They've been up a while now. There were morning cartoons, then *Sesame Street*, and the muffled roar of a vacuum at one point. Still, Nadine didn't move.

She arrived before the sun was up. There's a key on her chain for the back door. She could have let herself in and gone straight to the basement where there's a couch she's slept on several times when she's worked shifts for her brother-in-law's cartage company. A scratchy blue couch with lumps and springs that poke. The basement's unfinished and most of the walls are exposed, and the concrete floor is always frigid on her feet. The half bath still has no door. The kids aren't allowed down there but when Nadine stays over her sister Karen lets them nip down when Ross is out.

The screen door screeches open and Karen steps out with a pair of dirty pink rubber boots. She hangs them over the rail and bangs them together, dried chunks of mud drop to the yard.

"Jesus Christ," she says, turning to head back in. "I didn't see you there. Ross didn't say anything about calling you in."

"He hasn't."

"You come to run errands then?"

When she can afford it, Nadine drives into Brandon to stock up at the Kmart and the other box stores. Sometimes Karen will ditch the kids with Ross or a friend and the two of them will make a whole day of it. They'll stop for lunch at the pizza place on Broadway and get a pitcher, sometimes sit there right up until dinnertime.

"Stop it, Grady!" Candice yells again.

"Kids, cut it out right now or you'll go to your rooms," Karen hollers through the open door. "Grady's got pink eye so neither of them can go to daycare." She puts the boots, still filthy, on the corner of the deck. "They've been at it since the second they woke up."

"I heard." Nadine smiles without feeling it.

"How long've you been there?"

Nadine shrugs.

"What's going on?"

She doesn't have to tell Karen. She doesn't have to tell any-one about Aaron. And if she doesn't tell anyone, if she keeps the whole thing to herself, maybe it won't hurt as bad.

"Come inside to the kitchen," Karen says. "Ross is in the shower and I'm about to start breakfast."

"Auntie!" Candice makes a beeline for Nadine and she bends to hug her.

In the kitchen, Karen makes French toast and bacon. Candice sits on Nadine's lap while Grady puts on his latest G.I. Joe gear, a mask and ninja hood, and demonstrates some moves with each of the accompanying weapons, a crossbow with darts, a katana sword, throwing stars. Nadine feigns interest and goes through the motions of asking them about their friends, their latest favourite movies. By the time Aaron was their age, there were already indications that things were different. Neither of these two shows any of the same signs. In a gut reaction, Nadine lifts Candice from her lap and puts her down.

"No!" her niece protests and tries to climb back up.

"She's getting heavy," Nadine says to Karen as if to explain, but there's a catch in her voice.

"Leave your aunt alone now." Karen places the girl in her booster seat, sticky with dried juice, and gives her a handful of Froot Loops to occupy her. Karen eyes Nadine, prodding her to divulge.

"Daddy!" Candice shouts, mouth full of cereal, when Ross enters from the hallway, his frosted tips freshly gelled. He kisses the tops of his kids' heads and greets Nadine as he dishes him-self up at the stove. He eats half a slice of French toast with his fingers before even sitting at the table. As Karen serves the kids and brings Nadine a plate, Ross updates Karen on the latest issues at the cartage company. A late shipment, a problem driver who submitted incomplete weigh bills again, a missing crate of produce.

"But looks like we landed that contract with Cargill," he says, gulping back a glass of milk. "Plan to sign it on Wednesday." He turns to Nadine. "Could have some regular shifts for you in a month or so's time."

"Wouldn't that be nice?" Karen says to her.

Nadine nods. She wouldn't have to rush home so quickly between shifts anymore, and if the work turned into something more permanent down the line, maybe she could even find herself a small apartment in the city. Something more manageable. The possibility of that kind of simple life on her horizon causes a hiccup in her chest. Nadine covers her face to hide the emotion that's breaking out.

"Shit," Karen says, both confused and concerned. The kids turn to look at their aunt, and Nadine recovers quickly.

"It's okay. It's fine. There's just been a lot of stuff that's happened, but I'm okay." She smiles at her niece and nephew.

"You need a shift right now?" Ross asks. Everything comes down to cash for him.

"No." It comes out abrupt. "Thank you," she adds so she doesn't seem ungrateful.

"What's all *the stuff* that's happened?" Karen asks.

"There's been a lot of things happening lately with Aaron."

Ross immediately pushes back his chair and it screeches on the floor. He carries his dishes to the sink and drops them in, they rattle and clank. Karen looks down at the table. Aaron's always been off limits. As far as Nadine's aware, Candice and Grady don't even know they have a cousin. He's been a ghost in the family for a long while. The situation frustrated Nadine at first and there were many arguments, but as time went on Nadine gave in for her sister's sake. It was more important to her to keep her sister in her life. And if she was completely honest with herself, Nadine eventually came to like the arrangement. Because while in Brandon, she could pretend she had an entirely different life. An easier one. She regrets it now.

"I tried to help Aaron, but—"

"This isn't the time," Ross says. He doesn't return to the table but remains standing near the counter. The mood shifts and the kids pick up on it. They look from parent to parent, assessing.

Nadine continues. "It was our only option, and Aaron wanted it. He did."

"Kids, go play in the living room," Ross says.

"We can talk about this later," Karen says to Nadine.

"Now, kids." Ross pulls Candice from her chair.

"I'm not done," Grady says.

"Take it with you." Ross hands him the French toast still on his plate.

When they're gone, Ross turns to Karen. "Not in front of the kids."

"I know."

"In fact, not even in this house while they're in it." Ross pours himself a glass of orange juice and sits at the table. But nobody speaks, and the silence stretches thin.

Then Ross clears his throat. "Are you taking Grady to soccer registration this weekend?"

"I thought you were. To meet the coach and everything. But I can if you need," Karen says.

"Maybe. I may have to go in to the warehouse."

Nadine gets up, hooks her purse over her arm and walks out of the room.

Karen follows her to the front door. "Nadine, wait." Out on the porch, she lowers her voice. "He's heading to work shortly. Just stay, and we can talk when the kids have their nap."

But Nadine continues to her car with no idea where she'll go.

—

THE ROOM ECHOES. Bare walls and cheap, metal furniture. The judge's desk sits on a platform at the front and Al watches her sentence a man from another town for driving while impaired. Hardly any light spills in from the window in the room because of the large pine right outside. Its branches scratch the glass. This old building used to house the town newspaper shop in the fifties and sixties. When the newspaper shut down, the building remained empty until the former courthouse burned down in 1985. The seats meant for the public are empty. Al had thought the courtroom would be filled with townsfolk but was relieved when his lawyer, Clive Pugh, told him the judge had banned the public and the media to protect Aaron's privacy.

He met with Clive in a private room beforehand. Their meeting was short. Clive's advice was to plead not guilty, so they could go to a hearing. Al said no. He knows what he did, doesn't matter what the law thinks, he'll face whatever comes. He just wants it all to be over. Clive disagreed but also didn't press him. Every other time Al hired him, it had to do with the sale of his livestock or portions of his land. This was something else entirely, and though Clive maintained his professional air, he couldn't hide his discomfort. Both were glad when there was a knock on the door letting them know their time was up.

Al sits in a chair against the wall in a row with several other men and women. Most he doesn't know because they're from other towns and villages or the nearby reserves. Assault, possession, theft. All minor offences, but to Al they look liked hardened criminals.

Saltus has a travelling judge who drives from small town to small town on rotation. The younger judges all do this until they find a permanent opportunity in the city. This judge is not as young as they usually are. She's middle-aged and her blonde hair is big and wide. Another Hillary Clinton look-alike.

She calls up the next person. He was never told how long he'd have to wait but it's been over an hour already. He stares at his boots, dotted with flecks of green paint from this morning. He found two old spray cans in the basement from that time his mother wanted him to refurbish her lawn furniture. He was surprised they still worked, thought the paint would've long since dried up. The nozzle on one leaked, despite him tightening it, and almost half of what came out of it seemed to land on the ground and his boots. But he managed to cover all of the exposed metal on the truck.

The word's been used to describe him most of his life. He's not one, he's never had such inclinations. Even so, he doesn't think there's anything wrong with it. But maybe not going against it, not going against faggots, is the same thing as being one in many people's minds. Which is strange, but then he never understands things the way others do.

He suspects Raymond had such inclinations. He suspects that's what Raymond was trying to tell Al that Saturday in 1944. Al wishes he could have told Raymond that it was fine, that it didn't matter. But he was only fifteen and even though he felt that deep down, he didn't have the words to bring it to the surface.

There are so many other words that are submerged. So deep he still can't find them even now, nearing the end of his life. Words to describe himself. To describe who he is and how he feels about people. About love and sex. He wasn't even aware of it during that summer with Raymond. At that time, he told himself he was just a late bloomer. But the years passed. How can someone not want all those things you're supposed to want? A wife, sex, passionate kissing, being naked with another person. He'd have wanted a wife if they didn't have to be physical. He's always wanted to hold someone's hand. But intimacy with a woman wasn't possible without sex, and friendships with men weren't possible because he couldn't talk about sex.

But he let his guard down with Nadine and Aaron, and in doing so, he's put that poor boy at risk. He let himself forget that his life is always easier alone.

The judge finally calls Al's name and his lawyer motions for him to join him at the table near the front of the room. It looks like a table from the old elementary school. Narrow, low and meant for children.

She reviews his file for a minute or two before looking up. Her hair is like a helmet but her face isn't severe, it's more curious than judgmental. She addresses Clive, summarizing the case and reviewing the charge against Al. Then she asks, "How does your client plead?"

Clive looks at him, checking in to see if Al has changed his mind. He hasn't. "Guilty," Clive says.

The judge turns to Al. "Given you've had no other interferences with the law, I had contemplated a suspended sentence. But I'm also thinking of that poor boy whose life has been irreparably changed."

Al's skin prickles all over.

"I understand that the boy requested this surgery, if you can call it that, but he's just a boy. I don't know what you were thinking in agreeing to his request and in following through with it, but I don't think that matters. Whatever your intentions, they're irrelevant when thinking about that boy and his life. Having said that, I am giving you what I consider a very lenient sentence in this matter. Albert James Klassen, I am giving you a conditional sentence of ninety days. While this means you will be serving your time at home, a conditional sentence is still an imprisonment. Do you understand?"

Al nods.

"Let me be clear on another point too. Mr. Klassen, should that boy's condition worsen, or if there are any other complications that arise later, you may face additional charges and sentencing. Do you understand?"

Al nods again.

House arrest. He's allowed to leave for a few hours every Tuesday and Friday for errands and medical appointments, and he's allowed to do any necessary work on the farm. The rest of the time, he has to stay inside.

Al doesn't move from behind the desk. "Can I ask one question?" The judge waits. "How is he doing? Nobody has told me. Will he be all right?"

The judge looks down at the papers on her desk. There's a long silence. "You're right to worry. He has been through a very crude, very dangerous surgery, Mr. Klassen." She taps her fingers on his file, considering. "I will tell you that the hospital has confirmed he is out of danger and recovering."

Al looks back down at his green-flecked boots, the air falling out of him slowly.

"But now that you've asked this question, I feel the need to amend your sentence. The conditional sentence stands, with the addition that you do not have any further contact with that boy or his mother at any time, ever. Do you understand?" She raises her eyebrows and her helmet of hair finally moves. "Will you commit to it?"

Clive nods at him, as if encouraging.

"I will." Al's guided into the next room to start the paperwork that now follows. He'll never be able to make his proposal but the boy is okay. And that's all, that's everything. Oddly, he's looking forward to the next three months, to being able to shut everyone and everything out.

—

SHE SLICES ANOTHER ENVELOPE OPEN, date stamps the letter inside. The last of the morning's mail sorted. The fax machine rang a few times earlier so Lenore goes to grab that correspondence as well. When she's there, the machine starts up again and her eye is caught by the name on the sheet as it slides out. *Nadine Gourlay.* And underneath, an address in Beauville. She knows that town. She drove through it years ago when heading out to camp at Duck Mountain in Manitoba. She might have even stopped there to eat.

She searches for the file in the cabinet but it isn't there.

"Happens all the time," Bev tells her. "When you want the file, it's impossible to find. I'd imagine it's with Glen or Trevor."

"The mother was here yesterday, wasn't she?"

"She was."

"Did she go back to the hospital?"

"Must have. She wasn't charged with anything as far as I know." Bev looks at the clock. "Try looking for the file again after your lunch break. It'll turn up eventually."

It's past one already. Lenore grabs her jacket and purse.

THERE'S A SHARP SMELL OF BLEACH, but it's not the same as what they use at the Harvest Gold. This one's headier and thicker. She tastes it in her mouth and throat. She hovers in the hallway at the hospital, waiting for the nurse to leave the station, and as soon as it's clear, she nips down the staff only hallway and into Aaron's room.

He's up and leafing through an out-of-date *Chatelaine.*

"Hey," she says. "How are you feeling?"

He shrugs.

"You look good." It's true. There's more colour in his face and his hair's been washed, but he's distant and not at all interested in her being there.

"You didn't have to come back. They've already told me."

"Who told you what?"

"She left."

"Who left?"

"My mom. She left me here."

"No, she didn't," she says, but it's more of a question.

"They're working with a group home in Manitoba to find me a space."

"They?"

"Social Services. As soon as one opens up, they'll transfer me. Could be a couple of days, maybe more."

"I didn't know. Honestly, I thought I'd come back here to find both of you together." It doesn't make sense. "She didn't come here at all?"

He shakes his head.

"Did she go home?"

He shrugs. "They won't let me call."

"Aaron..." she says, but then is lost for other words.

"You don't have to stay."

"I don't have to be back at work until two."

"I just want to be alone."

—

JASE WAKES FROM A LONG NAP. He hears his dad in the garage, where he's been spending most of his time lately. His dad's trying to pretend that things are okay, but Jase knows he's not happy. Jase might be able to make things better, though. He might know how to fix it.

That night after everything had happened in the hotel room, the three of them came home and slept in the bed together. It was the closest they'd come to being a family in forever. They just needed something to remind them, even if that something was awful and someone got hurt.

Outside, it's still colder than it should be. Spring was on its way before but now it's like it's forgotten about them. The snow is gone, but nothing's really warming up. Jase zips up his jacket and hears his dad's music in the garage. It's not loud, but he can hear it because his dad always leaves the side door open. Jase wanders closer and hovers in the doorway. His dad's on the far side and bent over a table, working on an engine of some sort. Jase sees the lawn mower against the other wall.

"Dad?"

"Hey, Son. Feeling better?"

"Yes," he lies. "Can I help with something?"

"I'm taking this apart right now to use it for parts. It's a motor from an old mower. You want to learn how to do that?"

Jase doesn't want to but he nods anyway and walks over. His dad pulls up another stool for him and explains certain things about the motor. Valves, pistons, spark plugs. Jase tries to listen but he can't focus. He's too busy trying to figure other things out anyway.

"Could I ride the other mower again, Dad?"

"Again? I'm not working on that one now. It's all done."

"I know, but I just want to ride it. It was fun." He waits.

"Yeah, okay. Get on up there and I'll get the keys."

Jase's stomach buzzes. It's weird because he's been thinking about how to do this ever since he came home early from school for fighting, but it's different now that it's happening.

"You want to put the keys in too?" Sean holds them out and Jase nods.

The keys are heavier than he expected. Heavier and bigger than house keys, which is strange to him because a house is much bigger than a lawn mower. Jase slides the right key in and turns it. The mower starts up and his dad grins, proud of his work. Jase feels the machine vibrating, his whole body with it. He grips the steering wheel.

"Can I take it outside again?"

His dad looks at the closed garage doors. "One loop around the yard, okay? Want me to show you again?"

"I remember." It's one pedal to go and one pedal to stop. His heart races faster. He's surprised to be a little excited. He steps on the go pedal and the mower lurches forward. He quickly hits the other pedal and pops out of his seat for a second. His dad didn't see—he was already walking away. Jase catches his breath, reminds himself to be softer with his feet. His father presses the garage door opener that he keeps pinned to the wall above the table. The door starts to slide open, the grey daylight spills in across the stained floor. Jase puts his foot back on the go pedal, slowly and lightly. This time, the mower moves forward smoothly.

"Hold up, Son," his father shouts over the motor. "Let the door open all the way."

Jase gently brakes. He's miles away from the door but he listens to his father anyway. Then the door jams, it flaps up and down, and Jase creeps forward as it decides which way it wants to go. His dad steps toward the door and pushes it up over his head with effort. He turns, "Jesus!" He jumps out of the way, "Jase, I said hold up."

"Sorry." Jase slides under the door as it's still opening, narrowly missing his head. He is sorry, but he's also worried. This might be his only chance and he can't mess it up.

The wind is cold on his hands. Gloves would've been a good idea but it shouldn't take too long. Jase eyes the patch of trees at the one end of their property. Grey trunks thick and bunched together like they're standing guard. His foot presses down on the pedal a little harder and he speeds up. His ears feel the cold now too.

The mower rumbles across the lawn. He's getting closer, and he holds the steering wheel so tight his hands hurt.

"Stay away from the trees, okay?" His dad shouts from the open garage door. Jase is headed straight for one. Just a few feet more. "You hear me, Jase?"

There's a strain in his dad's voice, a note of worry. It's all it takes for Jase to veer left and drive alongside the line of trees.

"Good job, Son."

But it's not a good job. The plan's ruined. He slows the mower down so it's barely crawling. When he reaches a corner of the yard, Jase twists the steering wheel in a large, wide curve, not wanting to turn around just yet. He's screwed everything up and he doesn't want to look at his father.

"That's some nice driving," his dad shouts. "I'll have to let you take the car out sometime."

It's a joke and Jase should laugh, or at least smile, but it catches inside of him. Why does his father love him so much? It hurts too much to think about it.

"Bring it on in now."

Jase drives across the yard and tries to calm himself. He takes a few deep breaths and thinks of his superhero drawing on the table in his room. Last night before bed he finally picked the colours for the uniform and finished it. He has the whole picture done now. He still doesn't have the name but he knows it's close. It's floating in space somewhere, but it's floating toward him. Soon, it'll be here, he knows it. Maybe it'll just take longer than he wanted. He did it, though—he figured out what the superhero looks like, so he shouldn't be so worried all the time. Even now. He can be braver.

Jase wipes his nose on his jacket. He's calmer now, more in control. He looks back at the trees again. Even naked, without leaves, they look like soldiers. It makes him think of Aaron.

He steers the mower away from the garage and back around.

"I said bring it on in now."

"Just one more time."

"Jase, no."

He leans forward and focuses. From the corner of his eye he sees his father stepping out of the garage and into the yard.

"Turn the other way."

But his foot presses harder on the pedal, so hard that it won't go down any farther.

"Turn to the right, to the right!"

Jase ignores him, he has to. He's moving so fast, but there's a bump and the right side of the mower rises up and the left side angles down. He feels himself slide in the seat and he cranks the wheel without even thinking and slams on the brake. His chest clunks against the wheel as the mower jerks to a sudden stop. The air knocked from his lungs, Jase gulps for breath, his eyes watering as he does.

His father reaches him and pats his back gently. "It's okay now, you're okay. Breathe slowly."

The air rushes back into him and he feels like a balloon, filling up and expanding. Like he could lift up and take flight.

"I should've cleaned these branches up last fall after that storm."

Jase turns around and sees his father lifting a large dead branch from under a blanket of leaves. That's what he hit, that's what rocked him off course, and now the mower's wedged in tight between the trees.

This was all he had to do. One thing. But he can't get anything right. Why is he such a loser? It's like his mom and dad are losers too. They're a family of losers that can't ever win at anything. He hates them and himself. He hates everything.

"Let me get some of these out of the way and then I'll drive it back out." Sean hauls the branch out of the way, then grabs a few others, trying to clear a path. "You can turn it off for now."

He'll never get another chance. "I can do it."

"No, Jase, I'll take care of it. It's going to be tricky."

"I can do it."

"I said no." There's an edge in his voice that Jase rarely hears. "I saw you and you couldn't control it. At least you're not hurt and there's no damage but that's enough now."

He grabs another large branch and heaves it off to the side.

Jase puts the mower in reverse and takes his foot off the brake and presses the gas but it doesn't move. It's stuck on something, maybe another branch. He jams it down and then he's rocketing backwards, but in a curve because the steering wheel is still turned. He tries to straighten it and get it on course.

"Jase!"

There's another thud and Jase is knocked the other way this time. The back of the seat catches him but his head snaps back and he squeezes his eyelids shut. He hears his father grunt, even over the sound of the mower.

"Dad?"

There's no answer but Jase doesn't want to turn around. He pushes the switch out of reverse and back to its starting position. He doesn't turn it off. He can't. He climbs off the machine. Behind the mower, his dad is pinned up against a tree, but he's bent over, one hand still holding a tree branch, his head looking down.

Jase should step closer, lean in to hear what his father's saying, but he doesn't want to know. He just wants it all to be over now.

"Jase..." His dad's voice is wrong, it doesn't sound like him at all. Jase bolts, races back to the house. His family's needed help for a long time and now he finally gets to call.

"I'LL HAVE ANOTHER." Nadine pushes her empty glass toward the bartender, and he brings her another Bud. The Ace of Spades is a place she's always driven by on her way in and out of Brandon but has never been in. Squished between other cartage companies, a couple of used furniture stores and several peeler bars, it's a place where beer should be ordered in the bottle, not from the tap. Nadine doesn't care and drinks from the glass with someone else's lipstick stains on the rim.

A couple of old-timers sit in the corner near the VLTS. There's a table of what Nadine would bet are truck drivers and in-town couriers on a late lunch break, a couple of empty pitchers among their empty plates. In the other corner, two younger guys play pool. One with a paunch and an overly wet-looking perm, and the other with hair down to his shoulders and an eggshell-blue tank top, as if he stepped out of a hair band video. It's still mostly winter but he looks browned from the sun. Muscles made at the gym stretch taut as he leans over the table to make a shot. It's quick and smooth and the ball sinks into the pocket. He follows it up with two more and cleans the table. Raises his arms like Jesus and takes the bills that were lying on the table's ledge under a square of blue chalk.

"Another pitcher," he says at the bar. "Skunked him again. Always do."

Nadine raises her glass to him in congratulations.

"You want another?"

"I won't argue," she says.

"I always win anyway. At everything." He grins at her, then reaches over the bar, grabs a clean glass and pours himself some from the jug. Behind him, his friend racks up the balls and breaks them but the kid beside her doesn't move. Instead he waves his friend off and the guy starts a game by himself.

"You from around here?" he asks her.

"Sort of."

"I thought that was a yes or no question." He carries his glass and pitcher to the stool next to hers.

"What are you doing?"

"Thought you might want to chat." He leans on the bar and his tanned triceps twitch. She'd like to feel something if she could. The last time she slept with a man was when Aaron was a toddler. She'd gone out for a night at the bar with her friend Pam and left Aaron with Pam's sitter. A live rock cover band was playing at the local bar and they'd smoked a joint in the car before heading in. There were people from nearby towns, and even towns not so nearby because live bands that weren't local were rare. Especially ones that played the heavier stuff.

Earlier that day, Nadine and Pam went to the thrift store and bought extra-large T-shirts in the men's section and spent the afternoon cutting the sleeves and bottom sections up into strips and hanging coloured beads on the ends. Nadine cut hers so short that if she lifted her arms above her head, her black bra was visible. They drank vodka and grape juice before heading to the bar because they wanted to save money and it was all they had in the house. By the time they realized their tongues and teeth were purple, they were too buzzed to care.

"Whatcha got going on for the rest of the day?"

"Not much," says Nadine.

"Not much." He laughs at her non-answer. "All right, what are you doing this evening?"

"Not too sure yet."

"Right." That grin again. "Do you want plans for later?"

"I don't know about that."

"Why not?"

"Just don't think that'd work."

"What won't work?"

"Whatever you're thinking about."

"You don't know what I'm thinking about."

"So why don't you tell me?"

"That'd ruin the surprise, wouldn't it?"

"I'm not one for surprises anyway."

"You're one tough chick."

"I've been called worse."

"That was meant as a compliment."

His friend whistles behind him and points at his watch. The kid waves him off, and leans in closer to Nadine. "Since you're not giving me much here right now, why don't you give me your number and we'll see if you'll open up more later."

"I don't think so."

"Why not?"

"'Cause you're just a kid."

"I'm an adult, that's for sure."

"I'm more of one than you."

"I know, but I'm curious and that's not a bad thing."

She laughs, despite herself.

"So are you going to hand it over?"

"Hand what over?"

"Your number."

"Why don't you give me yours?"

"Sure, I'll give you mine but on one condition."

"What's that?"

He reaches back over the bar for a pen and writes his name, Dana, and his number, and slides it over to her. But when she tries to pick up it, he doesn't let go. "Yours first." He holds out the pen with his other hand.

"I might not be around tonight."

"That's okay, there's more than one night we got to work with."

Nadine takes the pen and scratches her name and number underneath his. He tears the napkin in half and hands her the half with his info on it. He reads hers.

"That's long distance."

"It is."

"So you're not from around here."

"Not yet."

"Okay, I got you. Well, I'd be happy to show you around town, Nadine." He pockets her number. "Here, have a little more on me." He fills her glass, then swivels on his stool and winks at her before heading back to the pool table. When he gets there, he pulls the torn napkin from his pocket and slaps it on the green felt tabletop.

The guy with the perm shakes his head. "Just barely under the wire."

"I still had almost half a minute to go."

"Bastard." The guy with the perm flops a ten on the table.

"You owe me a beer too."

"Why's that?"

"I filled her up."

"I don't got to pay for that."

"Damn straight you do." The kid turns and looks at Nadine, shrugging his shoulders. "It's not personal. I just always win."

She downs the last of her drink, not caring that she was just used for a bet. And basically the butt of a joke. As she heads out the door Dana says to his friend, "You never fucking learn."

All she remembers about that night out with Pam and her last fuck was that the guy's name was Mark and his jeans were suction-cup tight. He may have been out of her league, but they both knew it was only one night, and when they climbed into the back of his Chevy Monte Carlo she was on top and in control. She was almost thirty years old that night, and even though at that time she felt she was older and her life was settled now that she had a kid, it also felt like it was just beginning. And in a way it was, because it was right before the signs with Aaron began.

Will Aaron ever hit on someone like that, or be hit on? Will he ever have a night like she had back then where he feels powerful and complete and wild in the back seat of a car?

Three goddamn pints of beer and she doesn't feel a thing. She wants to be light-headed, to lose her footing, she wants her cheeks and her limbs to tingle. But instead she feels nothing. Things are too sharp, too clear and cutting. She drives to the next seedy bar she finds.

—

WHEN BEV'S OUT OF EARSHOT, Lenore picks up the fax with Nadine's contact information on it and dials the phone number. It rings and rings. After the ninth time, Bev returns to her desk and Lenore hangs up.

The Gourlay file still hasn't been returned, and Trevor tells her he doesn't have it. She slips into Glen's office. If she's not supposed to be in here, she can feign ignorance.

She finds the file easily enough and glances at the door before opening it. It contains pages and pages of notes, mostly in Roger's handwriting. There's a summary of the night at the hotel, and various other notes on interviews that were conducted. At the back, there's a set of forms. In the top left-hand corner is the provincial government's wheat sheaf, and just above it, the logo of the Department of Social Services. Her breath quickens as she reads through the forms. She's sure she understands them, but they still don't make sense.

She carries the forms and the file out to the main area. "Bev, what is this?"

Bev knows instantly what they are. "I'll be... Didn't know about that." She hands them back to Lenore. "They're Section 9 papers."

"But what do they mean?"

"It's what parents fill out when they voluntarily hand over their children to Social Services."

"When did that happen?"

Bev leans over her and looks at them again. "Yesterday, today? Can hardly tell from the chicken scratch, but that's

Roger's signature there." She points. "As witness." After a moment Bev asks, "You okay?"

"Yeah, I'm fine," Lenore lies.

—

As soon as al got home from his sentencing, instead of following the water trail out to the top of the valley, he went up to the spare room on the second floor, the room that was his bedroom as a child, and sat at the window. It was the best place in the house to view the valley. That was hours ago, and now the sun is beginning its descent on the horizon, a sliver of it already dipping down. Shadows stretch longer and longer until they reach the valley's edge and disappear, as if falling into the cavity below.

After Al had discovered Raymond in that makeshift nurse's uniform that weekend so long ago, he pieced some things together. He realized it wasn't Raymond's father who had called him to work on their farm that day. It was Raymond who'd called and left a message as if he was Mr. Nielsen.

Al spent the rest of that weekend worrying about Monday morning and returning to school. Things were damaged and he wanted to repair them. But how? It's not something he could ever bring up while they were at school, even if Raymond gave him the time of day. Al decided he would leave it until the following weekend, and maybe he'd bike out to Raymond's and talk to him then. But when Monday came around, Raymond actually waved to Al in the hallway and asked how his weekend was while he was ambling by Al with a group of his friends. And after school, Raymond honked goodbye as he passed Al in his car on his way home.

On Wednesday, Raymond asked Al if he wanted to play baseball with him and his friends after school. Al wanted to but he couldn't miss his school bus and had to decline. Raymond offered to drive him home after.

When Al arrived at the baseball field near the south end of town, a group of them were gathered behind one of the dugouts, deciding how they were going to divide themselves into two teams, which was now more challenging since Al brought the number of players to seven.

"I could just watch," Al told them. He wasn't confident in his athletic abilities, and no one argued with him. No one said anything at all, so he made his way to the wooden bleachers. Before reaching them, something chucked him on the shoulder from behind. He figured someone miscalculated a toss of the baseball, but it hurt like hell, and when Al turned, he saw it wasn't a ball at all but a large rock.

Al looked at the group of them, standing in a crowd together, watching him. Raymond said nothing. Then a guy on the edges threw another rock, which barely missed Al's right hip. Al knew he should've run, raced across the field back to town, but he was frozen. His legs so wobbly and woozy beneath him, if he tried to move he would've fallen.

The kid who threw the second rock rushed forward and shoved him, and that was all it took to get him to the ground.

"Faggot," the kid said, and kicked him in the thigh.

There was another kick to his stomach and Al curled up into a ball, held his knees against his chest and buried his face into them.

"We're gonna teach you a fuckin' lesson."

"Little shit!"

Someone got on top of him and started punching, but after a few hits, Al couldn't distinguish a punch from a kick. He wanted to call out Raymond's name, to ask him to stop, but at one point during the melee, when he was rolling over, Al saw Raymond towering over him, hands crunched into fists. His left foot pushing back slowly, as if aiming. Al caught his eye and he didn't see any remorse or regret in them.

Afterwards, when it was all over and everyone was gone, and Al finally managed to pick himself up off the ground, he found Raymond's plaid button-up still draped on one of the seats in the bleachers. Al used it to wipe the blood from his nose and mouth as he walked to the nearest store and asked the clerk to call his dad to come and pick him up.

Raymond had told everyone it was Al who had put on the nurse's uniform. That it was Al who'd made advances toward Raymond. And now it was Al's turn to feel betrayed. But with time, after the bruises faded and the scabs fell away, the emotions did too. Mostly.

The sun continues to descend, and Al waits until the valley is black in the distance and hardly visible at all before he rises and leaves the room.

—

"Good first day?" Trish follows Lenore into the bedroom and watches her rifle through her drawers.

"A little different than the Gold," Lenore answers, laughing.

"I bet." Trish sits on the end of the bed. "Lucky, though—you've got a whole different life now."

Lenore places a couple T-shirts on the bed, a few pairs of underwear. "We both do, I guess." She stops and looks at Trish. "I mean…"

"It's okay. I do." Trish picks up the T-shirts and folds them into neat squares. "Just not quite sure where it's headed yet but I'll figure it out." It's true. She has no idea what's next but she's not worrying about it right now. She's okay with this weird, neither-here-nor-there state she's in.

"And you, what did you do with your first day off in forever?" Lenore asks.

"I read an entire book. That Maeve Binchy novel that was in the stack on your nightstand. Can't remember the last time I read anything that wasn't for kids." She hadn't meant to bring Jase up, but there it was and she was okay with it. "It's been nothing but picture books and comics for the last while."

Lenore opens her closet and searches its floor. "I thought I had an old beach bag in here."

"Use mine," Trish gets her gym bag from the floor and pulls out her own items.

"You sure?"

Trish nods and Lenore packs her things into Trish's bag.

"Here," Lenore says, removing everything from the top drawer of one of her dressers and stuffing them in the lower ones, "you can use this."

"You don't need to do that."

"Well, I don't want your shit scattered all over my place, messing it up," Lenore says with a grin.

Trish places her things in the drawer and catches Lenore pulling a silky camisole and matching panties from another dresser and slipping them in the bag. There's a strained look on her face, though.

"Something up?"

Lenore zips up the bag and sits, thoughts whirring in her eyes. "I'm sorry I was being so judgmental about your decision to leave."

"I get it."

"As much as I think I know what it'd be like"—she pauses—"to be a mother. I don't."

Trish turns around and slowly pushes the drawer closed. She waits a moment before facing Lenore again.

"We have these ideas about what it's like, but..." Lenore says, then waves away the thought. "Never mind."

"But what?"

"At the station today, I found out that the boy from the hotel... his mother left him." She rises and slings the bag over her shoulder.

"What?"

"She signed him over to Social Services."

"She couldn't have. She wouldn't."

"I saw the paperwork."

"It must be a mistake. I spoke with her, the mother, after it happened, and I'm telling you, there's no way she would have done that."

"Maybe I misread something." Lenore shrugs it off and seems to disappear even further into her thoughts. In the kitchen, she pulls a key from a junk drawer and hands it to Trish. "Not like you need a key with that door, but here's one just in case."

"You headed to Roger's?"

"I don't know for how long or how often, or whatever, but we'll see."

"I'm happy for you."

"Me too."

But Trish picks up on a hesitancy of sorts as she follows Lenore to the door and locks it behind her.

—

WHEN LENORE GETS TO ROGER'S it's already dark, but he's out on the back deck with the barbecue.

"Dug it out of the garage this afternoon," he tells her, proud. "Salmon, in my homemade teriyaki sauce." A glass of white wine is already waiting for her. "It's chillier than I thought. If you want to wait inside, I'll bring this in. Almost done."

Lenore takes her bag inside and sees the kitchen table. Placemats, candles and a thin vase holding a single rose. It's such a cliché but she should still appreciate it. She decided this afternoon she wasn't going to bring up the papers, or Aaron and his mother. She was going to let things lie. It's not her life or her issue. And who is she to think she should get involved? What's done is done. She should just focus on her life and what's happening now. She finishes the glass of wine and refills it before Roger joins her.

"This is nice," she says, sitting at the table. "And there's no fire alarm."

He laughs, dishing up their plates. "How'd it go today?"

"I filed and that was pretty much it."

"Bev will love having you there but don't let her push it all off on you. She may try."

They barely talk throughout dinner. Lenore thinks of things to stay or ask but then doesn't. It's strained, and made worse because he doesn't seem to pick up on it. He pours her a Scotch after dinner and they settle on the couch and watch television. When she's into her second Scotch, his cluelessness really bothers her.

"I filed some paperwork for the Gourlay case," she says, and waits. But nothing. "What did she say to you when you met with her?"

"What do you mean?"

"When she signed her kid over into care. You were with her, weren't you?"

"I was."

"But you didn't tell me?"

"I didn't because she asked me not to. It was a difficult decision for her and it was a private one too." He picks up the remote and flicks up the volume.

Despite a small spot of fear blooming inside her, she pushes on. "I just find it hard to believe, that's all," she says. "She must've said something before signing."

"All she said was it was too much for her. That's it."

"Too much?"

"Don't you think she had to deal with a lot?"

"Yes, but—"

He cuts her off. "Do you know how many children with special needs and disabilities and whatnot are turned over to care because the parents can't cope?"

Lenore is about to respond when he cuts her off again. "A lot. I can tell you."

"But Aaron doesn't have a disability." She sees him raise his eyebrows even though he doesn't look up from the TV.

"When she signed the papers, did she know that he was okay?"

"That boy is not okay."

"He is. And despite the complication, he's still glad he had the procedure." Now Roger looks up at her, and the fear grows a little larger.

"That's talk around town."

"That's talk from his own mouth," she says. "I saw him at the hospital."

"Did you?"

"The day of your retirement, I returned the things they left at the hotel and he asked me to find out where she was. He was waiting for her and was anxious to get back home."

"Hmph," is all Roger says.

"I'll ask again. Did she know that he was fine when she signed those papers?"

Roger shakes his head. "I don't want to talk about this."

"Why? What aren't you telling me, Roger?"

He lets out a puff of air, a kind of uncomfortable sigh.

"I'm serious, Roger. What was the conversation between you two?"

"That's not something I can share with you."

"No?" And suddenly her fear is gone. Replaced by something else. Something that doesn't hold her back. "I could call her in Beauville to ask her myself. I have her number."

Roger eyes her, but it's impossible to tell what he's thinking.

"Did she think that Aaron was still in danger when you spoke to her?"

Roger gets up and pours himself another. "Listen, I'm done with work and don't need to talk about this anymore."

"I think you do." Her heart kicks in her chest.

"Won't do anyone any good."

"You don't think so?"

"What's done is done."

"That's all you have to say?"

He walks back to the couch and flips through the channels.

"Roger," she starts, her voice calmer, "I looked at the date on those papers. Those were signed the day after your retirement. You didn't go to the station that day." She pauses. "But you did go during the middle of the night." He continues to flip. "Which is also the night that she left town, isn't it?" Lenore moves to the armchair and sits on the edge, leaning forward on her elbows. "Roger, did you lie to her?"

He settles on a channel and balances the remote on the arm of the couch. Takes a drink. "I did what was best for that child."

The anger dissipates, just disappears in a flash. "How dare you?" she says before realizing the words are falling out of her mouth.

He doesn't even turn to look at her.

She rises, grabs the glass from his hand and throws it across the room. It hits the wall, splashing the paint and staining it a darker hue.

"Jesus," he says. "You need to calm down." He glares at her and for the first time there's anger in his eyes.

"There is only one thing I need to do." She grabs her jacket from the back of the chair and picks up her purse.

"You going home?"

"No." She makes her way to the door and he follows her. "I'm going to do what you couldn't." She walks out.

"Lenore." He stands in the doorway.

As she pulls away from house and is about to round the corner at the end of the block, she sees him in her rear-view—he's climbing into his own car in the driveway. She presses on the gas.

—

TRISH WAS PUTTING HER DIRTY DISHES in the sink when Sean called her from the hospital. He said everything was fine but he wanted to talk to her tonight.

When she gets there she checks in at the nurses' station and gets directions to Sean's room. She's not scared, but her neck feels like it's made of popsicle sticks, stiff and breakable. She reaches the door of his room, and through the small square of glass, sees him propped up in bed with a comic book. The bedside lamp is on, barely giving off enough light to read by. She pushes on the door.

"What happened?"

"It was an accident but we're fine."

"What kind of accident? Where's Jase?"

"He's okay, he's at home with my parents. They drove in from Shainley."

"Why didn't you call me?"

"The nurses wanted to," he says, sitting up and adjusting the pillows, wincing as he does, "but I told them not to. I have three cracked ribs and some bruising, it's nothing serious. Bed rest for a while and that's it."

"Were you at work?"

He shakes his head. "It happened at home in the garage. I was working and Jase came in to help. He wanted to ride Murray's lawn mower. I shouldn't have let him but I thought he might have fun. He's had a rough time lately." He says it gently, without blame. "It's not his fault, I wasn't watching closely enough. But that's not why I wanted to talk." He pauses. "Trish. What's your plan?"

"What do you mean?"

"You've left before and you've come back, but this time it feels different, and I think maybe it should be." He looks up at her. "I think this is all becoming too hard for Jase and we need to figure some things out."

"Okay."

"I don't know where to start."

"Me either."

"Do you plan on staying in town?"

"I think so. For a while anyway."

"If you are staying, do you still want to be a part of his life?"

She thinks about her response.

"Because if you don't, then you have to think about how that will impact him if you're still here. He's not going to stop coming to the Gold, you know that."

"I've thought about that but I can't quit my job. I can't leave yet."

"I've been doing some thinking this evening and I might have a solution." He flinches with pain as he shifts forward again. "I'm thinking Jase and I could move in with my parents for a while. I know Don will give me a good reference and Dad knows a few people in Shainley. Even if I don't find something right away, my parents will help out."

Shainley is a three-hour drive east. His mom works part-time at a law office, and his dad's retired but fills his time doing odd jobs as a handyman. She never knew them very well when they lived in Saltus but liked their company when they were around.

"And I think a change would be good for Jase," he says. "Don't you?"

"I think so."

"He might have a hard time at first but things will settle down. I just want to give him something stable."

"I know." She pauses, swallows hard. She wants to say something more, something big and meaningful, but nothing comes to her.

"I can't decide whether to wait until the end of the school year or to go next month during the Easter break. I'm thinking the sooner the better, but I'll talk to both schools first."

"Is there anything you need from me?"

"I don't think so. When we're gone, you can move back into the house and we can work all that out later."

They sit in silence for a long while, listening to the occasional footsteps coming and going in the hall outside the door. Then she finds the words. "I'm sorry."

IN THE HALLWAY, TRISH ALMOST MISSES the turn to the front doors. She's going over everything Sean told her in her head. In some way, it's exactly what she would've wished for. Sean and Jase together in a home that will support them, and in a town that will welcome them. But there's sadness there too. It's only natural. It's possible to miss something that never felt right in the first place. You get used to it, it grows on you. Grows into to you. Trish rubs her hands together, warming them. They'd grown cold and icy but she hadn't noticed until now. She pulls her purse from her shoulder and reaches in for her gloves. The entrance doors open before she finds them and Lenore strides in.

"What are you doing here?" Lenore asks, without slowing down.

"Sean had an accident." Trish automatically follows her, sensing something's up.

"Is he okay?"

Trish nods, she doesn't want to get into the details.

"Good. I may need your help." Lenore quickens her pace down the hall and Trish keeps up.

"With what?"

They near the nurses' station but it's empty.

"I don't think we'll have much time." Lenore pushes through the staff only door. Trish glances around before following. Trish has never seen Lenore like this before. Harried, a little scared, but all of it covered over with her usual determination. Lenore looks through the window of a door and her face shows a faint trace of sorrow. She knocks lightly and then opens the door. The room is dark inside, only a green light from a machine that doesn't appear to be connected to anything glows in the corner.

"Aaron?" Lenore whispers. She heads straight to the bed and pulls on the covers. He rolls over, waking. "Aaron. Do you want to go home?"

"What?" He wipes the spit from the corner of his mouth.

"Do you want to go home? Right now?"

He's fully awake and sits up. "I can't."

"Lenore?" Trish clues in to what Lenore's plans are.

"You can 'cause I'm going to take you."

"My mother doesn't want me to come home."

"That's not true. I'll explain in the car." Lenore pulls the dress out from the closet where she'd hung it up during her previous visit. "You want to put this on?"

"Lenore? What are you doing?" asks Trish.

She ignores her and pulls back Aaron's blankets all the way. "Come on, you have to hurry."

Aaron, hesitant and unsure, rises anyway and starts to remove his hospital gown. Lenore helps him. She pulls the dress over his arms and zips up the back. Flattens the sleeves across his shoulders with her palms. Aaron begins to cry, out of both fear and confusion. Lenore places a hand on the back of his neck and holds it there.

"It's okay, kiddo. We'll get you home now," Lenore says.

The moment stops Trish. A grieving boy, and this woman, her friend, comforting him so fiercely. It's a side of her Trish hasn't seen. The conversation with Sean is so fresh that her own grief rises to the surface, surprising her.

She hears running shoes squeaking in the hall. "We have to go," Trish says, her instinct to help kicking in. She steps into the hall and confronts the nurse, startling her.

"You shouldn't be in this hall," the nurse says.

"We're just leaving."

"We?" And as the nurse says it, Lenore steps out of the room, carrying Aaron's suitcase. Aaron's behind her, pulling on his jacket.

"What's going on?" the nurse asks in a stern voice, but there's a hint of fear as well.

"We're taking Aaron home."

Trish takes the suitcase from Lenore's hand so Lenore can help Aaron with his jacket.

"Home?"

"That's right. Excuse us." Lenore pushes past her.

Just as they reach the doors that lead to the nurses' station, they open. It's Roger. Though not in his uniform, he still carries that authoritative air. "Lenore, you can't do this," he says, blocking the doorway.

"The hell I can't."

"I'll call security," the nurse says, stepping around them and edging past Roger.

"Might as well call the station too," Lenore tells her, but then looks at Roger. "Let's get everything out in the open."

The nurse, sensing something else in the air, stops and looks at Roger for direction. But Roger only looks at Lenore.

"Go ahead. We'll see what Glen has to say," Lenore threatens.

But the nurse doesn't move, and neither does Roger. Lenore looks down toward the other end of the hall. "Can you bring my car around?" She hands Trish the keys and the suitcase and leads Aaron toward the emergency exit, its light bulb flickering behind the red glass. As she does, Roger follows them, leaving room for Trish to head back toward the main entrance where Lenore's car is parked.

Trish puts the suitcase in the back seat. She doesn't even know all the details of what's happening right now, but she has a few pieces of the puzzle and they're enough to know that she's not going to question Lenore. She slides forward in the driver's seat to reach the pedals. Lenore has almost three inches on her, though they've never measured. She feels like a kid stealing a parent's car. Her fingers grow stiff on the icy steering wheel. So many things are happening at once. So many big things. There's no time to sort through it all.

She does a slow U-turn in the parking lot and hits the concrete barrier in one of the parking stalls. Hears it scrape the edge of the bumper. She rounds the corner of the hospital and sees Lenore and Aaron waiting on the edges of the ambulance bay. Roger behind them, pacing. Trish pulls into the bay and leaves the keys in the ignition as Lenore walks Aaron around to the other side and helps him in.

"Are you coming with us?" Lenore asks her.

Trish pauses, but she's done all the escaping she needs to do and shakes her head.

Lenore simply nods and gets in the car.

"Lenore," Roger says, stepping closer. "You're not helping that boy at all. It's not right."

Lenore gets back out and strides up to Roger. "How dare you stand there and tell me what's right and what isn't after what you've done. Besides, what's right for you is not right for him." She pauses, then turns, climbing back into the car. "It's not right for me, either." The car pulls away.

Roger watches the car a moment, smacks his hand against his thigh, but Trish isn't sure if it's in anger or regret. He walks back in the emergency entrance but she stays outside in the bay.

Trish traces Lenore's red tail lights down the road and through the clutch of trees and bushes lining the far end of the hospital property. The night air is cool and crisp around her, bringing everything into clear relief. She should've hugged Lenore. If ever there was a time, tonight was it. Watching her footing over the icy patches on her way back to her car, Trish wonders how long it will be before she stops measuring her life by the number of mistakes she's made.

—

HIS SEMI IS THE MIDNIGHT-BLUE ONE with red racing stripes up its sides. Below each stripe in white lettering is his name and phone number, along with the double *O*s to indicate he's the owner and operator and not affiliated with any one company.

He's his own boss. Nadine climbs up into the cab through the driver's side door, and slides over to the passenger seat to make way for Garth, who grunts as he hauls himself up the steps and inside.

She spent most of the afternoon in bars. Just stopping for a drink here and there and leaving when she didn't spot anyone she thought she wanted, or when someone she did turned her down. The rejections never hurt, though. She just moved on. Late in the evening, when the alcohol was finally hitting her, and hitting her hard, she ordered a cheeseburger with fries and scarfed it down in record time. It was only then she realized how long it had been since she had a meal.

Garth was at the table across from her and wasn't someone she'd noticed at all until he commented on her ability to pack away the food and have nothing to show for it. The food helped her sober up but not entirely. She ordered another drink and one for Garth, and then joined him at his table. They small-talked for a while and there was nothing flirtatious about it, but when she told him what she wanted, he laughed at first, thinking it was a joke. He came around when he realized she was serious.

Nadine swoops a leg over his lap and knocks the air freshener and other items dangling from his rear-view, including a pewter Yorkshire terrier hanging on a strip of leather, and a Hawaiian lei. There's barely enough room for her between his belly and the steering wheel, but she wedges herself in and presses herself against him. Everything about him is round—his nose, his glasses, his neck. If he grew out a beard and had a few more years on him, he would make the perfect Santa.

Nadine removes his glasses and places them on the dash.

"You're sure about this?" he asks.

She kisses him and starts to grind herself against him, and she's aroused much quicker than she expected. She wasn't even sure she'd be able to orgasm but it happens before he's inside her, before she even has her jeans off. She shudders against him.

Nadine slides off him and pulls off her pants and shoes while he undoes his.

"I don't have any protection," he says. "I'm assuming you do, though."

"Shit," she says. His cock is hard and she wishes she could just lean over and blow him, but she's only done that a few times when she was much younger and was told on all occasions that she wasn't good at it. "I haven't been with anyone for a really long time. Years."

"That makes two of us then," he says and makes room for her to climb back on top.

The lack of room makes it difficult to find a rhythm, and after only a few moments she feels him going soft. She nips at his lip and pulls her shirt and bra up so he can feel her tits, but it doesn't work.

"Fuck," he says, apologetic. "I don't know what's going on."

"It's all right."

"Just rusty, I think."

"We can wait and try again."

"It's not like it doesn't feel good. It does. Honestly."

"Is there anything else I can do?"

"No, I was raring to go just a second ago. Thought I was about to come but then it just passed me by."

Nadine pulls her shirt down and moves off of him. Starts to dress.

"Shit."

"I'm sorry."

"It's not your fault at all." He zips up and pulls out his wallet, hands her a couple of twenties.

"I'm not a prostitute."

"No, I know, but you bought drinks, and I don't know where you're headed tonight but you should take a cab wherever you're going." He puts the money on the seat when she doesn't take it. "I'm sorry about that."

She pulls on her high-tops.

"I really did enjoy it, though."

Nadine picks up the cash and climbs out. She walks around to the front of the bar where her car is parked and drives a few blocks before realizing she's in no shape to do so. She pulls onto a residential street and gets into the back seat. She's not sad or angry or hurt. The only thing she sits with is the realization that she can never go back and be the person she wanted to be. She closes her eyes. When she wakes, she'll head home and face everything that's waiting for her.

—

BEFORE RETURNING TO LENORE's, Trish stops in at the Gold. She still has the keys to room 203 in her purse but doesn't want them anymore. There's no one at the front desk when she walks in.

She could put them back herself, but decides to go up to the second floor first.

The room is exactly as she left it, except it smells like soap. The stains are still there, a little more faint but obvious. They can use bleach on the mattress but they'll have to cut out the section of carpet and replace it entirely.

Trish turns and sees someone in the doorway watching her. Stacey Zerr.

"I'm sorry, I didn't mean to startle you."

"Thought you'd be gone by now. Off chasing the next story."

"Just leaving now." She gestures at the luggage sitting on the floor outside the room across the hall. "I've never covered a story like this before." She steps into the room uninvited. After taking a long scan of the room, Stacey finally looks at Trish and sees who she is. "We spoke the other night... You have the keys now?"

Trish looks at them in her hands but doesn't say anything.

Stacey moves in closer to the stain on the carpet.

"Can we film in here now?"

"Why?"

"Because our viewers would like to see it. They'd like to know what happened."

"You already told them what happened."

"But they haven't seen this."

"The bloody floor?"

"No. The truth. The location of the event, the room. Where it happened."

"Those are details, not the truth."

Stacey watches her, deciphering. "Were you working that night, on shift?"

Trish nods.

"What is the truth then?"

"You can film the room, just lock the door when you leave."
She exits, leaving Stacey alone inside. She'll never get the truth.
Trish's truth is different from Al's, and Al's from Jase's. Hers is
also different from the truth that Lenore's following right now,
and all the truths that lie ahead for Aaron.

—

HE ACTUALLY FELL ASLEEP. It was the first decent stretch Al's had
since everything happened. There's a kind of relief that comes
when you can stop wishing for something. When you let it go.

All the lights in the house are off but he makes his way to
the living room and settles in a chair in front of the window.
The stars in the sky are bright and light up the room. He could
stare at the prairie sky forever. He wishes the window was bigger,
that it stretched from one side of the house to the other. He's
thought about renovating for years, but there's so much in life
that never happens.

If it was warmer, he'd go and sit outside, but he contents
himself in the armchair. If he really wanted to, he could imagine
seeing Aaron outside the window, on the lawn, mingling in the
shadows from the trees that line the front yard. Why he'd be out
there at this time of night, Al doesn't know, but he can picture
him there. Moving with the branches and the breeze. It was fool-
ish of Al to think about them moving in. Dreaming was all it was
but the seed was planted anyway.

273

He hopes the boy doesn't regret it. As long as Aaron is okay, Al will be too.

He comes back to the small square frame around the window. It's keeping too much out and he wants more of the sky and the field. He wants to let it all in. To open everything up. The rooms too. Like the window, they're too small and too cramped. He doesn't need this many bedrooms anymore. What he needs is space. Wide open and unrestrained. He wants to start living bigger now.

There are some tools in the barn but there are more in the basement.

The first smash with the sledgehammer into the wall between the living room and spare bedroom sends dust and pieces of plaster flying. He still hasn't turned on the lights. Another smash. The impact reverberates through his whole body, a different kind of hum. Every single muscle is going to feel bruised and torn. And by the time the sun starts to rise in the morning, he'll still be at it.

—

THERE'S JUST THE SOUND of the car's engine. Its tires rushing along the pavement. Loud and rumbling. Some music, or even a talk show would be nice, but Aaron's asleep and Lenore doesn't want to wake him. He fell asleep right after they passed Wakamon. Until then, there was just awkward silence between them. Aaron didn't want to talk, and honestly, neither did she.

They were both stunned. Lenore still is. What a night. And there's still more to go.

She glances at the kid next to her. Head leaning against the window, balanced on one of Lenore's sweaters from the back seat, all scrunched up for a pillow. There's a tang of teenage sweat in the air. Kid probably hasn't been able to bathe since the surgery. Might still be a while before he can. He's curled up as best he can in the passenger seat, bony knees bent and protruding through his jeans, which he put on underneath the dress for warmth. There'd be something kind of hippyish about it if it wasn't for the running shoes and the vibrant windbreaker he's also wearing.

At the next major highway intersection, streetlamps mark the crossing. The light floods the car's interior and it's all bright white for a couple of seconds, and then dark again. It wakes Aaron.

"How far are we?"

"Nearing the border, I think. Not quite halfway." It's almost 2:30 a.m. and Lenore should be exhausted but she's wide awake, so awake it's like she'll never need to sleep again. "Do you want to stop at the next town and call your mom?"

Aaron shakes his head.

"I haven't called her myself. She doesn't know we're coming."

Aaron straightens in his seat, stretches his neck, and places Lenore's sweater across his legs like a blanket. Then he touches the condensation that gathered on the window from his breath while sleeping. Rubs his fingers through it until it's gone.

"How are you feeling? Physically."

Aaron puts his hands in his lap and pauses, taking an inventory of sorts. "I feel good."

"You sure?" Lenore looks at him quickly but it's long enough to see that Aaron's thoughts are elsewhere, and even in the darkness, his eyes are bright and there's a hint of a smile.

"If you do want to stop somewhere for a break, let me know." Lenore reaches over and turns on the radio. Whitney Houston followed by Eric Clapton and then a ton of commercials. "You can change the station."

"I like pretty much everything."

"That's unusual for a kid."

He shrugs. "Always have. Rap, grunge, pop, metal. Even country. There's something to like about all of it."

"Is that what you want to do when you're older? Something in music?"

"No. Or maybe. I don't know. When I was a lot younger, I used to want to be a nurse but now... maybe a veterinarian? I guess it all depends on where we move."

"You're moving?"

"That was the plan. Once we saved up enough, and once I was more transitioned, then we'd move to another place. I wanted to go to a city. Like Vancouver or Montreal, but Mom didn't think that was realistic." There's a long pause. "But all of that was before."

"Before what?"

"Before she left me there."

"But she didn't, your mother was lied to. I don't know exactly what was said or how it went down, but I can tell you that she made her decision based on wrong information. Okay?"

Aaron stares out the window.

"She was only trying to make the best decision she could based on the information she had. You can't blame her for that."

"I guess."

"You can't ask for anything more in a mother." The words catch in her throat as they come out. Aaron notices.

"Do you have kids?"

"Could never get my shit together enough for that." She laughs, but her eyes sting. Maybe she is more tired that she thought. "Almost, though."

"Really?"

Lenore waves it off and changes the subject. "What's the first thing you're going to do when you move to a new city?"

"My plan was to change my name right away," Aaron says. "I was going to change my name and get all my identification changed but I think I'll do that now. Like, right away."

"Yeah, to what?"

"It's not a big change, but I plan to spell my name with an *E*. And even though my middle name is Jesse, which is both a girl's name and a boy's name, I'm going to change it to Jane."

"Erin with an *E*. I like it. That's what I'll call you from now on—Erin with an *E*."

Erin grins beside her. Another top-forty song starts on the radio and Lenore turns it up. She focuses back on the long, narrow highway. Nothing but darkness in front of her. Empty and heavy at the same time. Erin starts to drift off again beside her and Lenore feels it too. Sudden and sharp. She's almost halfway there. They'll arrive just as the sun is about to come up. She can make it that long.

—

HE KNOWS HIS FATHER'S GOING to be okay, he'll be out in the next day or two, but Jase still doesn't want to come to the hospital to visit him. Even though it's Saturday, his grandma woke him early so they could come as soon as visiting hours started. When they get to his dad's room, his dad asks if they could have some time alone first and his grandma goes to get a coffee.

"How are you doing?" he asks Jase, like Jase is the one who's sick.

"Okay."

"I hope Grandma's behaving and listening to you. If she's not, don't be afraid to ground her."

"Dad," Jase says, laughing.

There's a few moments of silence.

"Do you have any comics in your school bag?"

"X-Men."

"Good. Why don't you bring your chair in close and read it to me?"

"Don't you want to read it?" It's always his dad who reads to him before bed.

"No, I'd like you to read it to me. You're getting really good."

Jase doesn't really want to but he says okay. He's not going to do all the voices that his dad does, he's only going to read it normal. For the first couple of pages he stumbles because it's weird, but then he forgets he's reading and just thinks about the story. When he's done, he closes the comic and taps it against his knees. His father watches him, smiling.

"I'm the luckiest father in the world, you know that, Jase? To have a son like you."

Jase stops tapping and looks away. How can he tell his dad what really happened?

"Jase? Come here." He pulls Jase to him even though it hurts him.

"I'm sorry, Dad. I didn't mean to." His chin quivers but he can't stop it.

"There's nothing to be sorry for, kid," Sean says. "You saved me, Son."

"I didn't."

"Yes, you did. You saved me."

Jase didn't save him the way a superhero would because a superhero would never have done that in the first place. But he knows that this is how his dad will remember it, and maybe that's okay.

"It's been real rough for a while now, Jase. I know it's been hard for you, but when I get out of here things are going to look up."

Jase doesn't lift his head from his father's chest but nods. He wants to fall asleep here, right in his dad's arms. But this time it's a good kind of sleep. He feels it.

—

ERIN'S BED SMELLS LIKE PEACHES and mint. Lenore stares at the glass of water that he must have brought her when she was asleep. When they got to the house, Erin unlocked the door with his key, but Nadine wasn't home. They were both exhausted and agreed to sleep first and figure out a plan to track her down when they woke up. Erin offered Lenore his room and Lenore didn't argue, accepting it as soon as it was offered. She doesn't know how much time has passed.

There are voices in the living room. It's a movie on TV, one she recognizes. *City Slickers.* She starts to drift again.

Two days after that final night at Daniel's, Lenore woke up in the hospital. She didn't remember anything in between. Her adoptive father was there, sleeping in the chair beside her. His neck hooked at an unnatural angle. She didn't wake him. Instead, she listened to his breath, to the sounds of footsteps in the hall nearing and then fading. There was a peacefulness that she didn't want to disturb, not knowing when she would feel it again.

Eventually, her father woke and called a doctor. A nurse came in first and checked her pulse and her temperature. Scratched some notes in her chart. Then the doctor arrived and Lenore's gut folded in on itself. He described to her the state she had been in when she arrived at the hospital. He told her everything the staff had done to revive her. And then he placed a hand on hers and told her that she had lost her baby. Almost twelve weeks, just nearing the end of her first trimester.

Her father cracked right there. Knees buckled under him and he sat on the edge of her bed to keep from falling to the floor. He pulled her in toward him and held her. "Oh, Lenore," he moaned out. "Why didn't you tell us?" He kissed the top of her head. "Why?" he asked again she didn't answer.

"I didn't know." Then she cried too, and he rocked her. But she was crying for different reasons. She was crying because she lied. That night after the powwow and the jingle dress dancer, and that needle over and over. That night she had known she was pregnant. She'd known for almost two weeks but was still figuring out what to do, who to tell. Or maybe she had been avoiding it altogether.

Lenore tries to pull herself up from the bed to join Erin in the living room, but everything is still too heavy. She sinks back into the sheets.

—

NADINE SEES THE STRANGE CAR parked out front as soon as she turns the corner. As she nears, the Saskatchewan licence plate catches her eye and she thinks the worst. But it's not the authorities. She unlocks the front door carefully and slowly enters. The sound of the TV carries down the hall. She follows it and finds her child asleep on the couch under the sleeping bag from the hall closet. Nadine puts both hands over her mouth and doesn't make a sound, but the tears come forth anyway.

She steps into the room and the floor creaks. Erin stirs.

"Mom?"

"You're home."

But before Erin can respond, Nadine kneels on the floor beside him and touches his leg, then his arm, his shoulder and head. "You're okay? You're all right?"

"I am."

"How'd you get here?"

"Lenore brought me—one of the waitresses from the hotel... She's in my room."

"I'm sorry, I'm sorry," Nadine says.

"Lenore told me what happened." Erin sits up, and Nadine climbs onto the couch beside him.

"I just... oh, god..." Nadine holds on tight. "I'm sorry."

"You don't have to be."

"I'm so glad you're home."

Neither of them pulls away, and instead they lean back into the couch while the movie plays.

"YOU HUNGRY?" NADINE ASKS when the credits roll.

"A little bit. I'm not sure what there is, though."

In the kitchen, they find half a loaf of bread in the freezer and defrost it in the microwave before toasting. Erin pulls out the peanut butter and honey from the cupboard and two jars of jam from the fridge while Nadine makes coffee. They eat three slices each.

"Should we wake her?" Nadine asks, motioning down the hall to Erin's room.

"Let's let her sleep."

"I'm not sure what to do next."

"Should we make an appointment to see the doctor?"

"Goertzen?"

"I guess." Erin shrugs.

"I'll call this morning." Nadine pauses. "And what about us?"

"What do you mean?"

"I've never asked you before and I should have. I'm sorry that I haven't..."

"Yeah?"

"What do you want me to call you?"

"It's still Erin, but with an *E*." He laughs. "That's what Lenore calls me, 'Erin with an *E*.'"

"I remember you told me your name. But..."

"Oh," Erin says, catching on, then looks away, thinking. "Yes, I'd like to try. Can we?"

"We can." Nadine sits up and clears her throat as if on stage. "Mom..."

"We agreed to try it."

"I know, but I don't want it to be a big deal."

Nadine clears her throat again, teasing.

"Please..." Erin says, groaning.

"No, no, I won't." Then Nadine turns serious. "But it is a big deal." She watches Erin for a moment. "It is a big deal... to have a daughter."

They both take in the moment, then Erin tosses a piece of crust at her.

"And still a little shit too," Nadine says, laughing.

—

"GET YOUR ASS IN HERE right now." It's the only thing Glen says when Roger answers the phone.

Roger looks at the clock. It's just after ten a.m. He pulls out the plug in the kitchen sink and wipes his hands on the dish-towel. The rest of the breakfast dishes can wait.

At the station, Bev's on the phone when he walks in. She's wearing a sweatshirt with some football team's logo on it and no makeup. She cups her hand over the mouthpiece. "This is a real mess, Roger. A real mess."

Roger looks at Glen's closed office door. "He's in a state."

"As he should be." Bev returns to her phone call.

Roger knocks on Glen's door.

"It's open!" Glen shouts a little too loudly. "Close it behind you," he says when he sees it's Roger. "Sit down."

Roger does, reading the level of tension in the room.

"Jesus Christ, Roger." Glen looks at him. "Jesus fucking Christ."

Roger sees the open file on Glen's desk, his own typed and handwritten notes. The Section 9 papers.

"What the fuck did you do?"

"What I had to, to keep that kid safe."

"Unbelievable." Glen rubs his forehead with both his hands. "I got an urgent call at home this morning from the detachment in Beauville. I called the mother back directly and had no idea what she was talking about. No fucking idea," Glen seethes at him. "I had to call Bev in to help me sort through this shit. When I finally understood the situation, I immediately called the local Social Services office and spoke with Ms. Schroeder. Thankfully, the copies of the Section 9 papers that you sent to her office hadn't been processed yet so I was able to stop it."

His plan could have worked. Lenore is the only reason why it didn't. He should be angry as hell with her but he's not.

284

"You've had a good career, Roger." Glen leans back and his chair squeaks. "You've never done anything untoward before, never been disciplined. And now this? Right at the end? I don't get it."

"Not sure there is anything to get."

"But there is, because what you've done impacts us all—this station, me, the whole bloody force. She could sue, for chrissakes."

"Will she?"

"Let's hope to god she doesn't."

There's a long silence, then Roger rises. "You need anything else?"

Glen waves him out of his office, and as Roger makes his way through the station to the doors, he nods goodbye to Bev as he passes, feeling oddly calm and wondering if he should feel anything different.

—

JASE CAREFULLY ROLLS UP HIS POSTER and ties it up with a piece of red yarn that he took from his grandmother's knitting bag. He told his grandmother he was going out to play with his friends at the schoolyard. She shouted from the kitchen that she'd be starting dinner soon and he should come home before five. She also reminded him that he needs to be in bed early tonight because tomorrow is Monday, but he doesn't care about school right now.

He was thinking about rabbits and snakes when he finished the picture. Butterflies too. He was thinking about how they can change. Rabbits change their colour in the spring and winter. Snakes leave their skin behind like dry paper on the ground; they just slide out of it. And butterflies, of course, were once caterpillars. And he was also thinking about how most people would like to change too, and that's what his superhero can do. He can change people into anyone they want to become. That's how he came up with his superhero's name. If people could be who they really want to be, they wouldn't have to hurt anyone else. Others might not understand the superpower just from the picture, but his mom will. At least he hopes she will. If she doesn't, then maybe one day he'll explain it to her.

—

ROGER'S IN THE GARAGE sorting through boxes and bins he's collected over the years. He's never been a hoarder, keeps only what he needs and was never sold on any of those gadgets and such that others always fall for. But he's surprised at the things he finds. A box of old dishes he was given by an older couple when he first moved to town because they thought a bachelor like him would need them. Camping gear that he bought shortly after arriving that he was sure he'd use more than he has. A set of golf clubs that don't look familiar to him at all. He was given a set by a former colleague, hoping Roger would take it up and join him on the course, but it's a sport Roger's never understood so he re-gifted that set as soon as he could. The set he holds now is a mystery to him.

The phone rings in the house and Roger barely gets to it before the machine kicks in. It's a collect call and he accepts the charges. "Hello?"

There's a beat before she responds, voice sure but quiet. "Hi." Then a tentative sigh. "I had to call collect, I'm sorry."

"Where are you?"

"Still in Manitoba." She doesn't say where, doesn't need to.

"Bev's been calling, wondering if you'll be in in the morning. Said she can't reach you at home." He pauses. "I guess you won't be going in."

"I won't be."

"You should call her. She'll likely look past a couple of missed days."

"I don't think I will."

"You'll go back to the Gold then?"

"No, I don't think I'll do that either."

"Then what are you going—"

"They're fine," she interrupts. "In case you were wondering."

"Oh."

"Is that all you have to say?" But there's no anger or accusation. "You could apologize," she says. "I won't put them on the phone, but you could send a letter or something." There's a long silence. "You could think about it."

"What are you doing, Lenore?"

"Not really sure, but that's okay."

"How long are you staying?"

"I'm leaving in a day or so. But I won't be back in Saltus for a while."

"I don't know what to say here."

"I just called to let you know they're okay."

"I understand that."

"You think about that letter."

"Lenore?"

But she hangs up.

Roger puts the receiver back and returns to the garage. He'll never write a letter to the kid or that mother. No point in even thinking about it. He knows what he did was right. When word gets out around town, not everyone will agree but that's okay. He can live with that. Just like Al has to live with what he's done. He wonders if Al's okay with what he did too.

Roger pulls on a pair of work gloves and sweeps out the area he just cleared. Dust motes rise in the air and catch in cobwebs. If he was to write a letter to anyone, it would be Lenore. He thinks about what it would say.

—

TRISH GETS OUT OF THE SHOWER and wonders how things will go from here on out. There are so many things to consider—she'll need to find a longer-term living arrangement. Even if Sean and Jase move to Shainley sooner rather than later, she doesn't want to live in their house. They'll have to find renters, or maybe sell it if they can. But will she stay in town? Should she move to the city? Or maybe go back to school? Can she even do this?

The doorbell rings as Trish is drying off. She pulls on Lenore's robe and heads to the front door. No one's there. She heads to the back door and no one's there either, but there is a scroll of paper rolling in the wind on the back step. Trish picks it up and carries it inside to the kitchen. She pulls on the string that binds it and lets the paper uncurl, spreads it open with her hands. It's Jase's superhero picture, now complete. The entire page is filled with colour. A yellow sun with fat rays stretches across the blue sky. Big, green trees grow between tall skyscrapers and over houses. The superhero flies through the air. His costume is orange and brown, which makes him appear dull against all the other things surrounding him but it also makes him stand out. There's a giant *T* on his chest, and across the top in big block letters, *Transformo*. On the streets below, two people look up at him and wave as he flies higher and away.

She places it on the kitchen counter and uses a butter knife and a bowl to keep it open on the flat surface. After a moment, she lifts her head to the light pouring in from the window above the sink. The sun is melting the frost from the trees. Everything's wet and glistening. Large, bouncy drops sway off the ends of branches just beginning to bud before they slide to the ground. It's the movement that catches her attention. His small figure peaking out from behind a tree across the street. He's a long way away and surely can't see through the gauzy curtains, but she reacts anyway. A searing rush of blood. Maybe it's because he's so far away, but she can already see the young man in him. He stares a long time, as if right at her, and something inside of her unlatches. She raises a hand and waves. He waves back, then shuffles off, and she lets out everything she's been holding in.

—

ROGER PULLS UP the long gravel driveway. Parks beside the truck that's licked with rust and nearing the end of its days. On the front lawn, a pile of old lumber, broken drywall and other refuse from the house. When he reaches the door, he hears the wail of a saw inside. Roger waits for a break in the noise before pressing the doorbell. Al answers in sweatpants and an old torn plaid shirt, a pair of safety goggles hanging around his neck. Bits of white dust and debris in his hair and speckling his skin.

"Yeah?"

"Can I come in?"

"Sure. Can't offer you a place to sit, though." Al opens the door and lets Roger follow him in. Once inside, Roger realizes that all that garbage on the front lawn is from the inside of the house—there's really not much left. Aside from the load-bearing walls, the rest have come down. Kitchen cupboards have been pulled off and there's nothing but a plastic sheet hanging from the ceiling to cover the toilet and shower. A couch, an armchair and some living room tables are stuffed in the corner with another plastic sheet draped over them.

"Why you here? Something else I need to do for my parole?"

Roger hesitates, taking in the scene. The place does not look livable.

They stand close to one another, surrounded by dust and slats, the exposed guts of the house.

"No, no. I'm actually fully retired now."

"Not the lawman anymore, just taking it easy?"

"I suppose so," Roger says. Then, "Thought you might want these back." He pulls the sheaf of letters from his pocket. "They made copies of them for the file, but these can come back to you. Don't know where the envelopes got to."

Al wipes his hands on a kerchief before taking them. Stuffs them into his back pocket.

"I also heard about that kid. Doing all right, apparently." Roger clears his throat and ambles about the room as if inspecting.

Al stares out the front room window, off in another world. Then he comes to and kicks scraps and other wreckage on the floor, making a pathway. "Wish I could offer you a seat."

"No, no. That's fine." But truthfully, Roger doesn't know how Al can stand it. "You made a real fucking mess," he says.

"Suppose I did. Didn't mean to." He picks up some pieces of laths, taps them together while he thinks. "I just wanted to try, you know." He hucks the broken pieces of wood onto the pile. "Maybe I was wrong."

The weight of the words lands. Roger holds them in his head a moment, then wanders about the house, wondering how Al will put everything back together. "It's a just a damn big project," he says, returning to the room.

"Take me some time, that's for sure," says Al.

"And a whole a lot of supplies."

"Yep."

"A lot from the city too."

Al nods.

"Living here with summer around the corner won't be so bad, but summers fly by. You know better than I do."

"I do."

"If you need, I could probably make a few runs to the city."
Roger lifts a few rolled-up pieces of carpet and carries them to
the pile on the lawn outside.

—

NADINE HAS HER ARM around Erin's waist. She's barely stopped
touching her daughter since she returned home. The two
of them sat cuddled on the couch over the last few days. In
between eating endless takeout and watching movies, they
discussed and made plans to move. Nadine finally agreed to
head west. Vancouver was too much for her, too big, too loud,
too many people, but she agreed to Victoria. Erin even started
packing up boxes.

Yesterday, Erin had a follow-up with her doctor in Winnipeg
and hormones will start shortly. She seems an entirely different person already from that night at the Gold. Taller,
bigger. Brighter.

"Come out to visit us when you can," Erin says to Lenore.

Lenore promises to. She's stayed for a couple of days while
she made her own plans. She called Trish and checked on her
savings account. She'll be fine for a while.

Lenore stops at the grocery store first and grabs juice, pre-
packaged sandwiches and fruit, and some crackers for snacking.
At the gas station she fills up and buys two road maps. One for
Manitoba and one for Saskatchewan. She always thought if
she moved anywhere, it would be somewhere with perpetual
warmth. Nevada, Arizona, New Mexico. But it's north where

she's headed. She's never liked the cold, but summer's just ahead, and maybe she'll leave before the winter sets in. Or maybe she'll develop a taste for it. Either way, she'll figure it out.

She turns on the highway and rolls the window down as she accelerates. The air rushes in and whips her hair. It's different than that time before when she stole Daniel's keys. That time she was running away, but now it's the opposite. There's so much ahead. Her heart thrums louder than the engine.

Acknowledgements

Deepest thanks to Nightwood Editions. Silas White and Emma Skagen, you are my knights in shining armour. It was a pleasure and a privilege to work with you, and I am infinitely grateful to you both for elevating this story with your thoughtful notes and insight, and to Angela Yen for designing a captivating and beautiful cover.

I also need to thank Coteau Books—where *Saltus* had a home before the company closed its doors. Amazing people worked there, including Dave Margoshes, who made this manuscript a better story, and me a better writer. I hope that every writer has a chance in their career to be treated as kindly and generously as I was by them. It was a small company with a big heart.

It was a humbling and terrifying experience to write this story and I sincerely want to thank my sensitivity reader, Jaye Kovach. She gently shared her knowledge and experience with me, and educated me in the most compassionate way possible, which is how all educational experiences should be. It was an honour to work with her.

There were many people I leaned on for research and information in various areas. In particular, I want to thank Alexis Kienlen, Stu Somerville, Jill Burkhardt, Natalie Huber and Luke Sitter.

Being a writer in Saskatchewan means you belong to a big supportive community. Thanks to the Saskatchewan Writers' Guild; the Sage Hill Writing Experience and the fellow writers in my workshops; the Saskatchewan Arts Board; the Saskatchewan Aboriginal Writers' Circle, Inc.; and, to my city's municipal government for generously supporting the writing community through its annual City of Regina Writing Award.

Lastly, and most importantly, thanks and love to my friends who helped me along the way. Harry, for stiff whisky and ankle socks. Jane, for shepherding this book through its earlier drafts with such expertise and passion. And Helen, simply, for everything.

Tara Gereaux's first book, *Size of a Fist* (Thistledown Press, 2015), was nominated for two 2016 Saskatchewan Book Awards. Her writing has been published in several literary magazines and has won awards, including the City of Regina Writing Award in 2016 and 2019. After graduating with an MFA in creative writing from the University of British Columbia, Tara worked as a story editor and writer in film and television for ten years. From the Qu'Appelle Valley in Saskatchewan and of Métis and European heritage, Tara lived in Vancouver for nearly two decades before returning to her home on the prairie. She lives in Regina on Treaty Four territory and the homeland of the Métis.